... OUT OF TOWN!

There was only one direction to go—east on the big highway. Jason Whitney was bitter. His lean, tough face was grim. Why hang around just to be convicted of a crime he didn't commit? The town was out to get him anyway. A few adolescent pranks, one or two gaudy nights, now they'd be blown up into larceny and embezzlement. Time to take off.

But one last telephone call—to Rose Allison, the only girl who had ever touched his troubled heart. He punched in the dime, dialed the number. Rose answered in her soft voice. All at once Jason blurted out his story. "I haven't done a thing. That's the truth. You can believe it or not." "I **believe** you, Jason! I'll **always** believe you!" She said it as if it were a vow.

SUNRISE

A triumphant novel of a fiery faith by
Grace Livingston Hill

GRACE LIVINGSTON HILL
SUNRISE

A NATIONAL GENERAL COMPANY

*This low-priced Bantam Book
has been completely reset in a type face
designed for easy reading, and was printed
from new plates. It contains the complete
text of the original hard-cover edition.*
NOT ONE WORD HAS BEEN OMITTED.

SUNRISE
*A Bantam Book / published by arrangement with
J. B. Lippincott Company*

PRINTING HISTORY
Lippincott edition published 1937
Bantam edition published December 1970
2nd printing
3rd printing

*Bantam Books are published by Bantam Books, Inc., a National
General company. Its trade-mark, consisting of the words "Bantam
Books" and the portrayal of a bantam, is registered in the United
States Patent Office and in other countries. Marca Registrada.
Bantam Books, Inc., 666 Fifth Avenue, New York, N.Y. 10019.*

PRINTED IN THE UNITED STATES OF AMERICA

CHAPTER I

At half past ten on Wednesday morning young Jason Whitney came out of the bank and walked down Main Street in the opposite direction from his home with a hard set look upon his face.

By eleven fifteen through some mysterious psychic wireless every boy on Main Street knew that Jason Whitney had lost his job in the bank and had disappeared down the highway toward the East.

When the noon whistle blew at the sawmill Charles Parsons drove up to the bank, got out of his old-fashioned car, and went into the bank to cash a check; when he drove home his brows were puckered thoughtfully. He put up the car in the garage and went into the kitchen. His wife Hannah was getting a nice lunch, ham and fried potatoes and a great thin slice of a mild raw onion on a lettuce leaf with slivers of green peppers and a pleasant tangy dressing.

He washed his hands at the sink in the kitchen, though they had a bathroom on the first floor as well as the second. He had always done that, and somehow the bathrooms had not been able to change his habits. Hannah never bothered him about it. She liked to see him contented, and she enjoyed her two bathrooms in a sweet content herself and kept them fit for kings and queens.

"Where is Rowan?" asked the young man's father as he sat down at the table.

"He went over to Bainbridge to see about exchanging his car for one he's heard of over there. He thinks this one is going to be an expense to him pretty soon," explained Rowan's mother.

1

"Anybody go with him?" asked the father sharply.

Hannah shook her head.

"No, he said he wanted to go alone. I suggested that Mrs. Morton might like to go to see her daughter, but he said no, he didn't want to be bothered. He wanted to be alone when he decided about the car."

Charles looked at his wife thoughtfully.

"You're sure he didn't pick up Jason Whitney somewhere?"

"Why, of course not, Father. Jason Whitney works in the bank and would be at work in the morning."

"Jason Whitney doesn't work in the bank any more!"

"Father! You don't mean he's quit?"

"No, he was fired!"

"What for?" said Hannah, aghast.

"I don't know. I didn't ask, but nobody seems to know or I'm sure I would have been told. Everybody downtown is agog to tell everything they can, and make up the rest, but they didn't have any reason to offer. Of course there'll be plenty of hearsay by night. But anyway, even if Jason Whitney hadn't been fired, I wouldn't put it past him to take a day off if he wanted to. What time did Rowan leave?"

"Half past eight. But it isn't like you, Father, to be so hard on Jason. He's only a boy you know, younger by two years than Rowan."

"He's old enough to know better than most of the things he does," said Charles shutting his lips together with a snap. "And I don't like to see our Rowan traveling with him continually."

"Now, Father, you don't think a mere boy like that can hurt our Rowan!"

"Nobody's beyond hurting. Those things are subtle! Unconscious influence is sometimes the worst influence of all. It undermines faith! And, Hannah, I don't see Rowan going to church quite as regularly as he used to. Last Sunday morning, do you know where he was?"

"No," said Hannah with an undisturbed look in her eyes.

"Well, I do," said Charles sharply. "He was walking East on the highway with Jason Whitney, down toward that disreputable Rowley joint, and if our son has taken to playing pool and drinking on Sunday morning with that worthless Jason Whitney instead of going to church I'll find a way to stop it or I'll disown him!"

"Father! You know you wouldn't do that! Even God doesn't do that! Not to His real own children!"

Charles' face softened almost imperceptibly.

"Well, I don't expect it'll come to that, of course," he said firmly. "I expect to be able to stop this nonsense without any such strenuous methods. But I've got my eyes open and I'm not letting anything like that go by again."

"Father, remember he's over twenty-one! You wouldn't have stood any such high-handedness when you were his age. He's a lot like you, you know."

"I'll remember. Hannah, but I intend to stop his tagging around with Jason Whitney!"

Hannah was still for a minute, watching the firm set of her husband's lips, then she spoke again, this time very gently.

"I guess you know why he does it, don't you?"

Charles looked up sharply.

"Does what?"

"Goes around with Jason Whitney. You know why he does it, don't you?"

"Well, why?" His tone bore a hint of impatience.

"For Jason's sister's sake."

"Well, that's no reason at all! If Rowan isn't man enough to win a girl without tagging around with her spoiled baby-brother he'd better lose her. Joyce Whitney is all right. She's a sweet girl, and I'd like to see our boy marry her, if she'll have him, when he gets a little more stable, but I don't see his companioning with Jason. Joyce can't help what her brother is, I suppose, but a man doesn't have to marry all a girl's relations."

"You married mine!" said Hannah quietly. "Look at Cousin Ephraim, how you've been patient with him, and helped him out of the very gutter, time and again."

"Oh, well—!" said Charles impatiently, "that was different!"

"How was it different? And Charles, you must remember Joyce *loves* her brother. Her mother left him in her care when she died."

"Well, why didn't she bring him up right then?" snorted Charles.

"Now, Charles, you know she was barely a child herself, and after the second Mrs. Whitney came she hadn't a chance. She packed them both off to school. And you know what Jason's father is, Charles. *Hard!* That's what he is. Jason hasn't ever had any love nor trust such as we've given Rowan. Jason hasn't had half a chance!"

"Well, that may all be true," said Charles looking a bit ashamed, "but that's no reason why our boy should go wrong in consequence."

"I don't believe he did!" said Hannah determinedly. "I don't believe he was playing pool nor drinking on Sunday morning! I don't believe he even went into that Rowley place unless it was to drag Jason out!"

"Well, mebbe I don't either," owned Charles, "but I mean to do more than just believe. I mean to *know!* It's my business as a father to know."

"Well—I *know!*" said Hannah firmly.

Charles looked at her with understanding in his eyes. Then he came over and stooped his tall height to kiss her forehead.

"Good little mother!" he murmured, like a benediction.

The news reached the Whitney home, a big old-fashioned white farmhouse on the outskirts of town, about half past twelve, when the grocery boy delivered some orders that had been telephoned.

"Seen Jason anywhere? It's high time he was here ta lunch!" asked Aunt Libby, an elderly white woman whom the second Mrs. Whitney had rescued from the poorhouse and put to work in her kitchen. Some of the neighbors wondered if it might not have been easier for Aunt Libby if she had stayed in the poorhouse.

"Yeah. I seen him 'bout two hours ago walkin' down the pike toward Rowley's."

"Aw, he wouldn't a ben walkin' down thetaway in the middle of the mornin'," said Aunt Libby proudly. "Jason works in the bank now."

"No, he don't! Not no more!" imparted the grocery boy. "He got fired this mornin'. Didn'tya know?"

"Aw, get away with yer kiddin'!" snapped Aunt Libby loftily, and vanished down cellar with her arms full of fruit jars.

Nevertheless her eyes were anxious as she came in to place the hot dishes on the table and ring the lunch bell.

"Where's Jason?" asked his stepmother grimly turning her small sharp eyes to the window and looking down the road. "Are they keeping him again at the bank? I'll have to phone them. I can't have my meal hours upset this way. It gives me indigestion." She walked heavily over to the telephone.

Aunt Libby gave a frightened glance toward Joyce who was just coming in the room and tried to speak so that she would not hear, but Joyce's ears were keen, and she heard every word.

"Sammy Rounds from the grocery says he got fired this morning!"

Jason's stepmother set the phone down hard on the table where it lived and whirled around as if the matter were some fault of Aunt Libby's.

"Exactly what I *thought* would happen!" she charged, fixing the cringing woman with a cold steel eye. "But you should never allow the help from the grocery to gossip to you about the family for which you work."

"I didn't—I just ast him ef he'd seen Jason—!" quavered Aunt Libby.

"Exactly what I say. Gossiping with the help from the grocery!" thundered Mrs. Whitney. "Don't do it again! That'll do! We'll serve ourselves today. You may go to the kitchen."

Aunt Libby went meekly out with anxious tears slipping weakly down her withered cheeks. She was fond of Jason. She slipped him cookies on the sly when he was late to meals and would have lost out on food according to his stepmother. Sometimes she even dared to make chocolate cake when it wasn't ordered, always revealing her wickedness when the senior Mr. Whitney was present because she knew he liked chocolate cake, and Mrs. Whitney wouldn't dare reprove her for it before him.

When the kitchen door was shut Mrs. Whitney turned upon Jason's sister:

"Well," she said ominously, "the fully expected has come to pass! Your darling brother has been dismissed from the bank! I was sure it would happen!"

"Don't you think we had better wait until we hear Jason's version? The grocery boy may not know anything about it. It may not be true!" said Joyce trying to appear unconcerned, although her face was white with anxiety.

"Jason's version!" laughed the stepmother contemptuously, "that's it! That's always it! Listen to Jason's version! And of course Jason's version is perfectly smooth. Well, you know what your father will say to Jason when he comes home."

"Perhaps," said Joyce a wild fear in her eyes, and a quaver in her voice, "perhaps he won't come home!"

"Ha!" sneered Mrs. Whitney contemptuously. "Not he! He'll come home all right. He loves his ease too much to leave home. Where would he get his bread and butter? I declare if I had my way your father would send him packing.

It's high time he did something to prove he is a man. You've spoiled him outrageously, Joyce. Always helping him to hide things from his father, always using your own pocket money to pay his debts. If you keep that up I'm going to advise your father not to let you have spending money. You'll have to learn that your brother isn't a little darling child any longer for you to moon over. He's a wild irresponsible young man, trailing off with all sorts, gambling away what little money his father dares give him, and drinking with a lot of low-down gangsters. I declare I'm ashamed to go among my friends any more, the things they find to tell me about my stepson."

"Do you discuss Jason with your friends?" asked Joyce in a stricken voice.

"How can I help it?" declared the woman in a raucous voice. "They force it upon me, pitying me, and laughing about his sins, trying to make light of them!"

Joyce was very white, and was gripping her hands together to keep them from shaking.

"But—I thought—!" great tears came into her eyes and she struggled to keep them back. She turned away quickly to hide them before they should fall.

"Well, you thought what?"

"You -were just reproving Aunt Libby for even hearing something she couldn't help hearing."

"She's a servant! That's not at all the same thing. Besides, are you presuming to *dictate* to me? To *criticize* me? Sit down and eat your lunch. There's no need in stretching out the meal to last the day. I want Aunt Libby to clean the silver this afternoon. And if Jason doesn't come till after we're done he goes lunchless till supper! Do you understand? No slipping him choice morsels on the side. I'm not going to have Jason upset everything for me any longer. I've stood enough from him, and if he's determined to be a disgrace to the family, very well, let him stand a few things himself! Sit down!"

Joyce struggled with her anger and her tears and sat down. It seemed a physical impossibility to eat, but there was no advantage in openly flouting her stepmother. She had tried it before and only made matters worse.

Mrs. Whitney, unhindered by responses from Joyce, went back to her favorite theme, which today she was pleased to call "Jason's Version," and harped on it. She rehashed everything that Jason had done, good or bad, and scourged them equally, until at last poor Joyce arose from the table in desperation:

"If you had only tried to make Jason a little happy sometimes," she protested with a sob, "perhaps he might not have been so unsatisfactory."

"Happy!" snorted Mrs. Whitney. *"Happy!* Make that young scapegrace happy? I wonder how you would have me go about it? Set up a pool table in my parlor, and invite a lot of gangsters here? Let them slop beer all over my furniture and call in a mob of girls from the street to dance with him? That's his idea of happiness, and I'm sure I—"

But Joyce had hurried up to her own room, shut the door, and flung herself upon her knees beside her bed, sobbing as if her heart would break.

About that time Rose Allison, shy pretty daughter of the minister, received a telephone call from Jason Whitney.

They had been classmates together in High School, though never very intimate. Just the day before, however, they had met on the street, Rose in a new pink dimity that gave her a willowy grace, and threw a soft glow upon her rounded cheeks. Jason had paused to lift his hat on his way to the bank. He had always liked Rose. She looked up shyly, and then because there seemed nothing more to say beyond good morning, Jason made as if to move on. Suddenly Rose lifted her earnest blue eyes and spoke hurriedly:

"Oh, Jason, I wish you'd do something for me!" There was something so wistful about her eyes, and she seemed so young and sweet, Jason was touched.

"Sure, I will, Kid, what is it?" he answered without hesitation, thrilled in spite of himself that she should appeal to him.

"Why, you see we have a meeting at our church tomorrow night, and each of us pledged to get ten people to come. I've tried as hard as I can and I can't get but nine. Would you be my tenth?"

"Great Caesar's ghost, Rose! *Church? Me?* I never go to church! It isn't in my line."

"I know," she said a little sadly, "I wish you did. I often wonder why you don't. We have pleasant times in church. But couldn't you come this once? I don't know another soul to ask."

"What is it?" he asked, hedging, trying to think of some good excuse. "Just prayer meeting?"

"No," said Rose eagerly, "it's in the church, not the prayer meeting room, and they've got a wonderful speaker from the city. He sings, too. My cousin heard him and she says he's wonderful. Says he's a man's man. I think you would like him."

Jason stood there in the sunshine looking down at her beautiful little face and something melted in his heart. He had an impulse to try and keep that smile on her face and that light in her eyes, and before he realized what he was going to do he had said:

"Sure, Kid, I'll do it! If you want it so much, I'll be there! What time? Eight? I'll be there!" and the great light that blazed in her face thrilled his heart again and made him wonder as he went his way. Rose Allison! Who knew she was like that? And a faint wistfulness passed over his own soul. Suppose he had been different. Suppose he had gone to Sunday School and church and grown up in the society of the young people of the church, and been a companion of a girl like that! Suppose he had a right to take her places, and send her flowers and candy! Would that in any way satisfy the great restlessness and craving that stirred his soul from day to day, prodding him to first one depredation or transgression and then another, without so far any adequate return?

Well, this once he would keep his word to her and go, even if it was dry as dust. Of course he wouldn't find anything interesting in church. But he would go and watch her from afar and try to figure out why she had asked him. Was it just what she had said, that she wanted so many scalps to hang at her belt when the prayer meeting reckoning came, or had there been some faint personal interest in himself?

He thought about that as he walked on to the bank and the idea was not unpleasant. There had been something in her look, in her smile that had seemed warm and friendly, almost as if she liked him, when she had asked him. And that lovely flush that came in her cheeks as she raised her long lashes and looked up pleadingly at him! His heart thrilled again. At that moment he couldn't remember that anybody, except his sister Joyce, had ever taken a personal interest in him. Not any girl had ever looked at him like that. Oh, there had been girls, girls looking archly, girls all painted up, and trying to be as blasé as the boys, girls with hidden meanings in their glances, girls that stirred the worst in him. But never a girl with a guileless look like this, a look of real friendly liking, too, that she was neither trying to conceal nor use to attract him. And he liked it. It sent a sweet keen pain through his heart, and made him wish he were worthy of a look like that. Of course he wasn't, but it wouldn't do any harm to please her this once anyway.

When he called up, Rose hadn't any idea where he was calling from, and her heart gave a little flutter. He hadn't forgotten all about her then. He was probably going to make some excuse, but anyway, he had remembered.

"Is that you, Rose?" His voice sounded manly and respectful. "Say, Kid, I can't keep my promise to you after all. I meant to. Honest I did! But a little something happened at the bank today and I'm leaving, see?"

"Oh! *Jason!* I'm sorry!" Her voice was full of genuine dismay. "You—haven't—*done* anything—to make them—?" Her voice trailed off fearsomely.

"No, not that, Rose! That's the truth! I haven't done a thing! But the poor fishes *think* I have, and that's just as bad. And the worst of it is I can't tell what I know, and so they've pinned it on me. Now you'll probably hear to the contrary, but that's the truth. You can believe it or not. I can't blame you if you don't."

"I *believe* you, Jason!" said the grave sweet voice of the girl. "I'll *always* believe you!" She said it as if it were a vow.

"Thanks a lot!" said Jason struggling with a lump in his throat. "And I'll always tell you the truth!" he answered back. "That is—" he added, "if I ever see you again! I'm beating it, Kid! I'm not sure I'll ever come back!"

"Ohh—*Jason!*" There were almost tears in the voice. "Please don't do that! Please stay at home and clear things up!"

"I can't, Kid, they won't clear up for me, ever, I guess. Not here anyway! I can't get a square deal! And nobody cares, except my sister. Not *any*body!"

"*I* care!" said Rose suddenly, almost unexpectedly to herself. There was a sweet dignity in her words. "I care, and I believe you!"

Jason's voice husked with sudden tears:

"Thanks awfully, a lot, Rose!" His own voice was serious and earnest. "I'll not forget you said that. I'll never forget you cared and you believed me! Sometime maybe I'll turn out to be something after all, *just for that!* And I'm mighty sorry I can't keep my promise to you tonight! I meant to, I really did. You didn't think I did, but I did! But I'll be thinking of you tonight! I'll be all alone and I'll be thinking of you. And if the time ever comes when I'm fit to come back, I'll let you know. Maybe sometime I'll let you know anyway. I'll think a lot about you, Kid. Good bye—*Rose—!*"

Rose turned away from the telephone with her eyes full of tears and went up to her room, and another girl went down on her knees beside her bed to pray for Jason.

At six o'clock the minister came home to supper. There were baked potatoes, creamed codfish, baked sweet apples and ginger bread. As he passed the butter to Rose he looked at her speculatively.

"By the way, Rosie, didn't you go to school with Jason Whitney?"

Rose's face flamed suddenly and then grew white. She arose precipitately and took the bread plate to refill it, saying as she went into the kitchen, "Yes Father."

When Rose came back with the bread plate her hand was trembling but she managed to set the plate down without being noticed, and slipped into her seat again. Her mother was busy with the younger children and did not notice how white her face was.

"Well, he seems to be in trouble again," said her father, as he scooped out his baked potato and put butter on it.

"Trouble?" asked Rose, trying not to seem too interested.

"Yes, they tell me he's been dismissed from the bank. It does seem too bad for his sister's sake at least. She is so fond of him, and so worried about him! But I'm afraid he is worthless. Or, perhaps I had better say, weak. He will go in bad company. And he's innately an idler. How was he in school? Do you remember?"

Rose looked down at her plate thoughtfully, trying to think back, remembering painfully instances in which Jason had been up for discipline.

"Why, I always thought he was a great deal misunderstood," she said at last. "If anything wrong was done the teachers just naturally blamed it on him, and several times I happened to know Corey Watkins was really the one who did it."

"Corey Watkins? Why, I thought he was the most exemplary boy! I always heard him spoken of in that way."

"You would. He was slick! He'd put the other fellows up to things and then he'd look so smug! I used to wish sometimes the teacher had a chance to sit down where I did!"

"Well, that's interesting! So you thought Jason Whitney was misunderstood. You thought he was a pretty good boy, did you?" The minister was studying his young daughter's face interestedly.

Rose looked down at her plate thoughtfully, and then she lifted her eyes boldly.

"No, Father, he wasn't always good. He did a lot of things, things that were against rules, you know, and all that. But he never did *mean* things like some of the other boys; like putting a hornet in the teacher's desk so she would get stung on her nose; or like putting a little garter snake in her lunch basket. He did fix a hat in the window over her head once where it would fall on her head during class and make everybody laugh, and he drew a funny picture of her on the blackboard the time she fell down in a mud-puddle. He got blamed for the snake, and the hornet, and for breaking up Tommy Beldon's bicycle that Rich Howland threw over the bridge, and even for stealing the money for the teacher's Christmas present, but never did find out who threw the hat down on her head, nor even who drew the picture on the blackboard."

The minister grinned appreciatively.

"Well, but didn't they find out eventually that Jason hadn't stolen the money, or broken the bicycle? Surely he defended himself."

"No, he didn't!" said Rose. "I asked him once why he didn't tell the teacher he didn't do it, and he just looked black and said if they wanted to think such rotten things about him they could. He wasn't going to tell them differently. So—I—well *I* went and told the teacher! But she wouldn't believe me. She told me girls had no way of finding out those things. She said a nice girl didn't know what boys like Jason would do, and that I mustn't try to defend him when the whole school board had investigated and said he did it. She said people would think I had a crush on him."

Rose's cheeks were very red now, and her father looked at her in astonishment.

"You don't say! I didn't suppose you ever looked twice at the boy. You never told us anything about it."

"I didn't think it was anything you'd especially care about," said Rose, suddenly realizing that she had been speaking out of the depths of her heart.

The minister studied her a moment in silence and then he said:

"Well, I'm sure I'm very glad to hear it, Jason had a very nice mother, and his sister is a rare girl. Perhaps he has been misunderstood in some directions. I know his father is a rather hard man. But it's a pity Jason doesn't go in better company."

Rose gave attention to her dinner and said no more, but her father watched her thoughtfully for some minutes, and decided that he would try to cultivate Jason Whitney's acquaintance and see if his child was right in her judgments.

"Doesn't Corey Watkins work in the bank, too?" he suddenly asked. Rose looked up startled, remembering what Jason had said over the telephone! "Why, yes!" she said with troubled wonder. Then she started to say more but thought better of it. That talk on the telephone had been something confidential. She couldn't bring herself to mention it even to her beloved father. Not now, anyway. But she sat by the window for a long time in the darkness that night, thinking about Jason and wondering if Corey Watkins had anything to do with his dismissal from the bank.

When Jason didn't come home to supper that night Joyce excused herself from eating, saying she had a headache, and Mrs. Whitney read her husband, newly returned from a business trip to New Fork, a lecture on training his son. Joyce could hear their loud voices arguing on what should have been done in the past and what ought to be done in the future, each blaming the other for the son's failings, the father bitterly, the wife triumphantly. It wasn't her fault. It was his and Joyce's fault.

And she told him just what course he ought to pursue when Jason came home at midnight or later, *probably drunk!* Not that Jason had ever come home yet in that condition, though he had often brought a smell of liquor on his breath. But she was assuming that all bars would be down now that Jason had allowed himself to lose his job at the bank. Such a nice job! So respectable, and so in keeping with the family traditions! That was the final note of the tempest—a wail!

Then Joyce, even in her far bedroom, could hear her father at the telephone, storming at the president of the bank, denouncing him and all the Board of Trustees. Then bitterly denouncing his son, coming even to the threat of disowning him as a good-for-naught. It was all very terrible to Joyce who had wept most of the afternoon, watching constantly out the window down the road for the brother who did not come. The little brother who had been put in her childish care! Her head was aching and she was both chilled and feverish. The rasping voice of her irritated father, the father whose nature and temper Jason had inherited, finally drove her from the house. She wandered down to the old pasture out of sight of the house entirely, hovering near the edge of the wood in the shadow of the trees, sitting on a fallen log and watching the dying colors of the sunset in the west, and wishing sorrowfully that she and Jason might go home to God where Mother was and be out of it all.

She sat there until the crimson faded into purple, and the gold died out from the folds of purple and changed into thunder color, then soft pearly gray of luminous evening with a star set out to watch the shadows creep into night. And all about her the little creatures set up a symphony, crickets, and tree toads, and little stirring things, slipping away to their homes, and a far nightingale sang a sharp clear note above it all. Then an owl hooted tentatively over her head, and took a preliminary curve or two above her, and it seemed that all things sad were in the sights and sounds. Night seemed to have claimed her life. Oh, God, will You not hear my prayer for Jason?

Over at the Parsons' farm the house was dark later than usual. Joyce watched until she saw a light pierce keenly through the darkness where their kitchen window must be, and then another in the dining room. It was not so far across the two pastures. But there was no light in the old barn that was now a garage. She had seen no car lights enter the Parsons' driveway. Where was Rowan? Did he know what had come to Jason?

And over in the Parsons' dining room Charles Parsons was sitting down to the table again, and looking at the empty place where his son should be.

"Hasn't Rowan got back from Bainbridge yet?" he asked with open worry in his voice.

"Not yet," said Hannah trying to keep her voice calm.

He was silent during the first part of the meal, trouble in his eyes.

"Jason hasn't come home either," he said significantly at last. "His stepmother telephoned down to the drugstore, just now while I was getting my evening paper, to know if he was there. She doesn't hesitate to broadcast his absence."

"No, she wouldn't," said Hannah quietly.

Nothing more was said until Charles finished his supper and shoved his chair back.

"I wish you'd tell Rowan I want him to wait up for me if I'm not here when he comes. This is Building Association night, you know, and I may be late."

"You'll be careful what you say to Rowan, Charles?"

"Yes, I'll be careful!" and he stooped and kissed his gray-haired wife and patted her shoulder, a grave smile in his eyes as he went out.

CHAPTER II

In the back room of Rowley's place five men were eating
an uninviting supper, waited upon by an ill-kempt woman
with straggling gray hair and a sodden face. She was wearing
men's shoes and she shuffled noisily about the wooden floor
as if driven by an unseen overseer.

Two of the men were young with hard dare-devil faces.
The others looked old in crime and had cruel mouths and
eyes that flinched at nothing.

"Anything happened today, Nance?"

"Naw!"

"Nobody come in?"

"Cuppla parties fer gas. Nobody else, only ceptin' Jase."

"Jase ben here? Whad'd'ee want? He knowed we was
away."

"Didn't want nuthin'. Jes' come in ta make a phone call!"

Rowley dropped his knife harshly.

"Jase made a phone call here, an' you didn't tell me!"

"Well, I'm tellin' ya now, ain't I?"

Rowley frowned.

"Who'd'ee call?"

"Jes' some gal. He was callin' off a date."

"Fer when?"

"Fer tanight!"

"Oh, well, then that's okay! More cabbage, Nance, an' be
quick about it! We got a lot ta do yet. What time was Jase in
here?"

"I couldn't say," said the old woman drawing a bored sigh.
"I was takin' a nap an' I didn't look at the clock."

"Well, next time you looks at the clock, see, Nance!"

threatened Rowley with a grim glance. "An' Nance, ef any-body asks where we was tonight, y'ur ta say we come in early an' et supper an' went straight ta bed. An' don't ya say an-uther thing, no matter how hard they press ya. See?"

"Jes's'you say!" answered Nance sullenly, and shuffled away to wash her dishes.

The night was dark, for the little thread of a moon that had appeared timidly not far from the single star, had slipped away early, too young to stay up late, and the star too, had pulled a cloud over its face.

But Joyce still sat there on her log watching up the road.

She did not see the side door of her home open, nor hear her stepmother calling:

"Joyce! Joyce! Come here! I want you!"

She was watching up the road!

Where was Jason?

At last she rose and slowly made her way across the pasture lot, and through the Parsons' meadow, not sure even yet that she was going to dare to go to the door and speak to Hannah Parsons. She longed so for some human being to speak to who would understand her. And Hannah was gentle and kind. But then what would Hannah understand? She couldn't tell her fears for her brother.

Nevertheless she made her way across the dewy grass, finally arriving at the pasture bars, and stood there leaning against a post watching Hannah's light in the kitchen window, when Rowan's car drove in.

Joyce waited in the shadow till Rowan came out and started to close the garage doors. Then she called softly through the darkness:

"Rowan! Rowan!"

He dropped his hold on the door instantly and came over to her.

"Joyce? You here? What's the matter?" he asked anxiously. He knew it would be no trifle that would bring shy Joyce Whitney in search of him.

"Rowan, have you seen Jason?" she asked in a whisper. "I was hoping he had been with you. He hasn't been home all day." Joyce's heart was beating so fast it almost seemed to stifle her. All the pent-up anxiety of the whole day was in her voice, and her hand stole to rest at the base of her throbbing throat. She looked up eagerly into the young man's eyes. Her own were luminous with unshed tears even in the darkness, and suddenly Rowan let down the bars and came and stood beside her, one hand resting comfortingly on her shoulder.

"No, I have not seen him," said Rowan gravely, and his voice was gentle as one talks to a little child. Its sympathy broke down the girl's self-control and her lips trembled.

"They say he has lost his position in the bank," she hurried on with her explanation, "and you know what that would mean to him! He knows father wouldn't stand for his losing another job, and—he—maybe wouldn't dare—come home!"

And now the tears rained down.

She put her hands up to brush them excitedly away.

"I thought perhaps—you might know where I could look for him! Nobody at home will do anything. They are angry! Very angry! And Jason would do anything when he gets frantic! I'm so worried. If I could only get word to him I'd go away with him myself. I have a little money of my own that would keep us till we could find something to do. Oh, isn't there any place you could suggest where I could look for him?"

A look almost of fear passed over Rowan's face.

"You say he's lost his job at the bank. Are you sure?"

"I guess it's true all right. My stepmother telephoned to Mr. Goodright. I don't know why. She didn't tell me what he said. She was very angry. But I know Jason. He wouldn't stay to face a thing like that."

"No," said Rowan thoughtfully, "I don't suppose he would. But I didn't think Goodright would turn him away. I thought—"

"Oh, Jason was probably to blame," said Jason's sister breaking down utterly and hiding her face in her hands for an instant. When she lifted her face, the one star had done away with her clouds and twinkled over Joyce's tears as she looked at the young man bravely, trying to conquer the tremble in her voice. "But—he's *my brother!* And I have to stand by him! Oh, don't you know *any* place where I could look for him?"

"Yes!" said Rowan crisply, his lips set, his whole body tense. "I think I know one place where he would go. He told me once—never mind! I'll find him. I'll bring him back to you! Oh don't cry, *dear!*"

And suddenly his arms went round her, he drew her close to himself, and laid his face tenderly down on hers kissing her wet lashes. Then his warm eager lips were on her own sweet trembling mouth, and he whispered softly with his lips against her hair:

"You are *precious!*"

One long moment more he held her close as she yielded her weary weakness to his strong arms, and then he let her go.

"I must go!" he said. "There wouldn't be a minute to spare if he is gone where I think. But I'll bring him back! You can trust me! I've got to go in the house for something before I start. Where will you go? Will you come in with Mother?"

"Oh no," said Joyce drawing back, "I must get right home! I'll have plenty to face as it is. Nobody must know I came here."

"Of course not!" said Rowan. "I ought to have thought of that!"

A moment more and Joyce was fleeing back through the pasture, her eyes starry with hope, and Rowan's kiss stinging sweetly upon her lips. It was the first time Rowan had kissed her. He had kissed her and said she was precious! But she mustn't think about that now. She must only think about her brother. The kiss had been a sort of seal from Rowan that he would help her. It was almost sacred. She must not think of it in any other way—not now, anyway.

She could feel his strong arms about her yet, as her feet flew on across the rough pasture, going with swiftness where they would have had difficulty in walking in the day, the thrill of her spirit carrying her on as if she had wings.

And Rowan, slipping off his shoes, was stealing up the back stairs, hoping to get away without his mother's knowing. Strange he should expect to, seeing he had hardly ever succeeded in getting away with anything like that in his life! Mother Hannah was a canny woman and had sharp ears.

He had a little money up in his room. He would need it, if things fell out as he expected.

He got the few things he was after and stuffed them in his pockets. He was on his way down again, his shoes in his hand, when he saw his mother standing at the foot of the back stairs in a shaft of light that came from the dining room door. She was smiling up at him.

"Your dinner is ready, laddie!" she said gently, not to startle him.

"Thanks, Mother!" he smiled at her embarrassedly just as when he was a little boy about to steal away on some forbidden project. "But I've got to go somewhere right away. I can't stop for dinner. It's something important, Mother! You'll *have* to trust me!"

Various emotions played over Hannah Parsons' face in the darkness of the kitchen, but what she said was:

"All right! Here's a sandwich to take with you! Put your shoes on and I'll have it in a paper bag!"

She stepped to the table in full view of him as he sat on the lower step of the stairs putting on his shoes. She swept four slices of bread with butter, laid two slices of hot beef within, reached to the cupboard drawer for a paper bag, and added a thick slice of maple cake. All in one motion it seemed, and Rowan, even in his absorption and haste, took thought to be glad of the kind of mother he had. He knew her heart was bursting with anxiety, but she would not ask him where he was going. It was her way. He was not a child any more. He knew, too, that he had often given her cause for anxiety, Yet here she was like a brave soldier sending him off with food into the unknown.

"When will you be back, laddie?" she asked in a voice that tried to be cheery.

"I can't tell, Mother." Rowan finished tying his shoe and stood up to take the lunch she had prepared.

"I—asked because your father said he wanted to see you. He asked that you stay up for him. Something important, he said. You know it's his Building Association night!"

Rowan was at the door with his hand on the knob, and she was not following him but her eyes were straining him to her very soul with yearning to protect him. He read the look:

"I can't be sure," he explained hurriedly. "I'll come back as soon as I can, and you and Father can trust me, Mother!"

He turned his head to look back and add:

"Tell Father it's something he would do if he were in my place. It's something I *must* do, and I *—can't explain!* If I don't get back tonight tell him I'll see him in the morning!"

"All right, my son!" Hannah Parsons' voice kept steady till the end, and she stepped to the window and looked out into the darkness as the rusty old car rattled away into the night again. He hadn't exchanged his car! Probably he was disappointed! Oh, she prayed that this thing he had to do was not any childish vengeful thing about his car, not any fancied dishonesty that must be avenged, not any unreasoning idea of crude honor.

"And Lord, don't let him be going to Rowley's, or anything like that!" she prayed. And yet it was straight toward Rowley's that Rowan Parsons was driving.

A girl with dark hair blowing about her face, stood out on her own back steps and listened to the clatter of his old machine, and pushed from her any doubt or dismay that pressed on her mind when she saw which way he was going. Remembering those strong arms that had been about her, that kiss on her lips, she would not doubt him. She would not let herself even think that perhaps Rowan and Jason had been mixed up together somehow in something—it was all so vague—a thing built up of sneers and looks and half-formed sentences, like the whiffle of a whiplash in air, writhing for a victim. So her eyes grew starry in the dark again as she rested on the word of Rowan that he would bring back her brother.

Did either of the two watchers who listened to the fading clatter of the old car have hint of premonition that the lad had fared afar, and that it would be long before he returned? If so the shadow was not dark enough to dim their thought of how he had looked and what he had said as he left them, and their hearts swelled with joy in him in spite of all their fears.

The wind had risen and was driving swift purple clouds across the dark sky when Joyce went into the house, seeking to steal upstairs to her room without seeing anybody. But her stepmother's ears were keen, and her voice was sharp.

"Joyce! That you at last? Come in here. Your father wants to see you!"

Joyce came into the sitting room, smoothing her hair back from her white face. Out there on the steps in the night she could feel Rowan's arms about her protectingly, hear his voice telling her she was precious, but in here in the bright lights that her stepmother loved she was all alone and must protect herself. Perhaps God was here, too, somewhere, but He always seemed very far away in that atmosphere. She told herself that she had no reason to cringe this way before her stepmother, but still she could not get away from the horror of her words. They seemed like acid in a wound.

Her father sat there stern and angry. He regarded her as somehow to blame for the state of things that had descended upon their household again.

"Well," said Mrs. Whitney leaning back in her wide rocker and swaying luxuriously back and forth as if the present occasion were one she enjoyed, "I suppose you've been out hunting darling baby-brother again. What success did you have this time? Gallivanting around in the dark in the country when most respectable young women are in homes carefully protected, or out under proper escort! What you think of yourself I'm sure I don't know. What the neighbors will think will be plenty. Wait till I hear it served up to me tomorrow over the phone, or at my bridge club. But don't let me interrupt you. Do tell us all the latest news!"

Joyce had grown very white and angry now, and she could not trust herself to speak. She gave her stepmother one long haughty furious look, turned wild eyes of appeal toward the implacable father who sat there in his silent anger Then realizing how hopeless it would be to appeal to him, she turned on her heel, dashed up the stairs, and down the hall to her room, locking the door and dropping on her knees beside the open window:

"O God," she prayed, "don't let her ever find out where I went. Please, *please* don't!"

And then she heard her father's heavy footsteps coming up the stairs.

"Joyce!" he thundered at her door.

"Yes, Father," she answered bravely, opening her door.

It was dark in her room. Only the weird light of the night at her window showed the clouds whirling tempestuously across a midnight blue. He stood blinking in the doorway with the brilliant light of the hall chandelier behind him, looking strangely baffled for an instant.

"Where is the light switch?" he roared. "Why are you here in the dark?"

She did not answer, but switched on the light and stood frail and white facing him, her big tragic eyes pleading with him for mercy.

"Where is your brother?" he roared, made savage by the vision of her sorrowful face. "And why should you be acting as if you were on a stage playing a tragedy? Where is Jason, I say?"

"I don't know," she answered.

"When did you last see him?" His eyes fixed her icily as if he thought she might be tempted to conceal something.

"At breakfast."

"How did he act?"

"Just as usual. He seemed quite happy. Was whistling as he went away."

"And when did you hear about this—this—outrageous—!"

he paused for a word and ended in blowing his nose resoundingly.

"When he didn't come home to lunch," answered Joyce as steadily as she could. "Aunt Libby asked the grocery boy if he had seen him, and he said no, and told her he wasn't at the bank anymore."

"And didn't you *do* anything about it? How did you know the grocery boy knew?"

"Mother called up the bank. She didn't tell me what they said."

Joyce turned slightly away from the merciless glance in her father's bitter eyes, and saw the star, shining amid the fitful clouds. It quieted her to know that somewhere out there was Rowan hunting for Jason. She couldn't tell her father that. It would only make him more angry. He resented Rowan. He tried to make out that it was Rowan's fault that Jason went with a lot of "rough-scuff" as he called the Rowley crowd. But it comforted her to know that Rowan was looking for him. And it comforted her to remember that he had told her she was precious, only she hurriedly tucked the thought far back in her mind lest her father should hunt it out of her —he had such a way of piercing the soul of his children with scathing words!

"Was there—any trouble—at breakfast—?" he began hesitantly and after a pause, speaking in a lower tone. "Did Jason have any altercations—with—" he cast a glance toward the head of the stairs—"that is—I mean, did anything happen—at breakfast?"

"No," said Joyce turning a pitying glance back at her father. Did he, too, feel those terrible family arguments, the sharp, barbed tongue of the woman whom he had married— or did he think it was all his children's fault? She looked speculatively at his bitter eyes and sour mouth. It seemed as if she faintly remembered other days in her childhood when those eyes were merry, not bitter, and the mouth pleasant and laughing. Always he had been a stern disciplinarian, but there had been times in her little girlhood when she loved her father greatly, and when they had beautiful hours together. But that was when her own mother was living.

She went a little nearer, feeling a sudden pity for him, which of course she must not express.

"No, Father," she said gently, "there was no unpleasantness at all. Everything was quite cheerful, and Jason went off in a good mood."

"And you have no idea what it's all about? You can't think of anywhere he could be, or why he should go off like this?"

"Mr. Whitney!" called his wife from the foot of the stairs. Her voice was like a fire siren, insistent, demanding, persistent, and she always called him "Mr. Whitney" when she knew his children were listening. It somehow seemed to give her the upper hand over the whole family.

"Why are you staying up there so long when you know I want to talk to you? Mr. Whitney!"

The father adjusted his voice to sternness.

"You say you don't know why he should be asked to resign his position, Joyce? Well, I'm quite sure it must have been his fault somehow, whatever the cause. It comes down to the same thing. You have so pampered him and petted him, so humored his every wish, that he is just a worthless lazy nobody. It is really all your fault! It only goes to show what a thankless task it is to rear children!" He turned and walked loudly downstairs, the noise of his footsteps blending with his wife's voluble words as he reached the floor below, and Joyce sank down by the window again. She drooped her head on her arms on the window sill, and suddenly remembered Rowan's arms about her and his lips kissing away her tears. Then something glad and new began to mingle with her prayers.

Over across the pastures Hannah Parsons got out the hardest task she could find and sat down to work late. She always did that when there was hard sailing ahead—something to fear or something to bear—she looked for the hardest task she could find and worked at it with all her might. It seemed to make the time go faster.

So now in her big rocker by the sitting room table, she sat and darned a lot of Rowan's old socks that she had almost decided were not worth darning. She had indeed considered cutting them up for polishing cloths.

But instead she set delicate, careful stitches as fine as weaving, that would not have hurt a baby's sensitive skin, and Rowan was no baby. She tried to smile as she darned away, thread after thread, clipping the ends off with her sharp scissors, inserting her capable hard-worked hand in the sock. No darning balls for her! She tried to think how pleased Rowan would be to have that particular pair of socks with the blue and white clocks resurrected. He had been sorry when they wore out. He liked them. She tried not to remember the glint of determination, the look of a knight about to go on a pilgrimage, in Rowan's eyes when he had told her this errand of his was important. Perhaps it was important. She longed with all her heart that her son should be a true knight and go on the right kind of errands, but he was young enough and eager enough to mistake values, and to think a matter of vindicating his own or some friend's rights a sufficient cause for sacrifice. She hoped and prayed that Rowan was not just going off on some hot-headed tangent. She must believe in him. When he looked like that and said she could trust him, she had always been justified in believing in him. Oh, she must believe in him! She could not sit here quietly and wait unless she did. There had been a noble look in his eyes when he went out, a look like his father when he was young!

Oh, she must not think about him that way. There was a tear streaking down, splashing on her glasses and obstructing her view. She could not sew and cry. Darning was very delicate work.

She took her glasses off and smiled across at the cat on its cushion as if the cat were a lady come to call, just to show herself she was not crying. She wiped off the splash on her cheeks and gave a quick dab at her eyes before she readjusted her glasses and took up her darning again.

Now, she must think about something else. She would turn her thoughts to Myra, her other child. Married these six years now and gone to live in a city a hundred miles away. Of course Hannah wasn't very happy about that either, because she had never fully trusted the man whom Myra married. And their little girl, now five years old, looked like him, which made it hard. Hannah had never been able to understand why Myra liked Mark Townsend. He wasn't their kind. A hard, compact man with shrewd eyes and a thin little tight mouth that could shut like a rat's. Of course she had never breathed that to Myra. She hadn't dared. For when she came out of her delusion and discovered that Myra had really fallen for this trig uninteresting little man with the hay-colored hair and the sharp sandy bristles on his upper lip, the marriage was a foregone conclusion, and she didn't want to say anything that she might have to live down the rest of her life. So she had shut her lips and lived through the wedding, and the going away, and had tried to keep the house cheery for Father and Rowan after her girl was gone. But it had been hard work, and many a night her pillow had been wet with slow silent tears, long after her dear Charles was sleeping soundly.

She hadn't even breathed her distrust to Charles after the first dismayed questionings. She hadn't been quite sure how he felt about it. He never said much, after that first hesitant sentence when they were alone.

"Seems as if that wasn't quite what we had expected for her, was it, Hannah? But I guess it must be all right. She seems to be set on it."

And Hannah had sighed and said, "Well, I don't know. I sometimes wonder whether the child isn't just in love with being in love, and having a home of her own. It doesn't seem possible she could love him, does it? She is such a lovely little thing, and he seems so much too old for her; though he really isn't, of course, in years."

"Well," said Charles with a companion sigh, "I suppose your folks said that about me when you were married!"

"They certainly did not!" flashed Hannah, and then laughed.

"Well, you know we think pretty much of our one girl!" said Charles, and sighed again. "But she seems happy. I guess it's all right."

So Hannah had made the best of her sorrow and done her weeping silently at night when it wouldn't hurt her man. But she had not ceased to miss her bright-haired girl who had been always singing around the house.

They didn't come home much after the marriage, only a day now and then. And Hannah always fancied that Myra had a nervous look whenever Mark was around, a fear lest she would offend him and call down upon herself a reprimand before them all. And the little granddaughter hadn't been much satisfaction, either. Her father seemed to own her so thoroughly that there was no room for any grandparents, not even in the ordinary way. If she gave her a cookie he would always turn out to be around and say, "Now, Ollie, you know your mother doesn't allow you to eat between meals!" Ollie! Such a silly name! But of course it was after his sister who died, and it was his child. He had a right to call her Pickles if he wanted to, she supposed. *Olive!* As if she were something to eat.

And presently Olive took on his attitude toward her grandmother and began answering her back, always belligerently. "You aren't my mother. My father don't want you to tell me

what I should do!" She wasn't even kissable! And Myra had
been so sweet and dear. When Hannah showed her affection
by a kiss the child would jerk away, and rub off the kiss
hard, with her fat hand, and say: "My daddy don't allow me
to be kissed!" And sometimes she would stick out her tongue
at her grandmother.

Hannah thought of Myra, her own five-year-old, sitting beside her there in her little chair with her own sewing, darning
a doll's diminutive sock. Sitting in the little rush-bottomed
chair, always wanting to do just what Mother was doing.
Charles had made her a little ironing board and bought her a
tiny iron, and a stove and dishes. How Charles loved to bring
things home for Myra! Her little Myra sitting in the little
chair, that was now up in the attic.

She had brought it down for Olive once, and the child
seemed to be almost pleased with it. But when she offered to
let her put it in the car and take it home with her Mark had
interposed. He said he didn't think it was worth taking, and
called her attention to a rush that was breaking. He said Ollie
had plenty of little chairs at home. And when the Grandmother suggested that it used to belong to the child's mother,
Mark only laughed and said they didn't want to train up their
child to be sentimental.

Suddenly Hannah felt another tear stealing down her cheek
and splashing on her glasses, and this wouldn't do at all. She
took off her glasses quickly and wiped them, and then laid
down her work while she went around briskly getting out
milk and bread to make a little milk toast and have it hot and
ready when Charles came in. It was almost time for him to
arrive. Eleven o'clock! He was usually home before that even
on Building Association nights. He liked a little bite to eat
when he was tired. He loved milk toast with plenty of butter,
piping hot, and maybe a glass of milk to drink along with it.
He hadn't eaten much supper. He had been worried about
Rowan, she could see.

And then she heard Charles coming up the front walk.
Dick Stebbins usually brought him home. She could hear the
car starting on again toward the Stebbins' farm.

She swept aside her darning, fixed a place at the table and
had it all ready for Charles when he came in.

He smiled at her and sat down.

"That looks good," he said, and then his eyes swept the
room.

"Rowan got back?"

"Yes, he got back," she said, "but he had to go again."

"Go again!" said Rowan's father blankly. "Where did he go?"

"Why, I don't know. He said he hadn't a minute to talk. But he said he would be back as soon as he could."

She spoke cheerfully, as if she were quite convinced there was nothing to worry about, but Charles paused in his eating and looked at her startled.

"But I don't understand, Hannah. Didn't you make him realize that I wanted to see him tonight, no matter how late it was?"

"Yes," said Hannah, "I told him, but he said tell you this was something you would do if you were in his place. I gathered that he felt it was something he was sure you would approve and want him to do."

"But I don't understand. Didn't he tell you what it was? Didn't he explain at all?"

"He said he couldn't, Charles. But— He said I could trust him! He said *we* could trust him. And he said if he didn't get back tonight he would see you in the morning."

Charles sat back and stared across the room, slowly sifting over what she had said. Then he studied the sweet, tired face of his wife, and suddenly his stern face broke into a wan smile.

"Well then, Hannah, I guess that's what we've got to do. I guess there isn't anything to do but trust our boy. And I'm pretty sure he can be trusted. He's been a good boy, a fairly good boy. Better than most! And we can't hamper our children too much, you know."

He finished with a sigh and went back to his toast, eating slowly, thoughtfully.

Just before they went up to bed he asked:

"You didn't see Jason about anywhere? He wasn't with Rowan when he went away?"

"Oh, no!" said Hannah with relief in her tone. "No, I'm quite sure of that. I noticed when he drove out the drive and there was only one in the car."

"He went in his car? The new one?"

"No, it was the old one, I think. It sounded just like it. But he was in such a hurry I didn't think to ask him about the car."

They went up to bed and said no more about it, and presently they knelt together to pray, hand in hand, and then lay down to sleep. And soon each thought the other was asleep, yet each was listening, hoping, alert for every car that passed on the highway, alive to every sound in the quiet stillness of their home.

And once, a little while before the dawn, they heard a car go speeding by at a tremendous pace, coming on with a roar, and flashing past and dying away in the distance. Both pairs of eyes flew silently open but there were no lights on that car! Strange! *No lights* on a dark night! Had they dreamed it?

And when the morning dawned at last it found them dozing off, but rousing at a knock at the door. Charles got up and put his head out of the window, mortified to find it a half hour later than his usual rising time.

"I thought I'd just stop by and tell ya the news," said a neighbor. "The bank was broken into last night and the watchman was found bound and gagged, and badly bruised from beating. They don't know if he will live. It was Sam Paisley, you know. The bugglers got away but they're after them. It might be that Rowley crowd you know. Is Rowan about? I thought he'd like to know."

"Why, no," said Rowan's father, swallowing hard, "Rowan's away!" a great fear gripped his heart. "On business!" he added. "I'm not sure what time he'll be home. Thank you for stopping! That's bad news. I'll have to get dressed and go down to see if there is anything I can do to help. Did they get much from the bank?"

"Don't know yet. They've gone after Mr. Goodright and the cashier. Well, I'll be getting on. They wanted me to stop and see if Jason Whitney is home yet!"

The neighbor passed on his way and Charles Parsons turned from the window and faced Hannah. Then each saw the stark question in one another's eyes, and each instantly smiled and flouted it with the smile.

Charles dressed rapidly, and Hannah hurried down and got a cup of coffee ready.

Charles drank it hastily and then turned to look back as he went out.

"Of course you understand, Hannah, that I trust Rowan utterly!" he said with one of his rare smiles.

"Of course!" said Hannah radiantly. *"Of course!"*

CHAPTER III

Si Aldrich, the neighbor bearing news of the bank robbery, went on to the Whitney farm.

Aunt Libby with a wet dishcloth in one hand opened the door, with Nathan Whitney standing just behind her in the shadows of the wide hall that ran from the front to the back of the house. Nathan's hair was on end and his face was bristling with belligerence, his eyes ready to do battle at the slightest provocation.

"Jason about anywhere, Aunt Libby?" asked Si, his keen little eyes peering into the shadows behind her and unexpectedly sighting Nathan Whitney.

Not that it bothered him any. Si rather relished an encounter with Nathan, especially under the circumstances, being the bearer of news that Nathan Whitney couldn't likely have heard yet.

Aunt Libby looked frightened and grasped the doorknob so hard with the hand that held the wet dishcloth that a stream of gray water dripped down from it to the neat linoleum.

"Why—n-no—!" she started to say, but Nathan brushed her aside like a fragment.

"Get to your kitchen, Aunt Libby!" he commanded. "Your bacon's burning! Can't you smell it?"

Aunt Libby cast a frightened look at Nathan, and a furtive one at Si, and scuttled away, not too far inside the kitchen door, lest she couldn't hear. Having nothing of her own she had set her starved little heart's love upon Jason, and now she felt it in her bones that Jason was in some kind of peril. Jason would have been surprised if he could have known

29

how Aunt Libby's heart yearned over him with all the love that would have been showered upon her own son if she had had one. She was trembling from head to foot, and the bacon burned on irreparably while she listened at the crack of the kitchen door.

"Mornin', Nate," grinned Si affably, twinkling his inquisitive little eyes innocently. "Jase up yet, ur am I too early?"

Nathan Whitney came and stood in the doorway, eyeing the early visitor suspiciously.

"Jason is away!" he said with dignity. "He is out of town!" he added as if to make the matter stronger. There was challenge in the very set of his under jaw and the glint of his stern eye.

Si's eyes came to a quick focus on the old man's face.

"Oh, *away*, is he? Out of town! You don't say! Well, now that's too bad! I just stepped up to tell him the news. if he hadn't heard it a'ready. I thought he might like to join in the search." He fixed his victim with a glance like a thin gimlet, and had the satisfaction of seeing him squirm.

"Jason went away yesterday morning to look for another position He's decided not to stay any longer with the bank," barked Jason's father "Even if he were home he wouldn't have time to join in any search. What's lost now? Widow Lamb's spotted cow, or has Riley Morton's pig run away again? I declare, if folks can't look after their own property and provide suitable fences I don't see why the whole neighborhood should be upset hunting for them."

"Wal I ain't heard of any of those events happenin' yet taday," said Si genially, "I was speakin' of the search fer the bank robbers!"

"Bank robbers!" Nathan Whitney's voice was suddenly weak and his face paled.

Si lost nothing of his expression.

"It's liable to be a murder case as well, too, if Sam Paisley don't come to before long When I left he was in a pretty bad way. Two doctors an' the 'pothecary workin' over him, ta say nothin' of the gym teacher down ta the school. They was the first on the scene D'ya mean ta say ya didn't hear the alarm? They rung it good an' loud!"

"I heard the fire alarm if that's what you mean," said Nathan, trying to look dignified and injured, "but I don't belong to the fire company. I looked out of the window but couldn't see a fire so why should I bother?"

"It wa'n't the fire alarm," said Si gustily, "that was the buggler alarm. Six blows! Don't ya mind? Wa'n't you at the last town meetin' when they agreed on the signals? Three on the south side an' two up here fer fire, four fer the east side includin' the fact'ry, five fer a drownin', six fer bugglery, and seven fer a lost child! And it was six good clear blows. But mebbe the wind was agin ya so ya couldn't hear."

"What time was it?"

Nathan Whitney was out on the porch now looking anxiously down the road toward the village, paling at the thought of what this might mean to his son.

" 'Long 'bout three ta four o'clock, I reckon, near's they cun tell. It was the Forbes brothers with their milk truck discovered it fust. They was drivin' inta town with a load of milk an' see Sam Paisley layin' there outside the bank right on his beat afront of the bank, with a dirty rag in his beak, a hole bashed in the back of his head, an' all trussed up like a Chrismus turkey. They think he mebbe hed some knockout drops too, he's sa long comin' to. Course he might be dead by this time. I didn't stay ta see. They wanted me ta get recruits fer the search. One thing they know, they cummed up this road. I heard 'em, but 'course I didn't know yet what had happened, ur I'd a stopped 'em. I always keep my ole gun loaded, an' anythin' suspicious I shoots! I don't care what 'tis, pig ur cow ur human, ef they's suspicious I shoots. Course I don't shoot ta kill. I shoots at their feet so they can't git away. Wal—you say Jason ain't about?"

He punctuated his question with a last keen look. He wanted to see Nathan Whitney squirm again. But Nathan Whitney didn't squirm twice, not for the same inquisitor.

"No," he said loftily, "Jason has gone seeking a position."

This was the statement he had agreed with himself in the wakeful watches of the night to give out in case Jason did not arrive at home in the morning. He had not known then how necessary it was going to become before morning was even well started on its way to a day.

The boring eyes still pierced his visage, but got no farther than the glint in Nathan's eyes.

"H'm! When d'ya 'xpec' him back?"

"Well, I'm not sure. It might be several days, or it might be even weeks. He has been wanting to take a little trip for some time, and of course as I said he is hunting the right kind of a job. He won't come back till he finds it, that's sure."

"H'm! Where's 'e gone?"

"A number of places," said Jason's father growing more haughty. "He'll probably bring up in New York before he gets back."

"H'm! N'York! Wal, that's a pity. Jason allus was good on a hunt. Ya might like ta wire him. Mebbe he'd come home sooner."

Si laughed, but there was a narrow, sinister look in his small eyes, and Nathan Whitney was both angry and frightened.

"Yes? Well," said Jason's father, "I guess you'll have to get along without my son this morning. Meantime, I guess I'd better get down and see just what has been happening anyway. Thanks for coming by, Si! See you again!" and Nathan Whitney backed into his hall and shut the door with a slam!

Si stood for several seconds staring thoughtfully at the closed door, a speculative twinkle growing in his little eyes. Then he said to himself slowly, in an undertone that could well have been heard inside the pantry window if one had been listening:

"Wal, I wunner what he would say ef he knew Jason's notebook was found on the floor in front of the busted safe? I wunner!" Then he turned and with leisurely gait marched down the road to the next farm to give the news and gather more facts.

Aunt Libby stood at the pantry window trembling so that she couldn't cut the bread. Instead she cut her finger and had to hurry into the kitchen and tie it up. Her lips were quite white as she tore a bit of linen rag from the edge of an old napkin in the dresser-drawer. Anybody who loved her would have been startled and maybe a bit frightened at her appearance. But there was no one who loved her, so her faintness passed, and she brushed the tears away from her eyes shamedly, washed her hands at the sink, and went back to cut the bread. But she could not forget those awful words that she had heard. They had found Jason's notebook in front of the safe that had been blown open!

As the morning went on and Aunt Libby stumbled about through her duties, the fear grew. Various rumors drifted back to the farm. Some said it was only a record of game scores from Rowley's, that notebook, and others—the grocery boy told Aunt Libby this in a hoarse whisper before he darted off with his empty basket—others hinted that it contained the serial numbers of valued papers and bonds that had been stolen from the safe!

Aunt Libby knew very little about financial matters, but her heart sensed there was something serious here, and she went about with ghastly face and a mind far from her work, wiping a furtive tear now and then. Other things besides bacon burned; these she took hastily as fast as it happened and buried them behind the old barn where not even the most industrious hen could ever scratch them up.

It was the lord of the manor himself who carried the news to his women folks. Breakfast was by no means a pleasant feast that morning when the lady of the house at last came down. Joyce, white and languid with dark circles under her eyes followed, reluctantly, and only on demand of her roaring father who would not be gainsayed.

While Nathan demanded bacon and roared at poor Aunt Libby, he told them the news. And while he was telling, and his wife was stridently saying it was no more than she expected, and that of course now everybody would say that Jason had broken into the bank for revenge, and his father was to blame for letting him go into a bank when he knew his capacity for getting into trouble, Joyce was weeping silently lifting a white stricken face in horror at her father's news. Then old Libby came trembling in with fresh bacon that was hardly cooked enough, and Nathan Whitney thundered his fist down on the table in his anger with such energy that the dishes rattled. Aunt Libby dropped the platter, bacon and all, and fled weeping to the kitchen for a brush and pan to take it up. The platter happened to be one of the second Mrs. Whitney's few wedding presents, which did not add to the pleasure of the scene, and Nathan Whitney arose thunderously and left his breakfast untasted, saying it was all everybody's fault but his, that this was anything but a happy home, and stamped into the hall to get his hat.

He came back before his wife had turned upon his daughter to continue the strife and gave stern orders as to how to answer any people who might come snooping around to question. They were to say that Jason had gone away indefinitely to hunt another job, probably in New York, and they were not to say *anything else!* Then he marched grimly away and Mrs. Whitney turned to deal with Joyce, reproaching her for carrying a long face and being the cause of her father's outbreak.

"Such children!" she said in a contemptuous tone. "No wonder your poor father is prematurely gray! Only two years my senior, and look at *my* hair!" she preened herself.

But then she discovered that Joyce had fled.

Meanwhile over across the meadows Hannah Parsons was down upon her knees beside her bed praying for her boy, and taking confidence about him from her Heavenly Father as she looked into His face and trusted everything to His care. She just handed it over deliberately, as something that she could do nothing about; knowing her Lord would work it out in the right way.

Then she arose with a quiet peace upon her face and went to Rowan's room to take account of stock and put everything in place for the day. Guessing there would be questionings later, perhaps investigations, she yet went about her work, putting her house in its best order, and taking her routine work as usual. She dared not think much about Rowan, only to trust him with God, keeping her eyes constantly above.

By and by when, or *if*, they came to ask about Rowan what was she to say? She sensed that there was more behind his going than he had said. She knew he trusted her not to talk. But if Rowan had guessed that a crime was to be perpetrated that night what would he have wanted her to say about his departure? Ah! she must rather ask herself, what would God want her to say? And she could trust God to teach her what to say. She must speak nothing but the truth of course, yet what was there to say?

And they came, later in the morning. The sheriff, apologetically, lifting his old felt hat and bowing respectfully to Hannah.

But there weren't many questions.

Merely the hour that Rowan had gone away, and whether he had a gun, and might they go up in his room and look around?

They were polite and kindly with it all. They were neighbors she had known for years. They spoke as if it were a mere form they were going through. They said Rowan's father had told them to come and look around. But something clutched at Hannah's heart, something seemed grasping her throat, and she couldn't get a deep breath. She answered their questions with serenity and wondered how she was able to go through with it. They went upstairs and looked around, but they didn't stay long. Hannah gave them a swift survey as they came down. They explained that they were looking for a certain kind of gun. Was she sure Rowan had no gun? And they looked at her sharply as she answered.

But Hannah could smile at that.

No, he never had a gun. She knew he wanted one, but for her sake he didn't get it. She was afraid of guns. Guns went off when you didn't expect them to and she didn't like to have them about. They had never had a gun in the house except an old revolutionary one that Charles' great-great grandfather had used in the war. It was up in the attic behind a trunk. Would they like her to get it?

They smiled sheepishly and went out to look around in the garage. They stopped again at the door to apologize again. They said Charles had suggested that they come and look, but Hannah knew that somebody else must have suggested first that there was possible reason for looking, or Charles never would have said it. The very attitude of the sheriff implied that! Someone, perhaps all of them, had suspected Rowan, her boy, of complicity in this awful deed, which would perhaps turn out to be murder!

"Father in Heaven, I'm putting my trust in You!" breathed Hannah softly in her heart, and turned her quiet eyes on the man who questioned her.

"No, Mr. Turner, I'm quite sure Rowan never had a gun hidden in the garage nor anywhere else. You are welcome to search all you want to."

Soon after they were gone the telephone rang. It was Charles.

"That you, Mother? Did Hop Turner come over there to look around?"

"Yes," said Hannah. "They've just gone."

"Well, you needn't worry. I wanted them to look around for themselves. I knew you'd understand. I tried to let you know they were coming, but something came up here so that I couldn't telephone any sooner. Sorry you had to be worried."

"I wasn't worried, Father." Her voice was strong and cheery.

"That's right. That's my girl!" said Charles with relief in his voice. "I knew I could trust you not to fret. You see, this thing is from the Lord somehow, and we've got to go through it triumphantly. I suppose it's one of our testings."

"Yes, Father, I thought about that," said Hannah. "Are you all right?"

"Yes, I'm all right!" was the hearty response. "But I've got to stay around here most of the day, and maybe into the night awhile. Being a director of the bank isn't all it's cracked up to be. They've been pretty hard hit."

"Oh, you mean money!" said Hannah in a tone as if that meant very little now. "You mean you may have to give up everything we own? But I won't mind that!"

"Well, Hannah, it may not come to that! But, of course, if it did, I know you'd take it like a soldier. However, we haven't gone as far as that. We've got to see how things come out. We've got to catch the thieves first. But I can't talk over the telephone. You just pray, Hannah. Any word from Rowan yet?"

"No," confidently.

"Well, that's all right," said Charles. "He'll come sooner or later and have an explanation. Now, you take things easy, Hannah. I may not be home till late tonight I'll take a bite down at the grocery. We're going over books and things."

"Books?" said Hannah startled. "Is there something wrong with the books?"

"We're making sure about everything, Hannah. Now, don't you go to getting up things to worry about."

"No, I won't!" said Hannah. "But Charles, you think maybe—?" Her voice trailed off in a worried little sigh.

"No, I don't think anything except that it's all going to be right in His good time. Now, Hannah you pray!"

Hannah turned from the instrument with a sigh and looked about her. Something she must do to keep her hands busy and her mind from dwelling on possibilities. She could go through the trunks in the attic, of course, and sort out things to send to Myra. Or she could clean the cellar. That was an idea. Clean the cellar!

She took three steps toward the cellar door and paused. Suppose those men should come back and find her cleaning the cellar! Might they not suspect her of clearing out something that she didn't want seen? No, best leave everything just as it was. It would be wisest to be seen going about her daily avocations as if nothing had happened. There were the yellow tomatoes glowing on the vines waiting to be picked! This would be the very day to make her yellow tomato preserves! Of course she hadn't intended to do it for three or four days yet, till she got her shelves cleaned in the cellar to receive them, but yellow tomato preserves were the very thing to be made today while her mind was upset. They required attention and skill and would be quite disarming if anyone came in. Hannah hated the thought of prying neighbors asking questions. She desired to keep her affairs to herself, and whatever anxieties she might have to bear, to bear them unannounced.

So she took her sunbonnet and a bright new preserving kettle and went to the garden, carrying a little wooden stool along to sit on as she picked down the row.

Down across the hollow in full sight of the tomato patch lived Widow Lamb, in a ramshackle cabin of three rooms and a leaky roof. Her cow had a habit of getting into the corn field and feasting now and then, just as Widow Lamb had a habit of getting into her neighbor's affairs and feasting her dreary soul on rare tidbits that were not meant for her.

And it wasn't long before Widow Lamb came over.

Hannah Parsons had filled two large baskets with the clear yellow globules, and taken them into the kitchen. She had washed them and put a great kettle full of them over the fire, and on the big white polished kitchen table she had spread out the other ingredients for her preserves. The big gray sugar jar, the ginger jar, the spices, the measuring cups and spoons, were all there at hand, and ranged along the wide oilcloth-covered shelf that ran from sink to stove were shining jars, and rings and covers lying in bowls of hot water; two long silver spoons to put in the jars so the hot stuff wouldn't break the jars when it was poured in, soup plates to put beneath the jars lest a drop should be spilled, though Hannah Parsons never spilled a drop when she was filling her jars. Everything was ready when that knock came at the door, and Hannah started a little. She had been almost happy for the moment thinking of everything she would need, trying to keep her mind busy so she wouldn't have to remember the robbery, and Rowan, her boy, away—where?

But instantly it all came back of course. Who was this now? The sheriff again? Or perhaps some other official to question her?

But she wiped her hands on the roller towel and tried to walk calmly to the door, though her heart was beating wildly. One thing she had resolved, that whoever came or whatever she was asked, she would not appear frightened. She would present to her suspicious public, if that was really what they were, a front of absolute trust in her son. And nobody, just *no*body should be able to make her wince or flinch. God was over all this and it was going to be made plain, and Rowan was going to be justified before his home town some time— God's time.

So she put a comfortable smile upon her face and opened the door. It was a relief to see only Widow Lamb. Of course it had been inevitable that she would come. Nothing grave or gay, of sickness or sorrow or festive occasion had passed without a visit of investigation from Mrs. Lamb.

"Good morning," she said, her quick little eyes darting about the big inviting kitchen, and searching the shadowy doorway of the dining room. "I've just run up to see if I could borrow a sprig of parsley for my soup. Mine didn't do so well this summer, and the last of it is gone. Somehow I don't think soup is so tasty without parsley."

"Of course!" said Hannah Parsons heartily. "Come right in and sit down. I have some fresh picked in my ice box, just brought it in a few minutes ago."

She set forth a rush-bottomed chair and was conscious as she stepped into her pantry to get the parsley, that her visitor went to the chair by way of the side of the kitchen next to the dining room, and paused long enough by the doorway to scan that room with a quick glance. Hannah was glad she had set the table for three as usual, in spite of the fact that she dared not hope that Rowan would be back for lunch. She knew her caller would take that in, and she could see it in her eyes that she had, as she came back with the parsley. Mrs. Lamb settled down in the chair and prepared to have a chat.

"What you doing?" she asked peering inquisitively toward the table, and then rising and lifting the lid of the preserve kettle to look within. "My goodness. Yellow tomats already? Why, I didn't know they were ripe enough yet for preserving."

"Yes," said Hannah with satisfaction, "they were lovely. I thought I'd get at it early. There's always so much pickling and preserving this time of year."

The guest stepped over to the table and picked up a plump yellow tomato.

"Seems 'zif they might a waited a wee bit, just a few days yet," she said, studying Hannah Parsons' face.

"Well, perhaps they might," agreed Hannah presently, "but it suited me to do them today so I picked them."

"You're making an awful lot," said the visitor.

"Yes, I usually make a good deal. Rowan is very fond of them, and his father isn't far behind in the amount he can eat. They do like spreadings on their bread. And then I always send some down to Myra, too."

The Widow Lamb surveyed her narrowly.

"H'm! You're expecting Rowan to be with you this winter, are you?"

"Well, so far as we know now that is the plan. He did talk of taking a post graduate course at the college, but I guess he's about given it up. He seems to think he wants to get to work."

"Didn't he go off yesterday? I thought I saw him drive out early in the morning."

"Yes," said Hannah patiently, "he went over to Bainbridge to see a car he heard about. He thought he might like to trade his for it."

"Oh, and he hasn't come back yet, has he?"

"Oh, yes," said Rowan's mother pleasantly, "he came back last night. Excuse me, I'm afraid that kettle is going to boil over."

"Why, I didn't see him come," said Widow Lamb. "I watched out the window till dark and I didn't see him come."

"Oh, can you see as far as our drive from your house?" asked Hannah innocently.

"Why, of course I can. I don't know what I'd do for company if it wasn't for watching my neighbors. I can see Whitney's house, and even a piece of Carroll's house beyond, especially in winter when the leaves are off the trees. I can tell what time their lights go out every night. And Jason Whitney's window is right in line with my bedroom window. I can always tell when Jason comes home late—or when he don't come home at all. I'm a real light sleeper you know, living alone as I do. I suppose it's a kind of self-protection keeps me wakeful. And Jason Whitney's light shines right into my eyes. Do you know, last night he never came home at all!"

"Oh, I don't see how you could tell that," said Hannah calmly. "He might have slept in some other room, or he might have even undressed in the dark if he came home late. Young folks do things like that sometimes."

"Oh, nothing like that in the Whitney house," said Widow Lamb with a dolorous shake of her head. "Nathan Whitney knows what goes on in his house. You can tell a lot about your neighbors, if you're used to their ways, even by when their lights go off and on. What time did you say it was that Rowan got home?"

"Why, I guess I didn't say," smiled Hannah. "I didn't take notice to the clock."

"Was Jason Whitney with him?"

"Why, no, I don't think so," said Hannah. "He didn't say anything about his being along."

"Well, you know what they're saying about Jason this morning, don't you?"

"Why, no," said Hannah cheerily, "I hadn't heard anybody say anything. But then you know people always will be talking. I wouldn't bother about gossip, Mrs. Lamb."

"Well, Hannah Parsons, there are some things one better bother about." She lowered her voice to a shrill whisper. "They're saying that Jason knew more'n a little about that robbery in the bank last night! They say he was with the Rowley crowd, *and some folks think it was him did the shooting!* They say he had a gun that the bullet they took out of Sam Paisley's side would fit!"

Hannah Parsons laughed.

"Oh, the idea!" she flouted gently. "That's ridiculous! Jason is a high-spirited boy, I know, but it's absurd anybody would say a thing like that about him. Why he's often been over here. We're very fond of Jason. He would no more break into a bank or shoot Sam Paisley than I would, Lizzie Lamb, and you know it. I don't think people ought to repeat foolish talk like that."

"Well, I thought I ought to tell you," said the Widow Lamb offendedly. "Jason working in the bank and all, the way he did, and just the day he was dismissed! And *your Rowan* going with him as much as he does, and sometimes going with that low-down Rowley crowd—I *thought you ought to be told!*"

For an instant Hannah's eyes flashed at her caller. Then she laughed again.

"Well, Mrs. Lamb," she said amusedly, "now you've got it off your mind suppose we talk about something else. Taste this preserve. Do you think it has ginger enough in it?"

The Widow Lamb took a good spoonful of the translucent preserve offered and smacked her lips.

"It's not so bad, is it?" she said. "Not that I'm overly fond of yellow tomats myself, but this seems to be real tasty. Well, now you speak of it, it might stand just a dear little bit more ginger, and cinnamon too. Let me have another taste. I wasn't thinking of cinnamon when I was tasting the last."

But finally the Widow Lamb went home bearing two hastily filled jars of preserve in a grape basket, and Hannah drew a sigh of relief.

All the afternoon they kept coming, neighbors who were curious, and neighbors who were anxious for Hannah, and wanted to see if she was worrying, and she met them all with a smile and sent them away with a pint jar of her delicious preserve, till they didn't know what to think.

And in between her callers Hannah Parsons would slip away to her bedroom and kneel beside her bed for a few minutes' look up into the face of her Heavenly Father, a breath of other-world air, and a bit of strengthening for the hard way she must go.

Then after the dusk came down, Joyce Whitney stole across the meadows like a wraith and slipped into the kitchen, her white face staring out of the shadows of the night when she opened the door. Her eyes were large with trouble, and Hannah Parsons turned from the stove where she was preparing a nice little supper in case either of her two dear men-folks came home, and took the girl close to her heart, folding her in loving hungry arms.

CHAPTER IV

Joyce Whitney had had a hard day. Beginning with the early morning when her father had raved about the house like a madman, there had been trouble and turmoil every hour. Nathan Whitney took himself off to the village to discover for himself just what had happened. He returned within the hour to question his womenfolk sternly and irascibly concerning every move that had been made the day before, especially anything that had to do with Jason, and then to shout orders at them all concerning what they were and what they were not to say when people came. They were all relieved when he went away again and his wife turned back to her own perplexities. For of all days for it to happen, this was the day when it was her yearly turn to entertain the bridge club, and they would begin to arrive by two o'clock.

Joyce always hated the event. It had happened three times in the past. Joyce didn't play bridge and wouldn't learn, which was another grievance that her stepmother had against her. But just because of this lack in her, her stepmother demanded twice as much service from her. There were the bridge tables to get ready, the sandwiches to make, the cakes to cut, and the parlor and the sitting room and the bedrooms must be in perfect order. Mrs. Whitney was proud of her big house and liked to show it off.

Joyce had just finished arranging a little side table with coffee cups and silver and a sugar bowl filled with loaf sugar when her father came rampaging in again. He flung his hat gustily down right in the midst of it all, jostling off a fine old china cup till it rolled from the edge and crashed in flinders on the floor, scattering lumps of sugar hither and yon. Then he let out a roar.

"What is all this tomfoolery getting in my way? Teacups in the parlor at a time like this! What do you think you are doing, I should like to know?"

He glared at his wife and then at Joyce who stood white and silent behind her stepmother.

His wife bristled and puffed up like a turkey cock.

"This is the day for my bridge club!" she said haughtily. "It is my turn to entertain them. What are you doing home at this hour of the day anyway? You are very much in the way!"

She stooped to pick up her precious cup and he glared at her.

"Indeed!" he said, "I'm in the way, am I? In my own house I'm in the way! Well, I like that! And you are presuming to go ahead and entertain your bridge club when my only son is in danger of being tried for murder, are you? Well, you'll find yourself mistaken. You'll entertain no bridge club in my house today! I didn't marry you to have you entertain the bridge club. Get this trash out of my way, and tell those gossiping old women there'll be no entertainment for them here today!"

Mrs Whitney was trembling and very angry.

"Nathan, do you realize to whom you are speaking? Ordering me around as if I were a servant, or a slave! Indeed I shall do nothing of the kind. Do you want the whole town talking about us any worse than they are now on account of your precious son? Don't you have sense enough to see that if we call off an affair that has been expected the neighbors will think there is something to all this? What we've got to do is to pay no attention to the whole thing, just go right ahead as if nothing was the matter. Tell people Jason has gone away to get another job. Tell them he didn't feel there was enough prospect for the future in this little bank and then they'll see what we care for all their hints and silly gossip. Joyce, pick up that sugar and dust it off. No, don't throw it away. The floor is perfectly clean and what they don't know won't hurt them when it's in tea. I can't waste all that sugar! Aunt Libby! Bring the dustpan and brush and take up this broken cup. Joyce, you'll have to take that linen cover off and iron it again. It's got all rumpled! And Mr. Whitney, I wish you'd go back to the village or somewhere. I didn't expect you to be around under foot and I've got all I can do to get ready for that club. Do you realize there will be thirty-two ladies here in a little while, Mr. Whitney?"

Nathan Whitney, realizing that his wife was probably right, as she usually made it appear, and in a panic at the thought of such an influx of women, seized his hat and went off again, slamming the door behind him loud enough to be heard across the meadows over at Parsons'. And Joyce, feeling sick at heart, gathered up the sugar, and made things as right as could be, but could not forget the anger and the panic and the actual fear in her father's eyes. Was her father really worrying about Jason at last, or was he just angry? Or —were things really worse than she had heard? Was it possible that they had some proof that would incriminate Jason? Oh, God! How mixed life was! What was the meaning of it all? Jason gone and Rowan gone, and no word from either! Father in Heaven give grace! Give strength! Strength not to sink down. Murder and robbery and perplexity, and only a dim memory of strong arms about her, like a dream, and tender lips on hers!

And with her brother under scorn, and distrust, she had to go on fixing silly bridge tables and prizes!

Her head ached in wild throbs, and she felt a great weakness upon her, but she must march on through the hours. She must dress up and smile when the guests came, for so her stepmother ordered, and it was the way to meet the criticism of course. She could recognize that herself, even though she was dazed with sorrow and apprehension.

Excitement and hurry brought the color to her white cheeks at the crucial moment when the members began to arrive, and though they stared at her unmercifully, she met their gaze with a smile, behind which her tortured eyes tried to look out gaily. But she was not doing it because her stepmother had ordered her to take off that woebegone look and act as if nothing was the matter. She was doing it for her brother's sake. People must not think such awful things of Jason. Jason never would have been a party to robbery. He never would have helped to shoot anybody, or beat or gag poor old Sam Paisley whom everybody honored.

What she really feared was that poor foolish Jason had compromised himself by going to Rowley's road house to play pool, and perhaps to dance with a lot of wild young girls. She didn't know that, she just feared it. And she feared that because of that they would be unable to clear him from other suspicion.

"Oh, Father!" she prayed, constantly, in her heart, "take Jason's cause and plead it for him. For our dear dead mother's sake who loved You, don't let my brother be thought guilty! Clear his name, and make him want to do right. For the Lord Jesus' sake who died for him, meet him now wherever he is and make him do the right thing!"

And between times she was showing the ladies up to the guest rooms to lay off their hats and wraps, listening to their exclamations over the new curtains her stepmother was so proud of, escorting them downstairs again, watching their prying glances backward into other rooms whose doors stood open.

"And is that your brother's room?" one bolder than the rest asked. Oh, they were not all cats, just curious, but Joyce was stabbed with every breath and look that showed they were thinking about Jason. She saw it as each one entered the house, that quick, searching look around, and then into her face, as if they would read more than was written behind her heart-breaking smile.

The afternoon dragged its interminable length along, and Joyce watched the intent faces over the game, glad at last for release from merciless inspection. And then came the refreshments, with endless cups of tea and coffee, passing of sandwiches and cake and bonbons. Would they never get enough? What were they waiting for anyway? It was getting dusk. She couldn't remember that they ever stayed so late before.

Her father came in while the last ones were lingering. He did not enter by the front door. She heard him stumbling unaccustomedly up the back stairs to his room. She heard a dull jar as he flung himself upon his bed. Poor Father! If she only dared go up and try to comfort him! But that would make her stepmother very angry. She never allowed them to be alone together any more without suffering for it.

If she only dared tell her father that Rowan had gone to find Jason. But that wouldn't do any good, for her father had no use for Rowan. He chose to say that Rowan had led Jason astray. Although he knew absolutely nothing against Rowan. Rowan had been away at college for the past four years, and had been at home now for only a few months. It was just because Rowan had graduated, and Jason had been sent home from college in disgrace at the end of his sophomore year that her father resented Rowan. He had been bitter about it ever since Jason came home and was put to work in the bank.

When the last guest had gone, Mrs. Whitney turned to Joyce complacently. She wanted to drain the last drop of satisfaction out of Joyce in a bit of reminiscing.

"Well, I thought it went off very well, didn't you, Joyce?" she said eyeing the weary girl.

"I thought it was ghastly!" said Joyce with a tremble in her voice, too tired and disheartened to dissemble any longer.

"You thought it was *what?*" said her stepmother instantly infuriated. "Just what about it was so ghastly? I ask you? I *demand* to know!"

Mrs. Whitney's voice was rising and her face showed excited red blotches on her cheeks. She too was tired, and Joyce was instantly sorry she had spoken. Why did she have to make more trouble? Hadn't they enough?

"Oh, all of it!" she answered wearily, just on the verge of tears. "All their prying eyes, their catty questions, and the way they asked when Jason was coming back!"

"Well, of course I expected that, after the way Jason had acted. But Mrs. Bartlett told me she thought I was a very brave woman to go right on and do my duty." Mrs. Whitney's voice was regaining its complacency. "I thought we carried it off very well indeed If you could just have roused yourself a little more from that lackadaisical attitude."

"Mother. did you know Father was upstairs?" said Joyce suddenly. "Do you think we'd better talk it over now?"

Mrs. Whitney was startled.

"What makes you think he is?" she asked sharply. "When did he come in?"

"He came in about five minutes ago. I heard him. He went up the back stairs as if he was very tired. I think from the sound that he lay down on his bed. I shouldn't wonder if he had one of his headaches!"

"Oh, you shouldn't wonder if he had a headache? Strange how your imagination always works for some of your own. You never wonder whether I have a headache, do you? Well, I have, a violent one! But no one thinks about me. I must go right on making allowances for everybody else! I must stop talking and—!"

But Joyce could bear no more and she had fled to her own room. A few minutes later when she heard her stepmother come upstairs to her father, she slipped downstairs again and out through the kitchen.

"Aunt Libby," she said as she paused in the doorway, "I'm going out for a little while to get some air. I can't stand it in the house any longer. You tell them if they ask about me that I don't want any more to eat tonight, please, and I'll be in pretty soon."

So she stole away into the darkness, and sat awhile as before, looking at the dying colors in the sky, and watching the light in Hannah Parsons' window, letting her eyes linger wistfully on the dark place where Rowan's window would be, watching the road for a possible car that might come. This was about the time that Rowan came home last night. Oh, that he would come now and bring Jason with him! How all her cares would roll away, and her heart would grow light!

And if he should come, would he ever put his arms about her and kiss her lips again, or was that only to comfort her in her trouble? It wasn't like Rowan to kiss her unmeaningly, but probably it was just to comfort her! She must not let herself get to cherishing that kiss, that thrill that swept over her with such ineffable joy when she thought of his arms about her. He was just being nice and comforting and it was out of all proportion for her to feel so happy about it. "God help me to be right about it!" she breathed softly.

But the night grew dark about her. It was eight o'clock. She could hear the absurd little cuckoo clock that Mrs. Whitney had insisted upon buying, coo out the hour from the parlor mantel. In a short time now they would begin to cry after her, and she would have to go in and account for herself. But she could not spend another night like last night without a word of comfort somewhere. Besides, she was worrying about Hannah! Had Hannah been hearing the rumors, and did she know that they included Rowan too in their ruthless hints? If she did Joyce knew how she would suffer. She had known and loved Hannah for years, ever since she was left a little motherless girl, with no other woman to go to for help and comfort and guidance. Hannah had been as much of a mother to her as any but an own mother could ever be. And since the advent of the second Mrs. Whitney, she had been a tower of strength to help and advise when things got unbearable. Always she gave sweet gentle advice, urging to patience, to forgiveness, to bearing all things!

Joyce could not bear to think that perhaps this dear

woman was enduring the same torture as herself. She must slip over there and look into her face at least, discover whether Rowan had told her where he was going, ask advice what to do in this trying situation.

So, like a shadow she flitted across the meadows again and came to stand where she had stood last night waiting for Rowan. But though she waited for almost an hour no Rowan came. There was the bleating of a young lamb, the bawling of a troubled cow, the stirring of the hens in the chicken house. Perhaps they dreamed of rats. She could hear the dogs howling over across the valley, and the neighing of the farmer's horse over at their own barn. The light gleamed sharply from the Widow Lamb's cottage down the hillside, and once the door opened widely and let out a flood of light, the Widow herself sharply defined against it as she stood looking up the hill. Joyce was glad that it was dark and she could not be seen. She withdrew hastily behind the garage, lest the eyes of Widow Lamb's prying little soul should search her out even in the darkness. Then over from behind the hill beyond the Widow's cottage a little piece of a ragged silver moon left over from the month came tottering up agedly and climbed the heaven. Joyce knew that her seclusion would soon be interrupted and that it was time for her to do something. So she crept stealthily to Hannah's door, tapped softly, lifted the latch and stole in.

"Dear child!" said Hannah softly looking with keen eyes at the white-faced girl. "I wondered where you were, and what was happening to you."

"We had a bridge party!" said Joyce making a wry face and venturing a tiny laugh that ended in a choking sob.

Instantly Hannah Parsons' arms were folded about her, and Joyce laid down her tired head on the motherly shoulder and thought how like her son's arms, were the mother's. She wondered, too, what Hannah would say if she knew that Rowan had held her close and kissed her before he left.

A long moment they stood in close embrace and then Joyce lifted her face showing wet lashes.

"Do you think my brother did that awful thing?" she asked softly, looking into the kindly old eyes that were yearning over her.

"Why, of course not, child!" said Hannah. "Not any more than you think my boy did it!" She watched the dear young face in her arms and was satisfied as she saw the sweet color flood the whiteness of her cheeks.

Then they both laughed and kissed each other tenderly.

"Of course!" lilted Joyce happily.

"Now, sit down, child, and let me get you something to eat. I don't believe you've eaten a thing all day."

"I can't remember," gurgled Joyce between laughter and tears.

"Well, what have you been doing with yourself all day? Don't you know when you go through hard things you have to eat to keep up your strength? Come, now, what have you been doing?"

"Having a bridge party, I tell you!" and now Joyce was laughing indeed. It was such a relief to be with somebody who understood, and who believed in Rowan and Jason.

"Land-a-massy!" said Hannah reverting to an ancient expletive that her own grandmother had used. "Now you don't mean to tell me!"

Hannah Parsons stood back amazed.

"Yes!" Joyce assured her solemnly. "Wasn't it awful?"

Hannah looked at the girl thoughtfully.

"I'm not sure but it was a good thing!" she said. "It certainly was a courageous thing for your stepmother to do. But then, of course, she wouldn't feel it the way you and I do. They weren't her sons or brothers. But I admire her courage. I certainly do. All I could think of to do was to make yellow tomato preserve, and I've been giving it all around the neighborhood all day. I think everyone in the immediate neighborhood has been here on some pretext or other, and gone away with a bottle. I'll have to buy a new supply of jars. Everyone except Miss Perkins. I'm expecting her in every minute if she can get her nephew to drive her over. If she comes you creep into the ironing board cupboard and hide."

"Oh, she was at our party!" said Joyce. "She'll be too tired to come tonight."

"All right, then eat your supper in peace. I'll expect her the first thing in the morning. I suppose she thought a bridge party was the best chance to find out things and she knew I wouldn't disappear in the night. Now, draw up to the table, child, and eat. Father hasn't come home yet. He's been down there all day at the bank, working. It seems they've discovered some crooked work, too, in the books. But you needn't start and look white. Jason wasn't a bookkeeper."

"No, he wasn't a bookkeeper," said Joyce with relief, "but you can't tell what they'll try to hang onto him. Everybody always had it in for my poor naughty little brother, and he seemed to think he had to live up to their idea of him. It made him so mad to be suspected of things, that he just went and did other things to make them think he was awful! I don't understand it in him, but I guess maybe that's like Father. Father always says he doesn't care what people think, but I can see he does."

"Yes, everybody cares," said Hannah wisely. "How is your father feeling about it?"

"Awful!" said Joyce. "He blames everybody, and blames Jason most of all for being what he is, and then if anybody blames Jason he turns right around and defends him."

"Of course he would," brooded Hannah. "He's his own son! It must be awfully hard for him."

"Thank you for saying that," said Joyce. "Everybody else is so hard on Father! Of course Father is hard on everybody, but then, I can't help feeling sorry for him."

"Yes," said Hannah, and then they were both still, knowing that they were both thinking of reasons why they were sorry for him, but reasons that they would never mention to one another.

Suddenly the girl looked up.

"You haven't—heard—from—Rowan yet?"

"No," said Hannah with a confident sigh, "but it's going to be all right! I'm sure. I've been praying all day, and I'm quite satisfied about it."

"Yes?" said Joyce wistfully, as if she wished she had such an assurance. "But—there's something I must tell you. I've been worrying all day whether I ought to let you know or not."

Hannah looked up with quick apprehension.

"Certainly tell, dear! You know there must be nothing between us two. Anything you say to me will be perfectly safe, you know."

"Of course," said Joyce with a flash of trust in her eyes. "It's not that. It's that—I am to blame—for Rowan being in this at all, I guess. Oh, I shouldn't have done it, but I didn't know what to do or whom to ask, and nobody was caring, not even Father! He was only angry at Jason."

A flicker of understanding came into the woman's eyes.

"Tell me everything, Joyce. I'll understand," she said quietly.

The girl drew a deep breath and looked up.

"Rowan didn't know Jason had gone off till I told him," she said. "I slipped over here last night just at dusk and waited by the fence for Rowan to drive in, and then I called to him, and asked him if he had seen Jason. That's all I meant to do. I never asked him to go after him. I had hoped that Jason went with him."

"Yes. that's what I thought it was." said Hannah with a sigh of relief. "I knew it was something good and right."

"Of course it would be!" said Joyce loyally. "But you act as if you knew all the time. Did Rowan tell you when he went into the house?"

"No, he didn't have time. He tried to get up to his room and down again without my seeing him. I expect he was afraid he'd have to take too much time to explain, of course I heard him. I haven't been listening for his step for twenty-one years without recognizing it, even when he takes his shoes off and goes upstairs in his stocking feet. But there I stood. So he just smiled and said he had to go out in a hurry and he couldn't tell me about it but I might trust him. So I've been trusting him. I gave him a couple of thrown-together sandwiches in a bag and he went. Just told me to explain to his father that it was something he would do if he were in his place, and went. I'm glad it was for you he went, Joyce. I'm glad he has gone after Jason. But—where do you suppose he has gone? How would he know where to find him?"

"He said he had an idea—" said Joyce. "I haven't been able to think where it would be. Something Jason had once said, I gathered. But I haven't dared think it through with so many rumors going around. I just wouldn't let such thoughts even pass through my mind. I am sure they didn't go to Rowley's. Everybody seems to think —! But what's the use? Rowan told me not to worry, that he would bring him back, and I'm not going to worry. Only, now and then I can't help thinking what if those Rowleys have somehow got it in for the boys and will do them some harm?"

"There, now, child, just you put them into the Father's care as I have. 'Casting all your care upon Him, for He careth for you.' That's what He's told us to do. You and I are both His children, his saved ones, and we have a right to rest on His promises and not be afraid."

"But does that count when we're trusting for the boys? I don't know about Rowan. He never talks much about such things, but I'm quite sure Jason isn't saved yet."

"I'm afraid Rowan isn't walking as close to the Lord as he should be," said his mother sadly. "When he was a little boy I used to be sure he was saved, but since he's grown up and been away to college he seems quite different, and I can't seem to get beneath his reserve. He joined the church, you know, when he was about fifteen, but I am not sure how much it meant to him. But I feel sure you and I have a right to pray, and to leave this whole matter in the Lord's hands. We cannot love our boys more than He loves them, and wherever, however, it all turns out, He is leading. We'll just pray, little girl, and God will work it out in His own way."

Joyce was still while she ate the tempting supper that Hannah had spread before her. At last she said hesitantly:

"It isn't that I can't trust God. It's just that I feel I was the cause of your suffering too. If I hadn't spoken to Rowan he never would have known about Jason, and he would have been safe at home with you now, and never have gone under that awful suspicion. Oh—-people are *so cruel!*"

She shuddered and closed her eyes from the thought of all the unspoken suspicions that had been flung at her that day.

"I know, dear! But that's something again that you didn't intend to do. You didn't know it would work out this way when you asked Rowan if he had seen your brother. But likely God meant to send Rowan all the time and He just used you as the instrument to give the message. I'm so glad you told me that you had talked with Rowan. Do you mind if I tell Father? I think it will ease his burden to know there was a real reason and it was not just a bit of his own impetuosity that took him away so suddenly."

"Of course, tell him," said Joyce. "I know he'll keep it to himself. I wouldn't like the town to know it. They would say —oh, they would say *horrible* things if they thought I went to a young man for help."

"I know, dear, and Father knows. We'll guard you as our own. And I'm sure my boy will keep his promise to you and bring back Jason if it is in his power. Now, you're not to worry any more. You must get some sleep and be ready to meet tomorrow calmly. I suppose you wouldn't want to stay here tonight? I'd love to keep you, and it is getting late."

"Oh, no, I must go!" said Joyce rising with sudden startled remembrance and glancing at the clock. "There would be an awful hue and cry if I didn't get back. They think I am walking about the meadow. I'll go quickly. Thank you for your dear comfort and the supper and—the—*assurance*. It's so good to know you understand. So good to know someone else is praying."

"I know, dear! And now go quickly. Suppose I go a ways with you. It's pretty dark in the meadow."

"I'm not afraid of the meadow," laughed Joyce sadly.

"And I daren't offer you the flashlight. Widow Lamb watches every light within sight. She would have you a burglar by morning surely if she saw a flashlight moving across lots. But I'll tell you what, you turn on the light in your room as soon as you get home and then I'll know you are all right!"

She stooped and kissed the girl and Joyce disappeared into the darkness, speeding across the meadow in the pale moonlight like a thing of the mist, and presently a light flashed on in the window of the room where Hannah knew Joyce slept. Then Hannah went in and shut her door, and stepping into the dark dining room slipped down on her knees beside a chair and breathed a prayer:

"I thank Thee, O my Father, that Thou hast sent me this added assurance. I trusted Thee, and I trusted Rowan, but it is nice to see the proofs, and I thank Thee, my Lord and my God."

Then she arose to get ready another nice little supper for her Charles in place of the one she had given to Joyce.

Two hours later she was rewarded at last by hearing the sound of the staid old family car coming up the hill, and she drew a breath of relief. Father was come at last.

CHAPTER V

Charles Parsons looked very weary when he came into the house. Hannah was startled by the thought that he looked years older, and his usual cheery smile was only a shadow of its former self.

"It's good to get home, Hannah," he said as he stooped and kissed her sweet anxious face.

"It's good to have you!" she said, laying her face on the rough sleeve of his coat for an instant. "It's been a hard day, I know. But now you're to sit down and eat some supper before you talk at all. You didn't stop for supper, did you? I knew you wouldn't."

"It tastes so much better at home," he pleaded wearily.

She was bustling back and forth from the kitchen stove.

"I know," she said as she put a steaming bowl of the soup he liked best before him, beef broth with barley, and plenty of carrots and onions.

"Ah!" he said sniffing the steam that rose. "That smells heartening!"

She brought him white bread of her own baking, and butter of her own making that smelled of the clover from which it was brewed. She brought a comb of honey from their own hives, and a dish of her yellow tomato preserve, a foaming glass of milk from their own cow, a piece of custard pie and some cottage cheese to which their own hens and cow had contributed, and contentedly he drew up his chair and ate, slowly, deliberately. Hannah sat down to watch him, not asking a question lest she worry him, though her whole soul was yearning to know the news.

At last he looked up and gave a sad little smile.

54

"Well," he said, "it's pretty bad. Worse even than I feared. Yes, it's been a pretty hard day!" and he sighed sadly.

"You mean money, Charles? *Our* money? Loss of money isn't the worst thing in the world. Don't let that worry you. We'll make out."

"No, not so much that. Though it may come to a loss if things can't be cleared up. But we've discovered things. Tampering with the books. Why, if this robbery hadn't happened we might not have found it out for months! And it looks bad. Really bad—!"

"You mean for Jason?"

Charles nodded.

"Yes," with a deep-drawn sigh, "and—well you might as well known the truth, Hannah, for you'll inevitably hear it from somebody if I don't tell you. For our boy too. You see, he's allowed himself to be associated with Jason."

Hannah was still for a minute thinking things out.

"Why do they pitch on Jason?" she said. "Was that why they dismissed him, because they had found something wrong with the books?"

"No, not that. They hadn't discovered it then. They dismissed him for fighting one of their very best men."

"Fighting?" said Hannah astonished.

"Yes, it seems he came in yesterday morning and went about his work as usual, and then suddenly there was a fight right there on the floor of the bank. Jason roared out 'You're a liar!' and knocked the other man down. It was some time before they could bring him to."

"Who was the other man?" asked Hannah thoughtfully.

"Corey Watkins. One of the most exemplary young men in the whole town!"

Hannah still looked thoughtful.

"Do you know, I never liked that fellow," she said half under her breath. "I never felt that he was really sincere. He always seems so slick."

"I know, Hannah, you take prejudices, and it doesn't help any that our Rowan blacked Corey's eye the first day they went to school together, and Corey went boohooing to the teacher and got Rowan a demerit for it. But you know they were only babies then, and you can't hold that against him. I know you and Rowan have always had it in for him, but you'll have to put your prejudices aside, for Goodright says he is absolutely dependable in every way and as honest as the day is long."

"I wonder——!" said Hannah Parsons with a worried look in her eyes.

"Well, anyhow, they think they've traced the trouble to Jason. It seems they found his notebook in front of the safe this morning, and they've found the same fingerprints on the pages of the ledger that were on the books. Of course they can't prove yet that the notebook was Jason's, although it looks that way. It had his name written in it. But they're going over to Whitney's and try for a set of Jason's fingerprints on something in his room. Poor Joyce! I suppose she'll suffer through this! I did my best to get them to omit that, to just wait a little and see whether we catch the thieves—it isn't conceivable that Jason did it alone, and of course that means an investigation of our boy when he gets back, but they were bent on it. In fact Corey Watkins' father practically insisted upon it. He is pretty well worked up against Jason of course on account of what he did to Corey. And then he always did have it in for Nathan Whitney. So things haven't been any too sweet."

"But I don't understand," said Hannah perplexed. "Do they think that Jason broke into the bank himself? He didn't have a key or anything, did he?"

"Oh, no! They didn't enter with a key, Mother. Burglars don't wait on keys. They know how to manipulate locks and bars. But you see Jason was seen to go down the road toward Rowley's as soon as he was dismissed from the bank, and they think he went right down and got help to get his revenge. And perhaps, too, to cover up what he had been doing to the books. You see, Hannah, there has been constant pilfering going on in the bank, and the books were being continually altered to cover it up, almost ever since Jason got his job there."

"It isn't possible that Jason did a thing like that, Charles!" said Hannah indignantly rising in her excitement and walking across to the window to stare out in the darkness toward the Whitney house across the meadows, that now showed a dim outline in the raggedy moonlight. "Charles, that's not possible! I know Jason Whitney. I've known him ever since he was a baby! Didn't I take care of him all the time his sweet little mother was slipping away to heaven? Don't I know his honest blue eyes? Don't I remember how he would always own up if he had been eating green apples, and how he once brought me a dime he had found under the step, when I knew he had very little money of his own and wanted to buy some candy? You can't tell me that a baby who started out being honest like that would get down to systematic pilfering from a bank before he was twenty-one! He had a nasty sullen temper like his irascible father, and he had a daredevil way of tossing his head back like a balky horse and saying he didn't care what people thought of him, but he wasn't dishonest, I'm sure and certain of that!"

Charles watched her with a sad kind of admiration.

"Well, Hannah, I'm sure I hope you're right, but I'm afraid it can't be proved," he said, "and I'm afraid it's going to go hard with Jason, whether he did or didn't have part in this robbery. I know you're pretty generally right in your insight into character, but I guess your heart has run away with your judgment this time. At any rate that very trait of Jason's that he won't try to set himself right in others' eyes is going to be his undoing. There won't be anybody else to take up for him, if he can't or won't defend himself."

"Rowan will!" said Hannah firmly, as if it were a settled thing.

Charles gave her a startled look.

"Has Rowan been home?"

Hannah shook her head.

"No, but Joyce has been here. She says it was her fault that Rowan is mixed up in this. She came over here last night just after dark and waited out by the fence till Rowan got back from Bainbridge to ask him if he knew where Jason was, and when she told him Jason had lost his job in the bank and hadn't been home to tell them, Rowan told her he would go and find him. He said he had an idea from something he said several months ago where he might have gone, and she wasn't to worry, he would find him and bring him back!"

Charles was watching her with alert eyes now, very thoughtfully.

"She said I might tell you, Father, but she didn't want anybody else to know she had been over here. Her stepmother would say shameful things to her if she found it out. I told her you would keep it to yourself."

Charles was silent for another thoughtful moment, then he said:

"Of course! Joyce mustn't be mixed up in this. And anyway it wouldn't help anybody to tell it. They would only think we had cooked it up between us. We'll keep it to ourselves—till Rowan comes back. That's the only thing that can

clear this thing up, to have Rowan come back—and Jason
too. And they will come back, of course, Mother! I'm glad
you told me this. It has cleared up any doubts that might
have been tempted to hover around if things get bad. Don't
you worry, little Mother. Rowan will come back!"

"Yes," said Hannah bravely, but with a quiver of her lip,
"of course he will—if—if—those awful Rowleys haven't shot
him or—something!"

"Now, Mother! Don't go to thinking up things like that!"
said Charles sharply. "Nothing like that could happen without it being found out by this time. If anybody had been shot
the police would have known it by now. They've been comb-
ing the country ever since the robbery."

"They might have carried him off and hidden him! If he
was trying to get Jason away from them, they might! Criminals, you know, do anything when they get desperate, Father!"

Hannah's voice was quivering now and the tears were coming softly down her cheeks.

"They are not such great criminals, those Rowleys!" said
Charles contemptuously. "They were only amateurs, I think.
They dropped one of the most important bundles of all the
papers they stole. One that would have done them the most
good, too. Did I tell you that? The little Paisley boy, Sam's
eldest, Tommy, isn't he? found it down in the ditch by the
road where it had been flung or dropped. He found it about
nine o'clock this morning. They must have come right up the
road past here, Hannah!"

"Yes," said Hannah as if she had known it all the time.
"That was they that drove by so furiously in the night without any tail light. I looked out of the window when they went
by."

"Yes," said Charles. "I did too, but I thought you were
asleep."

Hannah smiled till the tears trickled off into the nice pleasant wrinkles of her face and glistened there.

Charles smiled too.

"Now, Hannah, it's time we got to our knees. Where's the
Bible? Our Father knows just how we feel, and He's putting
every one of those tears into His bottle, and writing them
down in His book, and the time will come when He'll have
them in remembrance and make it all right! After all, our
boy seems to have gone on a legitimate errand, with no nonsense about it, and we ought to be thankful for it. We must

thank our Lord that He let us have that satisfaction. But I'm glad that we trusted Him before we knew everything. Glad we trusted our boy, too."

Charles got his Bible from the table where it usually lay and opened to their trouble psalm as they called it, the ninety-first.

"He that dwelleth in the secret place of the most High shall abide under the shadow of the Almighty. I will say of the Lord, He is my refuge and my fortress: my God; in Him will I trust Surely He shall deliver thee from the snare of the fowler, and from the noisome pestilence. He shall cover thee with His feathers, and under His wings shalt thou trust."

The tender words rang out in the quiet room where the two had sat so many nights together through the years, and often read them before when heavy sorrows were burdening them. Hannah remembered those other nights now, and Charles' voice, reading the words of trust just as he was reading them now. The night their first little baby lay dying and the doctor had told them there was no hope The night Rowan had been so sick and they thought he too was to be taken away. The night after Myra's wedding, when it had seemed to the two that this sorrow was almost worse than death. Ah, there had been other times, too, and always their Lord had sustained them!

As the wonderful promises followed one another climaxing with the triumphal ultimate hope, the two old saints remembered that they were not living for this life alone They were pilgrims journeying to a better country, where all their troubles were to be righted and all their tears wiped away.

And then they knelt side by side and hand in hand while Charles prayed, God standing close beside them, so that they could almost feel His hand upon their heads with a touch of assurance They had trusted before. They would go on trusting to the end, for their Heavenly Father had never yet failed them. The night might be dark now, but Day was promised, and their Guide could see in the dark as well as in the day, and "He knoweth the end from the beginning."

Next morning about eleven o'clock Myra arrived.

Myra had read a much distorted account of the bank robbery in her city paper, with suspicions so mixed with facts that one would have hardly recognized the story. Her brother's name was prominently woven into the tale, as being the son of her father, "a prominent citizen, one of the bank directors, and a respected elder of the church," etc.

It had been in the evening paper occupying a prominent place on the front page. Mark had brought it home and thrust it at Myra with a contemptuous:

"There! There's your lovely family! There's your high and mighty brother with his fine education and all his airs. Just a common robber and murderer! I *never* trusted him, but I certainly didn't expect *such* disgrace when I married you! Your father being such a religious man and all!"

Myra had read it with growing fear clutching at her heart, while fat little Olive reached for a couple of extra pieces of cake during her mother's preoccupation, and babbled:

"Who's a murderer, daddy? Did you mean Uncle Rowan? My uncle Rowan? Who's a thief an' a murderer? Will they have ta hang Uncle Rowan?"

Myra had turned and slapped her offspring soundly on her fat greedy little cheek, and jerked her down from the table, holding her wrist in a firm grasp and shaking the cake out of her clutching hands. Then she started toward the stairs pulling the howling child after her.

"No, I won't gooooo-to-bbbed!" howled Olive. "I was only asking mmm-my daddy a qqq-uest-ion! Daddy! Daddy!"

Mark took a quick stride and rescued the child summarily.

"Now, Myra, don't take your mad out on a baby!" he said in cutting contemptuous tones. "We've only one child and I don't intend to have her abused just because of your precious family!"

"My daddy won't let you send me ta bed when I only ast him a question!" wailed Olive belligerently. "My daddy'll kiss me an' hug me, won'tcha, Daddy? You shan't slap your little dirl! I'm Daddy's baby!"

Myra had escaped to her room while Mark consoled his child belowstairs by another piece of cake.

The evening afterward had not brought relief. Myra had cried all night and had taken the early morning train for her home, using money that she had hoarded for a new hat to pay for her ticket. Her husband's taunts had rankled in her soul all through the journey and she arrived at the farmhouse with swollen eyes and bottled up wrath enough to set on fire the course of nature in great shape. The disappointments of her life had seemed to culminate in this disgrace of her young brother, and she was ready to visit her suffering on any head that came in her way, even her beloved and much tried father and mother.

She burst into the big quiet kitchen where Hannah was

baking some delicate custards, along with her bread, to tempt Charles' appetite. She was weary with weeping, and exhausted with her long hot walk in the sun from the village, fairly running sometimes to escape kindly offers of lifts from neighbors, and to hide her swollen eyes from peering curious ones.

"Oh, Mother, what is this awful, *awful* thing that Rowan has done now!" she cried as she flung her arms about her mother's neck and buried her face in the comforting shoulder that had always been her refuge in childhood.

Hannah's arms went hungrily round her and she held her child close, her heart thrilling to have her thus once more, needing her. It had been so long since she had had her to herself. Always that watching Mark was about casting contempt at Myra for being sentimental. Acting as if Myra had always been *his*, and her parents had no right to even a look from her any more—and perhaps never had had. So Hannah held her girl close and smoothed her hair and said softly:

"There! There! My darling girl! Cry it out on Mother's neck. Dear child! Mother's so glad to have you!"

And suddenly Myra's arms held tightly to her in a great fierce hug that showed her own thwarted longings and repressed love, and Hannah was glad. She wished Charles were here to see this, and to share in it himself. Poor Charles. He sometimes said sadly:

"Seems as if our girl has sort of forgotten us. But I suppose that's to be expected now she has a home and a child of her own. Still it's sort of hard to feel she doesn't love us as she did!"

But she did! She *did!* Hannah could feel that straining clasp and exulted in it. Perhaps it was just that Myra had always been afraid of Mark's sarcastic remarks. Perhaps she was trying to be loyal to him and not have her parents see his faults. Dear child! She would learn some day through her own child, likely, that one could not hide things like that from a mother and father!

Myra presently gained control of herself and straightened up lifting her poor disfigured face with the tears upon it.

"Oh, Mother, what is it all about? Is it true that Rowan has disgraced us all? How could he? How *could* he, with all the care and training that has been given him?"

Hannah pushed her child gently into a chair and there was a look of gentle dignity upon her face, and almost reproof.

"Sit down, dear! You are overwrought. You don't realize

what you are saying. Your brother has not done anything wrong. How could you think he would? I had not realized that you would even have heard the talk that is going about. Quiet down and let me get you a wash rag to wash your face. Poor child! If I had thought you would hear all sorts of rumors I would have called you up and told you not to worry. Why didn't you call me at once if you were worried."

"Call you? And have all the neighbors on the line hear us? And besides, Mark would have thought it was awful for me to spend the money to telephone."

The tears were coming again and Hannah brought the nice cool cloth and put it over the swollen eyes and the hot forehead of her daughter.

"There, there, dear! You must have had a hard time! *I* understand."

But Myra was off again, working off all her overwrought nerves, and the stings of the years on her mother, without in the least realizing how much she was revealing.

"Mark says it is just what he expected!" she sobbed. "He says that he has always *known* Rowan was dishonest! He says he knows things about Rowan that we don't any of us *suspect,* and he won't tell me what they are!"

Hannah's lips shut with a sudden snap of anger, and her eyes flashed, but Myra was weeping too hard to see it, and Hannah had control of herself in a minute.

"Well, of course that isn't so," she said quietly. "Mark has had no opportunity to know anything about Rowan. We'll just have to forgive him for that. People get prejudices you know."

"Oh, but Mother, he says he knows this is so. He says Rowan will be tried for murder if Sam Paisley dies, and we all will be drawn into it and disgraced forever. He says that it is all your and father's fault. That you have been perfectly blind to what Rowan does and have humored him in everything—!" Myra was beside herself now, beyond her own control. The tortures of the years were having their revenge at last, and her nerves were tossing back her resentment on her poor tried mother. Just because she couldn't stand it all any more and wanted to get the burden off her own heart. Just because she wanted her mother to tell her it wasn't any of it true, and soothe her and make things all right and comfortable again, as she used to do for her when she was a little child.

"Look here, Myra!" said her mother suddenly in a stern

Mother-voice of command, "do you realize that you are talking about your own dear brother whom you have known intimately and loved all your life, long years before you ever saw Mark? Will you believe something against him said by a comparative *stranger?*"

Myra looked up startled and wailed:

"Yes, but Mother, he's my husband!"

They faced each other with consternation between them, as if suddenly the old sorrow had become a new peril looming up like a wall and shutting out any hope of comfort.

Then Hannah slowly lowered her glance to the floor and said in a sorrowful tone:

"Yes! I know—!" And there were volumes unuttered between those words.

Then after a minute she drew a deep breath and said kindly, but firmly:

"But even husbands can be mistaken! And yours certainly is!" Then after another pause she added:

"Everybody, of course, is human and liable to make mistakes. We've got to forgive and make allowances for that. But Myra, nothing, *nothing* excuses you for being disloyal to your brother! You need not answer Mark back, nor try to argue it out with him, but in your heart you must be loyal to your brother! It is unthinkable that you would not be!"

But Myra was weeping harder than ever.

"You always did stand up for Rowan! You humored him too much! Mark says you always loved him more than you did me! He says you were partial to Rowan!" It was the dregs of the rancor from Mark's daily nagging that Myra could not help flinging out, but Hannah did not quite see that at first and the words hurt her cruelly. She stood there aghast and looked at her child, with the saddest look on her face that a mother can wear.

"Be still!"

It was Charles who spoke, sternly, with the tone he had not used to his girl since she was a little child and had said "I won't!" to her mother once. He had come in without their hearing and stood looking at his daughter with outraged justice in his face.

"Don't you ever *dare* speak to your mother like that again, Myra!" he said again, into the startled silence that followed his first order.

Myra cowered, and covered her face with her hands, her weary shoulders sagging half in exhaustion, half in shame.

It was a tempestuous day, Myra half the time in hysterics, half the time saying bitter things about her brother.

But at last late in the afternoon, after much explanation, and alternate soothing and sternness, she took her leave, reluctant at the last.

"She is almost sick," said Hannah, looking up pitifully, as Charles came back from taking Myra to the train. Hannah's eyes were red with weeping the tears she had not shed over Rowan's disappearance.

"She *is* sick!" said Charles sternly. "If it hadn't been for her little girl I would have insisted on her staying over night at least, even though Mark raised the roof about it afterwards. She needs to be home and be taken care of! She is utterly run down under that man's persecutions. She doesn't dare call her soul her own! Our little girl! Oh, Hannah, I feel that I was very much to blame that I didn't look into his character and background more before we ever let her marry him. Oh, I wonder that any man dares to let his daughters marry! I was very much to blame."

"Now, Charles, don't blame yourself. You know we tried to make her see that she didn't know him very well."

"Yes, but we didn't try hard enough. We were too afraid that we would say something we would have to live down. We didn't want to be unfair to him, and we were unfair to our own child!"

"Well, Father, we thought we were doing the best we could, and it is too late to do anything now. We must just try to see what we can do for her."

"Yes, poor child!"

Then the two old saints went to their knees again, while the waters of sorrow deepened about them. They arose with the other-world light in their faces once more, to go on trusting.

Three days later, in the dead of night, Rowley's Road House burned to the ground, and poor old Nance, all alone and dead drunk on the dregs of the liquor the Rowleys left behind them, burned to death in her miserable bed in the lean-to.

CHAPTER VI

Nance, left alone, had gone on from hour to hour not knowing what to expect. She had sold gasoline to all who came until the gasoline gave out, and then because no more had been ordered she had to stop. The men had never allowed her to order gasoline.

She had sold drink until people stopped coming. Only travelers stopped at Rowley's after the night of the burglary. Strangely the townspeople came no more. Nance didn't understand it till a passing boy answered her questions and told her the rumors about Rowley's that were going about.

Vaguely she thought it over in her sodden mind as she went on mechanically with the things she had been hired to do. Having known sin and crime all her life familiarly, she was not surprised. She was dully resentful at being left here in a place of suspicion and peril, yet she was without initiation to do anything about it. At first she went on getting meals for no one because she had been told with oaths that she was always to have a meal ready to serve to them. But by and by when she had eaten up all the meals and there was very little left to make meals with, as the Rowleys had left no great amount of supplies when they decamped, she cunningly realized that there was still liquor, and no one to prevent her helping herself.

So she drew from the small stock on hand and drank till she was beyond fear, and then she prepared herself more drink, and lighting a candle, because she had been forbidden to leave the electric light burning all night in her dreary lean-to room, she set it on the floor near her bed, and lay down with her bottle to drink and sleep. The boy had told her that the Road House was under suspicion. He had said the police were likely going to raid it tomorrow and take her to court to tell all she knew. Nance knew that she must not tell anything except what the men had told her to. She knew that they were somewhere, and that wherever they were they had ways of meting out vengeance to her if she failed to obey their commands. It made no difference even if they had gone to far wilds, they would somehow reach out long arms of gangdom and get her. She did not want to be questioned. She did not mean to be questioned.

So she drank heavily and slept.

The night was very dark around Rowley's. Even the ragged moon was behind a cloud, and only the night creatures made dreary sounds.

The weird little flickering spent candle reached up licking tongues of yellow flame now and then as its tallow dripped lower, and lower, and Nance upon her bed drank, and muttered, and slept heavily, flinging a scrawny arm out till the cover of her couch slipped down, down, and the candle could at last lick out its hungry tongue and reach it. Then it leaped up in triumph and blazed along the bedding, enveloping the unconscious woman, flaring high along the wall, devouring as it leapt, gaining fury, as it swept higher, till it roared and swung upward, bursting into a rosy cloud that lit the heavens for miles about.

Then, too late, the watchman in the village saw the light and sent in the alarm. Bells began to ring, and firemen rushed from their homes. A belated engine got under way and went wildly to the fray, startled citizens pulled on quick garments and went flying in noisy cars to the scene. But Nance would not be there for questioning when the police came in the morning. Through fire she had passed to a higher tribunal.

The rickety old buildings made a beautiful blaze and were quickly consumed. The place was a furnace when the fire company arrived, and beyond all hope of being saved.

Vaguely aware of a woman who had been one of the dwellers at Rowley's, the townspeople tried their best to enter and rescue her if she was still there. The boy who had talked with her the day before insisted she must be there. But entrance was impossible. They called aloud to know if anyone was inside, but no answer came. Nance was lying very still, her spirit gone.

The roof was crashing in now, the rickety walls tottering. Iron beds appeared like weird skeletons, toppling on crazy floors that stood at strange angles. Tables and chairs and bottles were revealed, starkly reminding of revelry long past, hinting rudely of the life that had been lived behind those commonplace walls. The assembled townspeople looked and shuddered.

As soon as possible they soaked the place with water, drenching steaming floors till one could walk within on heavy shoes and not be burned. The lean-to had been largely buried beneath falling debris and it was not until late in the afternoon that they found the pitiful group of charred bones that was all that poor old Nance had left behind her in a world that had perhaps sinned against her as much as she had sinned.

They buried her sorrowfully down in the meadow behind the site of the house where she had labored, and they put a rude cross to mark the place.

It was the next morning that they discovered the hiding place beneath the old floor of the lean-to, directly under Nance's bed. And it was quite by accident that they came upon it.

Because of the robbery and the consequent suspicion that hung over the Road House, the police kept vigilant watch since the fire, and had carefully searched for a safe where at least some of the booty might be hidden.

They had indeed found a safe, a small inexpensive affair that was hardly worth using as a safe, for two men could easily have carried it off, root and branch. But they found in it only a few unimportant papers, and a small pile of change, the money that Nance had taken in from the sale of gas and beer. Nothing that had the least possible bearing upon the robbery.

Disappointed, after poking around among the ashes, the police had withdrawn. There remained only two or three firemen to guard the smoking remains and keep the village children from getting on fire.

The great blistered gas pumps stood starkly in front of the ruins, their charred hose like writhing serpents, disconnected and scattered over the ground. Electric light wires sprawled in slimy network of mud and water and ashes. Broken bulbs of red and blue and yellow that had garlanded Rowley's Road House in its better days appeared like dirty berries here and there in the grass. Small boys were discovering them and bulging their pockets full of mementoes of the dramatic event, the most dramatic event that had come into their young knowledge! Not only fire, but robbery, perhaps murder —for Sam Paisley was not yet out of danger—and a woman had burned to death! No dime novel or movie house could equal that for thrill.

It was while walking there among the debris, penetrating toward the lean-to, throwing burnt ends of beams out of the way, and poking among the ashes, that Jack Connelly the fire chief came upon a great iron cover! It had a heavy ring in the middle, sunk even with its surface so that it would not protrude above its smoothness. Perhaps he would not even have noticed it, covered as it was with ashes, if his foot as it kicked aside the rubble had not given back a hollow sound, like an echo.

He looked down startled and stepped again, then stamped. It was unmistakable. There was an empty space below it. What did that mean?

He took a shovel and cleared the place about it for several feet, and there it was. An iron cover with a cement rim about it!

He stooped and lifted the ring from its socket and pulled the heavy lid up, but his strength was not enough to swing it free alone and he had to call another man to help him lift it and swing it away from the opening. Then he turned his flashlight down and saw a hollowed place like a small room, and over in the far corner of the darkness a large safe sunk in the wall!

He shut off the light and turned to his companion.

"Bob, this here is something else! It may be something and then again it may not be! Send the kid down to tell them per-lice ta come back. I ain't agonta be responsible fer lookin' inta this alone."

A moment more and a motorcycle shot down the road toward the village, and presently with blare of horn and siren a red car came rushing back filled with policemen, nearly all the little village boasted.

The combination of the safe baffled them for hours, and in the end they had to use dynamite to get it open. But when the contents were finally brought to the light of day they found all the booty that had been stolen from the bank except a few hundred dollars in small bills and change that the robbers had evidently taken with them.

Hastily the bank representatives were sent for, the treasure brought back to the bank again, and then the work of checking it up began in earnest.

Meantime the search went on for the criminals, for now they definitely knew whom to look for—at least, they knew three of them, they said in covert whispers, with downward glances, and significant tones.

Charles Parsons, seeing some of these glances, and hearing now and then a whisper, felt his heart sink, for he knew what they were thinking. Even men who were his friends and who respected him too much to speak out their thoughts were thinking that somehow Jason Whitney and Rowan Parsons were mixed up in the whole thing, if not as the actual perpetrators of the deed, at least as accomplices. If not, why didn't they come home? They must know what had happened, wherever they might be. The story of the robbery and the probable slaying of a good citizen must have penetrated anywhere they might have hidden. Was it not broadcast on the radio? Was it not blazoned in headlines in the city papers? They could not fail to see it or hear it, and if they were innocent surely they would have sense enough to come home and say so! Both of them were too well educated and too intelligent not to know that to stay away was the worst thing they could do.

So Charles came home at night and tried to smile bravely.

"We've got most of the money back in the bank, Hannah," he said with a sigh of relief, which yet had in it a tinge of sadness, "but they still think our boys were to blame for it."

He had come to calling them *"our* boys" now. He seemed to have forgotten his grudge against Jason.

"Well," said Hannah with her brave smile, "what does it matter? They can't arrest them while they're away, and when they come back they can surely prove they were not guilty. God has them hidden somewhere for his own good purpose."

"Yes, I was thinking that," said Charles. "God has let us know that there isn't a shadow of doubt about them as far as any criminal connection with that robbery is concerned, and that's a great thing. He has been tender of us. And for some reason He wants us to bear this obliquy, at least for awhile."

Hannah looked up thoughtfully.

"Yes. I'm thankful. But you know, Charles, we aren't *sure* ourselves about Jason. We're sure that Rowan went out to find and save Jason, but how do we know but Jason was in on this thing? How do you know but our Rowan suspected that, and went out to try and persuade him out of it, and perhaps they both got caught in the net and couldn't get away alive? Jason was in the bank, you know, and you said somebody had been tampering with the books."

"I know, but I've been looking into the matter pretty thoroughly and I'm convinced that Jason had nothing to do with it. I've inquired into details most definitely. I am pretty sure I have settled it that the last tampering which included quite a large sum, several hundred dollars, more than had been attempted at any one time before, was taken that very morning that Jason was dismissed, and after he left the bank. The weight of the testimony is that Jason had had no possible opportunity at the books that morning. Though it's true one man does think he saw him looking over one of the books very early when he first came in, and says he looked confused when he looked at him. But Mr. Goodright is very sure that was not possible. He says he was watching the boy from the time he came in, knowing what he must presently say to him."

"Who was the one man, Charles?"

"Well, it was Corey Watkins, if you must know," smiled Charles half sheepishly. "Of course that won't count with you, but it certainly does with everyone else connected with the bank. Corey Watkins, they say, is the most conscientious and the most exact, and the most observing man working for them."

"H'm!" said Hannah thoughtfully, and said no more.

There was a long silence and at last Charles said:

"Well, of course you might be right, Hannah!"

Hannah looked up in surprise.

"Why, I didn't say anything!"

"No, but you looked it," smiled her husband. "But anyway, Hannah, I don't think any more that Jason was in this bank business. I believe he went away to find another job or to hide his heart. Goodright has been telling me what he said to him, and how cut up and angry the boy was. He says he almost felt he might have done him an injustice. He even offered to let Jason have another trial, it seems, but Jason declined it and left with his head high. He said if Mr. Goodright thought he was capable of doing some of those things that he had charged him with that he didn't want to work for him another hour, and he got up and went out without even denying what was charged. Of course that looks bad for him. And yet Mr. Goodright is inclined to believe in him, I am sure. I think even yet he would give him another chance if he would come back in spite of his proud rejection of his help."

"But it was just like Jason," said Hannah. "I know how he held his dark head, and how narrow and angry his fiery eyes got. He was like that when he was a child. And he comes truly by it. He's his father all over again."

"Yes," sighed Charles. "And Nathan is feeling this. He looks twenty years older than he did a week ago. The poor man hasn't any Saviour to lean on. I don't suppose he'd even own that he's feeling it, either, except in anger at the boy. Well, poor man! Hannah, we've a great deal to be thankful for that we have such a wonderful God, and that His word is so full of dependable promises."

Hannah gave her husband a bright smile and went on with her work.

But the rumors continued and grew as they went the rounds of the town, and more and more of them drifted back to the parsonage, and to the ears of Rose Allison.

"Gee!" said her young brother Bob at the lunch table, talking with his mouth full of bread and jelly, "Gee! They're sayin' now that Jase Whitney was the one that showed the Rowleys the combination of the safe, and gave 'em the high sign when Sam Paisley was at the other side of the block. They say they're almost sure he was the one that hit Sam on the head with a piece a' lead pipe. I don't b'lieve it. Jase is a good egg. He wouldn't do a thing like that!"

Rose looked up startled and opened her mouth to speak, then closed it again. Finally she decided to speak.

"No, I don't believe it either!" she said firmly. But she did not give her reason for thinking so.

Late that afternoon Bob was lying in the old-fashioned hammock on the front porch close under the windows of his father's study, conning his history for the next day's lesson. His father had told him very firmly that if he didn't have that long string of dates perfectly before supper he couldn't go out that night to a Boy Scout entertainment he was eager to attend, so he had taken time off from a ball game and was studying hard, rolled up in the fringes of the hammock, his eyes shut, saying over and over the dates. "Columbus discovered America in fourteen-ninety-two—"

Rose had been up in her room standing at the window staring out at a faraway hill, without seeing it, struggling with a natural reticence. But at last she made a decision and hurried down to her father's study. She knew he had come in a few minutes before from parishional calls, and it never bothered him as much to be interrupted in the afternoon as it did in the morning when he was usually studying or writing a new sermon.

Rose tapped at the door and stepped in.

"Father, are you too busy to talk to me a minute? There's something I think maybe I ought to tell you."

Bob pricked up his ears. She wasn't going to tell Dad about that window he broke with his baseball at school, was she? Aw, Gee, wha'd she wanta do that for? He was goin' ta pay for it with his own money. He'd already told the superintendent so. Gee! That wasn't like Rose ta go squealing. She was a good sport. She didn't tell tales.

He remained motionless in the hammock and listened. If she looked out of the window she wouldn't know there was a soul in the hammock, it was so still and looked so flat.

But Rose was not looking out of the window. She came over and stood with her back to it and her hands behind her on the window sill.

"Father, I don't know whether this is important or not, but it seemed to me I'd better tell you. It isn't anything much, and might not have anything to do with the case, but I can't seem to get away from worrying about it."

"All right. Say on, little girl!"

"Well, Father, you know I was trying to get my quota of people to come to the meeting the other night, and I had them all but one, I just couldn't seem to think of another one to ask that somebody else hadn't asked."

The father wasn't paying much attention to her. He had his eyes on the evening paper which he had just brought in, but he nodded rather absent-mindedly, and she went on.

"That was the day before the night of the robbery," she said.

At the word robbery her father looked up sharply. He didn't want his sweet young daughter connected in any way with this crime, even in any trifling incident, and he gave instant attention. And out in the hammock Bob listened breathlessly.

"Well, Father, I was on my way down to the post office and I saw Jason Whitney coming along on his way to the bank. The thought came to me that maybe I might ask him. I didn't suppose it would do any good, but I didn't see how it could do any harm either, and I didn't know another soul to ask, so when he stopped and said good morning I thought maybe I should ask him."

"Does he usually stop to say good morning to you?" Mr.

Allison was watching his lovely daughter intently, and noticing with a sudden qualm how fast she was growing into young womanhood. There was a soft flush on her cheek as she talked and her eyes were cast down as if she were a trifle embarrassed.

"No, he never did before. I don't know why he did. I don't think he meant to. He acted as if he was going right on and then all of a sudden he stopped. You know we used to sit across the aisle in high school, though we never knew each other very well. He didn't pay much attention to girls just then. So when he stopped I thought maybe that showed I should ask him. So I did."

"He turned you down, I suppose?"

"No," said Rose, "not exactly. I said, 'Oh, Jason, I wish you'd do something for me!' And he said, 'Sure, I will, Kid, what is it?' And then I told him about the meetings and how we had each pledged to ask so many and I had them all but one. And he said, 'Great Caesar's ghost, Rose. *Church? I* never go to church. It isn't in my line!' So then I told him about the speaker and he stood still a minute and looked at me sort of thoughtfully, and finally he said: 'Sure, Kid, I'll do it,' and then he lifted his hat again and went on."

"But he didn't come, did he?" asked the father amusedly. He was much relieved that Rose's worry had been merely a matter of inviting an old schoolmate to meeting, nothing really to do with the robbery. Poor fellow! How different things might have been if he had come instead of—well, where was he anyway? Did he believe that Jason Whitney had taken part in a robbery or not? He wasn't sure. But he watched his daughter's face as she went on.

"No, Father, but he called me up."

"He called you up? On the telephone?" The father's swivel chair came smartly down to the level and he sat up straight and looked at Rose. "He *took the liberty* of calling you up! When?"

"Why, I guess it was just a little while after he had been fired from the bank. The dining room clock was striking twelve when he began to talk I remember because I had to ask him over again. I couldn't hear. But you know the dining room clock is almost always a little slow. You ought to fix it. It was half an hour slow all last week."

"Well, get on. What did he say? I don't suppose he intended to come any of the time."

"Yes, he did. I really think he did. He said he'd meant to

keep his promise to me but he couldn't because something had happened at the bank that morning and he was leaving town."

"He said that to you?" The father looked startled and thoughtful.

"Yes, he said just that, and I said I was sorry. And then before I stopped to think I said, 'Oh, Jason, you haven't done anything to make them dismiss you, have you?' And his voice got real bitter the way it used to do in school when the teacher found fault with him, and he said, 'No, Rose, I haven't, and that's the truth, but the poor fishes think I have and that's just as bad. And the worst of it is I can't tell what I know so they've pinned everything on me. They'll tell you to the contrary and I can't blame you if you believe them instead of me, but it's true!' "

The father was still, considering her for a moment.

"And what did you say to that, Rose?"

Rose hadn't expected to be asked that, and her face got white and embarrassed and then she lifted honest eyes and looked at her father with a sweet young dignity, lifting her chin a bit.

"I said I would believe him, I said I would *always* believe him!"

She looked straight into her father's eyes with a gentle kind of defiance ready to meet even his condemnation, as if she believed what she had done was right. He watched her in astonishment. The little girl was becoming a woman, and he admired the way she spoke. He did not condemn her. After a minute he said:

"And was that all, dear?"

Her eyes became thoughtful, and lovely color suddenly flooded her face again.

"No, Father. He said 'Thanks a lot' sort of as if he was crying, and then after a second he said 'And I'll *always* tell *you* the *truth!*' and then he was still almost a whole minute and he added in a very low tone: 'If I ever see you again! I'm beating it, Kid, and I'm not sure I'm ever coming back. I can't get a square deal here, and nobody cares, nobody but my sister, and she can't do anything about it.' "

Rose stopped there. Somehow the rest was too sacred even for her father to know. She couldn't bring it out that she had said she cared too. Her father might take it in a different way from what she meant it. And anyway, it had nothing to do with the whole case.

"We said good-bye," she added simply and stood waiting a moment.

"And what has troubled you about this, Rose?" asked her father.

"Well it's what he said about being blamed for what somebody else had done, and not being able to tell. I just got to thinking that Corey Watkins is in the bank too, and how he used to do things and let Jason be the goat, and I wondered—"

Mr. Allison studied her thoughtfully.

"But Corey is a young man now, daughter, and he has the respect and confidence of everybody concerned. I asked about him only yesterday because of what you had told me about his tricks in school that Jason got blamed for, but I find that he has been most exemplary in the bank, in the church, everywhere. He is quite a church worker over at the Second Church."

"Yes," said Rose quite unmoved. "He always was. He's always been exemplary, and Jason has got the blame."

There was silence in the room for a long minute while the minister studied his young daughter's face again. Then she lifted her eyes and spoke once more.

"Then you don't think I ought to tell them that he talked to me, and said he was going away? I thought perhaps you would think I should go and tell Mr. Goodright."

"Oh, no!" said the minister quickly. "I don't want you to get mixed up in this thing. Anything you could possibly say would be utterly misunderstood and cause terrible gossip, especially just now."

"I know," said Rose with a sigh, partly troubled and partly relieved. Her tone showed that she fully understood what would be said.

"No, child! Don't breathe a word. If anything at all is to be said I would be the one to say it, but I can't see how it could possibly do any good. They would only say you were a romantic girl, and that girls always defended good-looking young men."

"I know!" said Rose again. "I didn't want to, but I thought maybe I should."

"Well, dear, I'm glad you told me, and if anything comes up that your bit of evidence can help I'll let it be known some way, but at present I can't see how it would help. And anyway, you can't just go and cast aspersions upon some other young man without a bit of evidence. And without that what point would there be to your testimony? Only a statement from the young man himself that he wasn't getting a square deal, which wouldn't mean a thing to them, nor change their opinion."

"I know," she said sadly as she left him and went her way.

Poor child! She had thought it all out, and yet she was willing to go and tell them, if it was the right thing to do. What a good little thing she was! And how sweet she looked when she was confessing that she had told Jason Whitney she would believe him!

He found himself profoundly thankful that Jason Whitney was gone away. No telling what complication might have arisen out of this so simple and sweet beginning if he had stayed. Suppose he had come to meeting. Suppose he had been converted and become a trustworthy person? Well, even such impossible things as that had happened through the years, and the grace of God was able to save even Jason Whitney. But he must watch his sweet little girl. She was growing into a woman, and she was certainly a winsome lass.

Then the minister went into retirement behind his newspaper and forgot the whole matter for the time being.

But out under the window in the hammock there was a motionless young person who was not forgetting what he had just heard, and he lay still and thought it over, lay so still that he was even afraid he might go to sleep. He didn't want anybody to know that he had heard what he had heard.

CHAPTER VII

Bob Allison lay motionless for as much as five whole minutes, thinking. He was perhaps doing the most intensive thinking about one single thing of his whole lifetime.

He had always had trouble in concentrating, there were so many interesting topics to divert his mind, especially when he was trying to study.

But just now he was putting his whole eager young soul into concentrating, and it brought about a state of bodily quiescence that would have alarmed his mother if she had happened to be where she could watch him. Nothing save absolute oblivion in sleep had ever before made young Robert Allison lie so still.

For it happened that Jason Whitney had been Bob Allison's hero since kindergarten days.

It was Jason Whitney who had taken the trouble at odd moments before and after school, to teach Bob how to pitch a ball better than any of the other boys in his grade. It was Jason who made snow men for him, and taken him sometimes on his bike to school, and once took him along when he went fishing. Bob adored the very ground Jason walked on.

And now Jason had been driven from his job, and his home, into a cold unsympathetic world, with a cloud of suspicions hanging over his past, and a dark uncertain future before him. Bob felt that he had to do something about it.

Bob had been quick to register another name mentioned by his sister in her confidential talk with their father. Corey Watkins had been for years as much hated by Bob as Jason had been adored. His aversion to Corey Watkins was much more deeply seated than even his love for Jason Whitney,

77

and dated back to the time when he was only three years old and had gone to visit high school with his sister Rose. They were out in the yard at recess time, and Rose was talking to some of her friends with her back turned. Corey had come along and persuaded the infant Bobbie to pick up a nice soft yellow bumblebee in his chubby hand and stroke its yellow fur. When sudden disillusionment had come and he howled, bringing Rose and the teacher to instant rescue, Corey had told them that it was Jason who had perpetrated the trick. Bob had never forgotten that. He could feel the sting in his hand yet whenever he saw the smug look on Corey Watkins' face.

And Corey Watkins was a pain in the neck, even though he was grown up. Corey was slick, and of course it was he who had done anything in the bank that ought not to have been done. And he had let Jason be the goat. Bob knew very many other instances when this had been the case. He wondered why grown people were always so stupid, and petted the wrong people. Mr. Goodright was likely that way, too. He probably didn't know Corey was that kind of a guy, and he ought to be enlightened. Bob felt himself constituted to be the enlightener. There was nobody else who could very well do it, so he must.

He could see that it wouldn't do for Rose to go to Mr. Goodright and tell what she knew. Everybody might hear of it and think she had a case on Jason. Of course Rose couldn't do anything. His father had been right about that.

And his father was a minister, and a minister had to be careful about hurting people's feelings. Mrs. Watkins was a member of the church. No, his father couldn't warn the bank. He would have to do it himself. And even he mustn't let them know who he was. He was too young. They wouldn't pay any attention to just a kid's warning, not unless he had seen something definite to tell. Of course there was the time Rose had been so sick and Father was away, and his mother had sent him to the drugstore for medicine at midnight. He had seen Corey Watkins come out of a side door in the bank and go around through the alley instead of going up Main Street which was the short way to the Watkins home. Still, of course, that didn't exactly prove anything. But somehow he had got to show up Corey Watkins to the world, or to the bank anyway, and bring back his idol, Jason, to his rightful place among his fellow townsmen where he would be no longer misjudged, but understood and admired as was right and proper. Having decided this much it did not take him long to decide what to do. Mr. Goodright, the president of the bank should be informed of the injustice he had done in dismissing Jason from his place in the bank and retaining Corey Watkins. Another half second sufficed to decide Bob how to right this wrong. He would himself write a letter to Mr. Goodright informing him of the mistake he was making in retaining Corey and dismissing Jason, and he would sign it "a well-wisher of the bank" or something like that.

Having reached this conclusion and feeling that the whole matter was already on its way to being set right, Bob opened one eye and glanced briefly at the page where his forefinger was inserted in the much thumbed history he held. Softly his lips mumbled over the stale old phrases. "Christopher Columbus discovered America in 1492," on down through a long list that he had been droning over more or less all afternoon with only half his mind upon it. Now he was wholly concentrated and he had the fourteen long lines perfectly in five minutes, so that he was sure he would not forget them.

Then softly he flung open the red fringes of the hammock which enveloped him, stealthily swung first one leg and then the other free, and slid down noiselessly to the porch floor, thence continuously to the grass in front. He stole around the house, issuing a moment later from the other side and mounting the front steps whistling, "My country 'tis of thee," a trifle off key, but gaily.

He knocked at his father's study door, and entering, produced his history triumphantly.

"I'm ready to recite," he announced, and glibly hurled the facts of history at his preoccupied father, who smiled his satisfaction, his eyes upon his evening paper, and signified that Bob was now free to attend the evening entertainment of the Boy Scouts.

Bob retired from the room silently, not with his usual grin when a penance was completed, and softly ascended the stairs to his room. He had intended chasing the cat, tying a worm to her tail, and then setting her free in the chicken yard among the hens, but that was before graver matters engrossed his mind.

Almost stealthily he entered his room and pushed the bolt on the door so that he would not be interrupted. Then the better to act the part he had now to play he removed his shoes and stocking-footed went over to the bed and got a pillow, placing it in the desk chair to still a chronic creak that the seat sometimes emitted. He sat gravely down and got out his writing materials.

Sheet after sheet of his Christmas writing paper he rejected because of the emblems they bore, and they were numerous. There was the first kindergarten paper with a row of little children hand in hand going to school with their school bags and slates. That was the first paper he ever got, and he had once admired it. How silly it looked to him now. And there was the animal paper. Some had kittens, some puppies, some ponies, and some a group of cows, but all those were childish and would not do for grave matters like this. And there was the baseball paper with batters and catchers and pitchers all in suitable costumes. He put them aside. There was nothing left but the last paper from his tenth birthday that displayed his initials in red and blue and gold letters! And that wouldn't do either! He was going to sign this note "a well-wisher." It wasn't necessary for them to know his name. It would carry more weight, he felt sure, if it appeared to be written by some man.

So finally he ventured forth stealthily to his mother's desk in her room and filched a sheet of her plain note paper.

He went at his task vigorously, forming each letter with care, trying to keep the lines even and not let them run uphill. His clear round schoolboy hand was very characterful. Now and then he rubbed his smudgy hand across his eyes wearily and sighed. It was unwonted that he should apply himself so intensively to a task like this. Several times he almost gave it up, but he plodded on, and by the time the supper bell rang he had completed his letter. It was a bit smeary, but very plainly decipherable.

Mr. Goodright,
President of the Bank.

Dear Sir:

You had better watch your step. You've got a slick guy in your bank and you'd be surprised if you knew who he was. I can't name him because it wouldn't be honorable to tell tales. Jason Whitney is a noble young man who took the blame for another, and you ought to try and get him back when you get rid of the other man. You won't have any trouble in spotting the crook if you just pick out the one you're sure he isn't, and then watch him hard. But remember he is slick. He had it in for Jason since he was a kid.

Very truly yours
A Well-Wisher

Bob took some of his treasured money saved for marbles and went to the office for a stamp to mail his letter, thereby arriving late at supper with unwashen hands and uncombed hair, incurring a reprimand. But he felt that that was the penalty of being noble and trying to set wrongs right, so he suffered in silence.

Even at the Boy Scout entertainment that evening he was preoccupied, and felt like a noble elderly person set apart to higher things than laughing over childish tricks put up for amusement. His deep-set admiration for Jason Whitney, and his great longing to do something to set him right in the eyes of the world, stimulated him like an intoxicating drink. He kept wondering all the evening how long it would be before his letter began to take effect. He regretted deeply that he had to go to school in the morning and could not hover around and watch to see if anything was happening at the bank after that letter would have been received. It was a great bore this having to go to school after one reached the age of discretion and had been called to noble endeavors.

Still, he enjoyed the entertainment fairly well in spite of his distraught mind, and managed to write down one or two tricks on a scrubby card he found in his pocket. He went home tired and happy, casting a knowing look toward the postoffice as he went by as to a fellow conspirator. That night he dreamed that Jason was restored to the fellowship of the town, and all saw what a wise and noble young man he was, and how utterly despicable was the one who had tried to cause his downfall.

The next morning when Mr. Goodright received that letter he read it with much amusement, slowly, and with a relish. Then he turned to the front page and read it again, carefully, deliberately, thoughtfully. Finally he folded it away in a second envelope and locked it into a secret drawer in his desk. Then he took a pencil and wrote a list of all the employees of the bank, from the least unto the greatest. Slowly, thoughtfully, he went down the list checking off the names, numbering them in the order he had checked them, and paused, noting with astonishment the first name he had checked off. Then he sat back and stared for fully five minutes at the blank wall ahead of him.

Was this a game or something serious? Was it some friend of Jason who was trying to get revenge? Was it—no, it couldn't be Jason himself. He took out the letter again from its hiding and looked at the formation of each letter, each word. Surely that was a child, or at least a very young person. No grown person could have imitated a schoolboy's writing as well as that—or—could it be a school girl? No, there was something altogether boyish about it.

The bank president went to a cabinet and took out a drawer where were filed the specimens of handwriting of all the employees in the bank and spent several minutes in absorbed contemplation of the formation of the letters. Finally he locked Bob's letter away again, and got up and walked the length of the room several times, his hands behind him.

It was absurd, of course, to pay any attention to an anonymous letter, especially one that came so obviously from a boy, for there was "boy" written all over that missive, and yet there was something in the Bible about "out of the mouth of babies." There might be something in it well worth considerering, perhaps even worth acting upon, especially if there should be any further signs of tampering with the books.

The president went back to the perplexities of the day, but every little while that schoolboy letter kept coming to mind, and as he chanced to see the different employees under him he kept applying the test the boy had given, and smiling, with albeit a grave look in his eyes.

And then, when Charles Parsons came in late in the afternoon, he unlocked his secret drawer and took the letter out and showed it to him.

"What do you think of that, Charlie?"

There was a twinkle in Charles Parsons' eyes as he handed the letter back but his voice was grave as he answered:

"There might be something in it, you know, Jamie. It is sometimes permitted to boys to see and know things that their elders cannot find out. You mind the time when you and I peeked in the back windows of the greengrocery one night and saw Mr. Buxton fitting a false bottom to his peck measure so it wouldn't hold quite a peck; and the time we caught the temperance lecturer taking a drink at the hotel bar; and the time we hid in the bushes and caught Sam Downes kissing the milkmaid at Browers when he was supposed to be taking the minister's daughter to choir rehearsal? You know, Jamie, a boy gets around a lot, and learns to read character sometimes rather better than his elders. I wouldn't ignore the warning, if you can call it a warning that doesn't tell you what it warns against."

"Yes," said James Goodright. "That's it. I wish I had the

little rascal here that wrote that letter and I'd choke it out of him who it is he means."

Charles Parsons grinned.

"You wouldn't have let anybody choke a thing like that out of you, Jamie, when you were that age. You know you wouldn't! Not if you choked for it."

"No, I suppose not," said the banker. "And after all, perhaps that's why it has worried me all day, the very fact that he didn't mention a name. There isn't anything that I can do about it."

"Except follow the advice of the letter," said Charles gravely.

"Well, I have!" said the banker. "I wrote a list and narrowed it down to two, and I've been worrying all day about which of the two it could be. And yet, of course, it isn't fair to either of them to pay any attention to it at all. I have perfect confidence in every man in the bank."

"Yes," said Charles, "and yet it must have been somebody. If it still goes on, if it wasn't Jason, then we can say it must *be* somebody here. Of course you didn't suspect any deliberate work when you dismissed Jason, you say. You thought the discrepancies were carelessness."

"Yes, that's it," said the banker passing a hand wearily over his eyes. "I certainly wish that this matter was cleared up. Of course it's a great weight off my mind that we got back most of our property and none of our trustees are going to have to be brought down to poverty, but I certainly wish I understood it all. There is something back of it that I cannot understand, Charlie. It isn't just an ordinary bank robbery. There has been some inside work. I'm sure of that. I suppose I must have precipitated matters by dismissing Jason Whitney, but—I was all out of patience."

"I wouldn't be so sure!" said Charles. "We haven't got this thing figured out yet, Jamie. It's a matter to pray over, I'm thinking."

The banker drew a deep sigh.

"Yes, I suppose so, Charlie. You attend to the praying end, won't you? You were always better at that than I. Charlie, what's become of your boy Rowan? And what's all this whispering about him that I hear?"

Charles Parsons turned his deep eyes on his friend.

"If you want to know what I think, Jamie," he said gravely, "I think he's gone after Jason to try and bring him back."

The banker studied his friend's face for awhile and then he said, "Well, Charlie, I sincerely hope he has! I'm glad you trust your boy. You know him better than I do. And time will tell. Well, anyway, Charlie, we're standing by each other, just as we always did."

"God bless you for that, Jamie," said Charles, grasping his friend's hand.

"Well, that goes without saying, of course," said the banker. "I know you, and I trust you better than my own soul."

"Better be careful, Jamie," said Charles with a wry smile, "you know what the letter warns, that you're to watch the one you trust the most, or something like that."

"Well, that's not you, Charlie Parsons. I'd stake my soul on that! But I certainly do wish they'd catch one of those Rowleys and put him through the third degree. Then I think we'd know a little something at least. But don't say anything about this letter to anyone."

"Of course not," said Charles. And after a few more words they parted.

Two hours later word came flashing over the wires that one of the Rowley gang had been shot down by police in a western city and killed, and a second Rowley had been captured and taken to the police station, while several others who had been a part of the outfit at Rowley's Road House, had escaped westward.

The town and countryside held its breath for a few hours and looked at one another with horror in their eyes. They had never supposed that stark things like robbery and shootings would come to their quiet town. They gave pause to think of the dark-browed man who had presided over the gas station and over the Road House, and who had gone in and out among them hostilely, having little to say to anyone. It was easy to think of him as a gangster, a public enemy, but it was appalling to think they had harbored him quietly now for nearly two years and not known a peril in their midst. And now he had met his end, ignominiously, as should be, in an alley, with his feet lying pitifully straight on the cobble stones as the evening papers pictured him. What a leveler death was! How it suddenly took the power from villains and brought their evil machinations to an end!

And the other Rowley brother captured! They drew a breath of relief, and then turned to face the rest of the story. "The others had escaped." *Who were the others?*

A later edition of the paper stated that one of those who

had been with the Rowleys when taken was Pete Bundon, a notorious escaped convict. They thought of him, a thickset, ugly jowled man, uncouth, and with a beetling brow and cruel eyes. But somehow by this time it did not seem so important to the town as the question, Who were the others who had escaped? The next paper narrowed it down to three in all who had been in the gang when discovered, Pete Bundon and two others, not as yet identified.

Wild, fearful eyes looked into one another and dared not ask that question, "Who?" Two fathers lay wide-eyed and stared at the dark all night, saw that question in unfriendly eyes and trembled for the future. A mother, and a tender sister lay and waited for the morning, with tears upon their lashes, and firm quivering lips that prayed. And a girl lay all alone in a little cottage bed in the parsonage room, and cried her heart out into her pillow, setting her lips in a firm believing line. Never! Never would she believe such a thing! Never though the whole world said he was a criminal. She *knew!* And if necessary she would tell what she knew!

But no one had dared to voice the question yet. The slaying of Rowley was too new. The capture of the other ought to reveal something—though that kind never told on each other!

And then the morning came, and a nasty little snake of a reporter who had come down to the scene of the burglary the night before and sneaked around among certain townspeople, came out with a story that froze the hearts of all who knew and loved either Jason Whitney or Rowan Parsons.

"It is said," the scathing paragraph read, "that Jason Whitney had long been in partnership with the Rowley brothers, having spent much time in their Road House, supposedly playing pool and dancing with the kind of women who infest such places, and that his job in the bank which dated back several months had made it easy for the thieves to effect an entrance. In fact it is pretty well established now that young Whitney was inside the bank at the time of the robbery, though he had that day been dismissed from employment there. A notebook of his had been dropped in front of the broken safe, and gave ample proof of his presence at the time of the robbery.

"Closely connected with young Whitney was his intimate friend, Rowan Parsons, who is supposed to have spent the day of the robbery in Bainbridge making preparations for a good getaway for all concerned. Both Parsons and Whitney disappeared the night of the robbery and have not been heard from since. It is supposed that these two accomplices were with the gang when it was first sighted in the alley, when Pete Bundon was recognized by an old prison pal of his who had been pardoned out for good conduct, and that they made good their escape during the shooting. It is confidently expected that all three will be captured within the next twenty-four hours, as word has gone out with warning in every direction and a cordon of police is drawn about the whole area, so that final escape is practically cut off."

The people of the town read the paragraphs aghast and terror filled their eyes. Even the worst gossip of the town had not dreamed of anything so crude and bald and blatant as these printed words. Those who had harbored the worst thoughts concerning the two young men, were somehow shamefaced and guilty that such things should really be printed against one who belonged among them.

Joyce Whitney read the paper first, white-lipped and trembling, and hid it before her father should come down and her bitter tongued stepmother, and then she crept through the morning sunlight, shivering, and hurried across the meadows to the Parsons' house to knock timidly at the door.

Hannah opened the door and her face was grave and sad, but not stricken.

"Oh, have you seen the paper?" whispered Joyce, and then saw that Rowan's father was reading it.

"Oh, what shall we do?" she cried in a despairing voice as she dropped into a chair, too weak to stand.

"Do?" said Hannah Parsons. "Do? We're going to trust and not be afraid!"

"Do, dear child?" said Charles lifting his eyes with a look of triumph. "Don't you know what our God has said? 'No weapon that is formed against thee shall prosper; and every tongue that shall rise against thee in judgment thou shalt condemn. This is the heritage of the servants of the Lord, and their righteousness is of me, saith the Lord.' What we are going to do, child, is just to wait God's time and He will set all right again. This is for some good purpose, and we are just going to trust Him!"

CHAPTER VIII

Rose Allison went to the village store for more sugar. Her
mother was putting up the peaches that grew on the old
gnarled bitter peach tree in the parsonage back yard, and
they always took a lot of sugar to make them taste like
peaches. Some years they seemed worse than others, and
had to be pickled to make them edible at all.

While she waited for sugar and cinnamon she could not
help overhearing the talk around her. It was midmorning and
many of the housewives of the town and countryside were in
the store. The spaces in front of the counter were pretty well
filled. Women with big market baskets were poking around
among the piles of cereals and crackers, looking at lists, and
gazing up to the shelves behind the counters.

Close beside Rose, Mrs. Alcott and Mrs. Brisbane were
standing, awaiting their turns. Rose gazed around the store
and sighed. It would be a long time before her turn came,
there were so many ahead of her. Her head ached and her
feet were tired too, for she had been standing up by the sink
peeling peaches all the morning. Then she heard a name spoken just behind her. That was Mrs. Baker and Miss Ginny
Hollis. No need to turn around to see. Their voices were unmistakable.

"Have you heard how Joyce Whitney is?"

That was Miss Hollis.

"Why, no. Is she sick? I hadn't heard, but I'm not surprised. I should think she'd want to hide her head somewhere
and never come out again! What an awful thing it is to have
a scapegrace brother!"

Mrs. Baker's voice was raucous and penetrating. She was

slightly deaf and talked the louder because she seemed to feel
that all womankind had a like affliction. Several people
turned quickly to listen, and stopped their own conversation
as they looked toward Mrs. Baker.

"Oh, well, I don't know that she's sick. I just saw the doctor stop there as I was coming by just now, and I figured it
out that she must be. There wasn't anybody else to be sick. I
had just been talking with Mrs. Whitney over the telephone
and she seemed all right, so I supposed it must be Joyce. Her
father never calls Dr. Babb. He always gets Dr. Fulton. Besides, Joyce looked awfully peaked at the card party, didn't
you think so?"

Her voice was necessarily raised to accommodate Mrs.
Baker's dull ears, but she compromised by husking it into a
resonant whisper, which the whole store could hear. And suddenly the store became very quiet, with only now and then a
question from a purchaser. "How much is that a pound?" or
"You can give me half of one of those watermelons. Oh, you
don't cut them? Well, I don't want any then. Only half our
family eats watermelon anyway."

"Well, yes," said Mrs. Baker, "now you speak of it I remember she did look peaked. But then who wouldn't with a
gangster for a brother? I declare I think that Jason Whitney
ought to be strung up, disgracing a decent family the way
he's done. A pity he hadn't died when his poor mother did, I
say! There might have been some chance for him then, or for
the rest of the family anyway. So you think Joyce is sick?
Well, I must tell Mrs. Petrie. She was a friend of the first
Mrs. Whitney, you know, and she's always interested to know
about the family. Now that she can't get out any more she
sort of depends upon me for the news. By the way, did you
take notice to Mr. Whitney stealing around to the back door
before the party broke up and then stomping up the back
stairs?"

"Yes, I did!" said Miss Ginny. "He slipped in behind the
syringa bushes and went past the window where I sat. Pitiful,
isn't it, how hard his poor wife has to work to have a little
pleasure? Other men come *in* when they get home while
we're breaking up, and pass the time of day and all that, have
their little joke, and flatter the ladies. But not Nathan Whitney! He skulks into the house and stamps around upstairs.
Makes everybody know he's come home and wants his house
to himself. I certainly am glad *I* never married!" and Miss
Ginny tossed her head independently.

"Well, I didn't think so much of it that day," said Mrs. Baker. "Of course he must have been terribly worked up and all. When one has a son like that—you know—"

Mrs. Baker shook her head ominously.

"Oh, what do they think about Jason now?" asked Miss Ginny avidly. "Have they found out anything more?"

"Well, not definitely. But I heard Cal Green say that he thought they had the shooting pretty well tied up to Jason. You see they're about certain he did the most of the planning, though they do say—" her voice lowered into a sepulchral whisper—"that Rowan Parsons was really at the bottom of it all. He furnished the brains I guess. But Jason did the actual deed, they seem pretty sure. At least Cal Green said so, and his wife's cousin is living over at Talbuts, right across the corner from the bank, and if anybody would know they would."

"Rowan Parsons! Oh, what a pity! And he's so well educated! And so good looking! It really doesn't pay to educate children, does it? You never know how they're going to turn out. That's what I always say, it's a risk, having children! But Rowan Parsons! Who would ever have thought it! What makes them think so? Did they have evidence?"

"Well, I really don't know. But they all seem to think it's so! I guess because he and Jason Whitney went off together early that morning. That is, they say Rowan was waiting for Jason at Rowley's, just think of it, of all places! Poor Hannah Parsons! Her only son! And now they're telling that Rowan was in Bainbridge getting a car ready for them all to get away in."

"But I thought Jason was in the bank until half past ten that morning. How could he go to Bainbridge if he was in the bank?"

"Well, that's so, it must be that Rowan was waiting for him in Rowley's all that time."

"Well, but Rowan didn't know that Jason was going to be dismissed, surely?"

Mrs. Baker turned puzzled eyes on her inquisitor and looked annoyed.

"Oh, well, I don't know just how it was, but I know that Jason Whitney was in the thick of it all day, for everybody says so, and not a soul has heard a word from him or seen a hide of him since he marched out of that bank at ten-thirty on Wednesday morning! Not even his poor sick sister! No, Mr. Prentiss! Not that end of the steak. I want the little end.

At the prices you charge I can't afford the big end of the sirloin."

Rose had turned sharply around and almost cried out when Mrs. Baker said that no one had heard from Jason since he walked out of the bank at ten-thirty! Just in time she remembered and closed her lips, but she gave the woman an indignant look before she turned away, and drew a sharp breath. What cats these women were! To think they would talk that way about Jason!

But Miss Ginny was not through with the conversation yet. Mrs. Baker had turned away to follow the butcher till he cut her steak to fit her pocketbook, so Miss Ginny turned to the other two women beside Rose, Mrs. Alcott and Mrs. Brisbane.

"Such a pity, isn't it?" she said with sympathy in her voice. "Poor Joyce Whitney! First to lose her mother, and then to have a brother like that! Did you hear Mrs. Baker say just now that Jason hasn't sent Joyce any word since he was dismissed from the bank?"

"Oh, yes, we heard it," said Mrs. Brisbane. "One couldn't very well miss hearing it," and she gave a sly wink at Mrs. Alcott. "But what I want to know is, where did she find out all these details? Do the police report to her? However, I suppose it's all more or less true. Everybody seems to think so, anyway. Yes, poor Joyce! She hasn't a very pleasant life. I understand she and Mrs. Whitney don't get on so well together."

"Well, look at the way she does," said Miss Ginny. "Mrs. Whitney had the loveliest card party on Wednesday and Joyce wouldn't play at all. She never will. She won't even learn. And Mrs. Whitney had to invite an extra to make out the tables because Mrs. Pettibone was sick."

"Wasn't Joyce at the party at all?" asked Mrs. Alcott curiously.

"Oh, yes, she was there, that is, she took us upstairs to lay off our things, and she helped pass and pour at the end when the refreshments came on. But she didn't really enter into things the way Mrs. Baker's daughters do."

"Well, I think Joyce is to be pitied!" said Mrs. Brisbane. "She's like her mother, quiet and retiring, and her mother never went out to parties much. She was just a sweet homebody, and Joyce is going to be another one if they let her alone. I don't know but it's a relief. No lipstick and permanent waves on her!"

"She doesn't need any!" said Mrs. Alcott. "Her hair was born permanent, and looks wonderful, and as for lipstick, her lips are red enough by nature!"

"Not now," said Miss Ginny primly. "You ought to have seen her Wednesday. She was white as a sheet!"

"Well, she had a right to be if all you say is true!" said Mrs. Alcott. "Her only brother lost his job, and you know what her father is, worse than a northeast storm if anything goes wrong. And if she hadn't heard from her brother that made it that much worse. Though I doubt myself whether that is true. He probably phoned them!"

"No!" said Miss Ginny Hollis sharply, "I had it from the best of sources that he did not, and I for one am sorry for Joyce, even if she is so sort of hold-offish. She really can't expect much in the future if her brother is found guilty, and this should turn out to be a murder case as they are afraid now it will. You know nobody would marry a girl whose brother was a murderer, or a robber."

"Perhaps she doesn't want to get married," said Mrs. Brisbane cheerfully, with a significant look toward Miss Hollis. "Some don't!"

"Well, I think she ought to get married," said Mrs. Alcott complacently, as if she would be willing to arrange it if all were agreeable. "There's that nice Corey Watkins! Why doesn't she take him? They would make a nice pair. She's attractive enough and I've often seen him looking at her in church. It really would be better for her to marry, especially now since this has happened about her brother."

Rose's package was brought just then and she turned swiftly away. She felt that if she stayed another minute she would surely burst forth with indignant remonstrance, minister's daughter though she was. Those horrid women! She had never known how cruel they could be until now that they had turned their tongues on people that she liked. And to think they would talk that way about Jason's sweet sister Joyce! It was unthinkable! How she would like to be free just for once to stand out there in the middle of the store and tell them just what she thought of them, just what they were, and then tell them that they were all mistaken. That she knew that Jason had not been at Bainbridge, nor even with Rowan, anywhere. She was sure he had been alone when he telephoned her in the first despair of his dismissal. She was not quite sure how it was that she knew that, but somehow the conviction was strong and deep in her.

She tried to reason it out now as she walked slowly toward the parsonage. Well, it had been his tone. He had been confiding in her. He had needed sympathy. If Rowan had been with him and they had been engaged in the devilish things the town seemed to think, Jason would have had no time to turn back and telephone to a girl to whom he had given but a casual promise that she had never really expected him to keep. He would have been too busy to think of her.

Of course those catty women wouldn't believe that even if they knew it, but Rose *knew* it was true.

And then she fell to wondering if Joyce had something like that to comfort her. Could it be true that Jason had not telephoned his sister? She wished she knew. If he hadn't perhaps it would help if she told Joyce what Jason had said to her about leaving town. Would Father object to her doing that?

She thought about it all the morning while she helped her mother to finish the peaches, and when her father was sitting on the porch after lunch she slipped out beside him.

"Father," she said, sitting down on the arm of a big porch rocker, "they say that Joyce Whitney is sick, and they say she hasn't had any word from Jason at all."

"It probably isn't true. They are saying all sorts of things. Who told you she was sick?"

"Nobody told me. The women in the store were talking about it this morning. But I was thinking if it was true that she had not had any word from him maybe I ought to tell her that he phoned me."

"No!" said her father sharply, "I don't see that that's necessary. Besides, she might resent your speaking about it."

"She wouldn't," said Rose. "She's sweet. I thought I'd take some flowers and go over and say I heard she was sick, and then if she said anything maybe I could just tell her about Jason. I wouldn't, of course, if the way didn't open."

The minister looked at his sweet earnest young daughter yearningly.

"Take her the flowers if you like, child, but don't talk about Jason. I wouldn't like to have that old bear of a father of hers know that his scalawag of a son had even spoken to my girl!"

She was very still and serious for several minutes, rocking slowly back and forth and staring off at the clouds in a lazy blue sky. Then she said softly:

"Father, it wouldn't be anything like that. Mr. Whitney

would not know. But, I thought perhaps the Lord would like
me to tell Joyce!"

The father was very still now, his elbow on the chair arm,
his head resting against his hand, his eyes looking down, then
he said gravely:

"If that's the case, Rose, go. But go in the strength of the
Lord, not in your own strength."

"All right," she breathed softly.

She kissed him gravely and went away. He could hear her
up in her room getting ready to go out, but it was a long time
before she came down. The sun had gone lower in the west,
and her father had gone out to make parishional calls.

She wore the little pink dimity she had had on the day she
met Jason and asked him to meeting, and she went and
picked both hands full of pansies before she walked down the
street and out the highway toward the Whitney place.

Rose was four years younger than Joyce. She had never
been very intimate with her. For a few Sundays Joyce had
taught the Sunday School class she was in. She had always
shyly smiled whenever they met. It was going to be a little
awkward to explain her coming. As she walked out the edge
of the highway she tried to plan what she would say. Suppose
nobody was home but Mrs. Whitney? She never had liked
Mrs. Whitney. So her shy steps faltered by the way. Yet
somehow she was driven on.

It was Aunt Libby who opened the door, however. Mrs.
Whitney had betaken herself out of the gossip of home to
visit her sister seventy miles away.

"Is Joyce Whitney here?" asked Rose, almost hoping by
now that she wasn't.

"Well, she is an' she isn't!" said Aunt Libby with a quick
look around, and her habitual furtiveness, as if there were always a watcher dogging her steps.

"I heard she was sick," said Rose taking courage.

"Well, she ain't so good," said Aunt Libby under her
breath. "I had the doctor in this morning myself, seeing Mrs.
Whitney was away and couldn't mind. I ben havin' a misery
in my side fer several weeks an' I ain't hed time justa stop an'
see what was ailin' me. So I phoned him up an' he come. An'
I wanted Joyce ta let him look her over, too, but she
wouldn't. She said doctors couldn't do her no good! Just like
that! Poor thing, she's that worried! She ain't hed a word
from Jason yet, you know, an' it's just awful with folks

comin' here day in an' day out astin' questions which you ain't allowed to answer. The master he won't have no word said. It hurts a body to be that unfriendly—"

"Yes?" said Rose hopefully. "Well, I wonder if I could see Joyce just a minute or two. She wouldn't mind me, would she? I've brought her some flowers. I heard she was sick and I brought her some pansies!"

"Ain't they purty!" said Aunt Libby wistfully. "We don't have no flowers around here much. Mrs. Whitney, she don't care for 'em. But Joyce, she goes up in the woods and picks wild ones and takes 'em up to her room. She'd put 'em on the table, only Mrs. Whitney, she calls 'em weeds. Joyce is out there now in the grape arbor settin'. She stays out there a good deal so she won't have to see all the folks that come, an' hear 'em talk. It's just awful the things they say about Jason. It breaks my heart—"

"I know," said Rose sympathetically, "I think so too. It makes me angry. Do you suppose it would bother Joyce if I went out there and took her these pansies?"

Aunt Libby gave another of her frightened looks back of her and hesitated.

"I don't guess it would," she said doubtfully. She liked dramatic entrances. She loved bringing things to a climax. These two pretty young things sort of belonged together. Of course she had been set to keep watch and keep out visitors, but this young thing in pink dimity was different.

"Suppose you just walk around the house that side till you come on the path that leads to the arbor. You'll find the way. And then she won't think I sent you."

Rose gave Aunt Libby an understanding smile and went as she was bidden, presently arriving at the entrance to the grape arbor, a long deep trellis covered thickly with great grape leaves, and drooping bunches of purple fruit with the soft blue bloom on them. It was cool and dark there, a sweet quiet gloom where green shadows and purple lights prevailed.

Down at the far end there was a light bench painted white and there Joyce sat slumped sadly with her face in her hands.

Rose paused in dismay. Joyce was crying and she would be intruding! It was not right. She must go away. She would leave the flowers with Aunt Libby and go away.

She turned, but her light step crunched on the gravel of the path, and Joyce lifted her head startled.

"Oh, please excuse me!" said Rose looking frightened. "I didn't mean to intrude. I heard you were sick and I brought you some flowers! But I'll leave them in the house and go away. I know you don't want to be bothered with me now."

"No, don't go away!" said Joyce yearningly. "I am glad you came. It was dear of you! I'm not sick, but I'm very sad, and—I'm so alone!"

Suddenly Rose put the flowers down on the bench and sat down beside Joyce, putting her arms softly around the older girl's neck.

"I'm so sorry!" breathed Rose. "I love you!"

And suddenly Joyce was crying with her face in Rose's neck. Rose held her close and began to cry with her. There was a big wet spot on Rose's nice pink dimity shoulder, wet with hot tears.

"You know," said Joyce at last, lifting her tear-wet face in apology, "I haven't—heard—from my brother yet, and—people are saying such dreadful things about him!"

"I know," said Rose holding her tight, "they are awful! And it's all silly, what they are saying. Jason wouldn't do any of those things! Of course he wouldn't. I know Jason," and she held her pretty tear-wet face up bravely. "We went to school together, you know. He sat right across the aisle from me the whole last year. We were seniors together. Jason wasn't like that! He was splendid! He didn't do mean things. He only did funny things!"

"Oh, thank you for saying that, dear!" said Joyce with a trembling smile on her lips. "I know he wasn't like that, but I didn't know anybody else knew it. Even Father couldn't always understand him. You see everything is against him—a lot of evidence. And he hasn't been heard from. If I could only hear just a word from him. If I could only know he is safe."

"Of course he's safe!" said Rose with the confidence of an older person. "He's gone away to find a better job and get a square deal. He felt he couldn't start fresh in this old town and he's gone away to begin over again. I know, for he told me so!"

"He *told* you so!" Joyce echoed the words in sudden startled wonder and delight. "You mean you saw him? You talked with him?"

"No, I didn't see him, but I talked with him. He called me up on the telephone. That's why I came over. I thought you ought to know."

"He called you up on the telephone? Oh, *when* did he call you?"

"Wednesday noon! Father didn't want me to say anything to anybody. He didn't think it had any bearing on the case, and he thought people would misunderstand."

"They would, of course," said Joyce quickly. "Oh, people are terrible! But of course they need not know. But please go on. How did he come to call you up? I did not even know you were friends."

"We weren't," said Rose quickly. "Only schoolmates. We never talked much to each other, only to say good morning, and once he brought a bunch of wild roses to school, just three or four of them and laid them on my desk. Just grinned and laid them on my desk! I thanked him and smiled, and that was all. We never talked even after that, only when we had to ask where a lesson was or something. But last week Friday I was walking along the street and he came from the other direction, and when we met he stopped and said good morning. He acted as if he was going to say something else, and when he didn't I spoke. I asked him if he wouldn't be the tenth one on my list to come to the big rally in the church Wednesday night. I had only nine people and I'd promised to ask ten. We all did. But I somehow couldn't think of a tenth that nobody else had asked. I don't know why I suddenly asked him. I didn't expect him to come. I knew he never came to our church. But I was embarrassed and wanted to say something, so I asked him."

"And what did he say?" the sister asked eagerly.

"Why, he said, '*Me,* Go to church? *I* never go to church!' and then I guess I looked disappointed so he asked what it was, just prayer-meeting? And I told him about the rally with the wonderful speaker from New York, and all of a sudden he said, 'All right, Kid, I'll come if it will please you.' "

"And then he went away!" said the sister sadly. "Oh if he had only stayed and gone to that meeting! How wonderful that would have been! That was Wednesday night, wasn't it? Oh, that might have saved all this awfulness! But then, even if he had been here, he might not have come. He might have had some excuse. Boys are that way sometimes. Maybe he didn't even intend to come when he promised."

There was a quiver of tears about her voice, but Rose spoke quickly.

"Yes, I think he really meant to come. He said he did when he called me up."

"You mean he called you up after that?"

"Yes, he called me up to tell me he couldn't come, and he said he had really meant to come and was sorry he couldn't, but that something had happened down at the bank and he was leaving. And then before I thought what I was doing I said, 'Oh, Jason, you haven't done anything to make them—' and then I stopped. I was frightened that I had suggested such a thing. But he took me right up and said, no, he hadn't done anything wrong, but the poor fishes thought he had, and that was just as bad. And he said the worst of it was he couldn't tell all he knew, and so they had pinned it all on him, and there was no use his staying here, he couldn't get a square deal anywhere!"

"That is true!" said Joyce with a little moan. "Nobody stood up for him anywhere!"

"I know," said Rose. "I'm sorry! But I thought it might make a little difference to you to know he said he hadn't done anything wrong. Of course I knew you believed in him. But I thought it might help a little to know what he said."

"It does!" said Joyce. "It helps a great deal, and it was sweet of you to come. It was precious!" And then suddenly her heart thrilled with the thought of the last time that word had been used in her hearing, and about herself.

"But you are precious yourself," said Rose gravely. "That's why I wanted to come. Father thought I might be intruding, but I felt I should come."

"Your father knows?"

"Yes. I didn't know what to do and I asked him. He is a very understanding father. He won't tell anybody else."

"Oh, I'm glad he knows!" said Joyce suddenly. "Of course he would keep it to himself for your sake if for no other reason. But I'm glad one good man knows."

"He believes in him, too," said Rose thoughtfully. "I'm sure he does."

"Well, that is a comfort," said Joyce. "Even if he didn't quite believe in him, it would be good just to know he was willing to think any good at all of him, to even consider it. It seems as if very few others are. Just the Parsons. I don't know any others."

"Oh, I'm glad the Parsons believe in him," said Rose happily. "I always liked them. And Rowan, too, though I never knew him so well. He's been away at college. But—I don't believe Rowan had anything to do with all this burglary business either."

"No, he didn't!" said Joyce emphatically. "I happen to know that he didn't! I can't tell you all about it now, but I know, and sometime I hope I can tell you."

"Well, I'm glad about that too. Rowan was Jason's friend. I know he used to like him when he was in high school. I've heard Jason talking to the boys at recess and telling them what Rowan could do in athletics and things."

"Yes," said Joyce, a soft color stealing into her pale face. "He always made a hero out of Rowan. And that's what makes it so outrageous what they are saying about them both!"

"I know," said Rose. "I was down at the store this morning getting some things for mother and I heard some of those women talking. I wanted to turn around and shake them till they couldn't get their breath. I felt very wicked. It seemed as if I could do something awful to them, and they were just laughing and babbling on. Some of them had been up to your mother's tea or something."

"I know," said Joyce, "that ghastly bridge party. But I suppose it doesn't matter, since we know what they are saying is not true."

"Yes, but it's awful that they can go on saying those things when we—when you are just suffering about it all."

"Well, I'm not going to suffer!" said Joyce trying to speak brightly. "I'm going to try and look up and rejoice. I certainly ought to be thankful to God, and thankful to you for bringing me this word. I never doubted Jason. I knew he hadn't broken into the bank nor shot Mr. Paisley, but it is good to know his own word concerning his dismissal from the bank. It takes away a great horror that was beginning to fill my mind. I know now there must be some explanation of his absence and his silence, and probably he doesn't know all that has happened here, and wouldn't realize how I would agonize over him."

"Yes," said Rose, "he spoke of you. I almost forgot that part."

"He spoke of me?" said Joyce her eyes lighting with hope.

"Yes, he said that nobody cared anything about him or believed in him except his sister."

"Oh! How sweet it is to know that! He's always been shy of affection. I didn't know whether he cared or not."

"He does!" said Rose with deep conviction. "I could tell by his voice. He was feeling pretty badly. He said he was beating it and he didn't know as he would ever come back, but then after a minute he said if the time ever came when he felt he was fit to come back he'd let me know."

Rose's voice was very low as she told this. It seemed too much her own to let another hear it, and yet she knew the sister would treasure it. It surely showed that Jason had no idea at that time of committing any crime.

They both sat very still for a moment thinking this over. Then Joyce suddenly threw her arms about Rose and drew her close to her.

"You dear little girl!" she said. "You have comforted me a lot! You have brought me a word that shows the very best side of my dear brother, and it seems to lift me above the things that people are saying and help me to bear it all. I guess God is going to work it all out somehow, and I'm going to trust Him."

"Yes," said Rose softly, "I guess God knows how to straighten this all out."

The two girls sat together very silently for a few minutes with their arms about one another, and then Joyce gathered up the cool velvet pansies and buried her hot face in them, breathing in their delicate spicy fragrance.

"I shall never forget what you have done for me!" said Joyce at last as Rose got up to go. "You have given me more assurance to hold up my head among the terrible kindness of my neighbors."

Then suddenly from the house came the clarion voice of Mrs. Whitney:

"Joyce, Joyce! Where on earth are you! For pity's sake come into the house. I want you at once!"

Mrs. Whitney had thought of something, and had come home to prevent it. It had occurred to her that during her absence Joyce might somehow get in touch with her brother and bring the renegade home to harbor him, to hide him perhaps, and that *must not be!* So she had taken the first train home to prevent it.

"Joyce, Joyce! Where are you?" the voice clanged on impatiently.

The two girls huddled together in the dim recesses of the arbor, looked into each other's eyes for an instant, reading each other's thoughts, and then suddenly they smiled, a soft quiet smile that passed like a flash of understanding from the eyes of one to the other.

"It's all right," whispered Rose, "I was just going anyway. You just let me slip around the other side of the house, the way I came, and she'll never know I was here. Good-bye. I've loved being with you."

Joyce stooped suddenly and kissed her. Then Rose stole out from the back of the arbor and around behind the trees, skirting the house behind the shrubbery; she climbed nimbly over a fence and was on the highway.

Joyce laid her pansies down in the grass in a hidden spot in the arbor till she could retrieve them after dark and carry them to her own room. Then she turned and went swiftly in to answer the summons.

CHAPTER IX

That night Corey Watkins came to call on Joyce.

She had slipped out to the grape arbor to get her pansies and she heard the steps coming up the walk, and poor tired old Aunt Libby shuffling to the door.

It would likely be some of her stepmother's friends, and at first she thought she could stay out in the arbor. And then there came a sudden panic lest they would stay all evening and she would be called and would have to go in. She felt she just could not go in tonight and talk with anybody, and answer any more of those awful questions her stepmother's friends asked her because they were afraid to ask Mrs. Whitney. It would be better to go straight to bed.

So she scooped up the cool velvety flowers, and flew back into the kitchen door and up the back stairs swiftly, silently, before Aunt Libby had got the chain and bolt fairly off the front door.

She locked her door, slipped her flowers into the washbowl and undressed in the dark. If anybody called for her she would be in bed with a headache. That was perfectly true. She had had a headache all the afternoon. It almost seemed as if she had had it continuously since Jason went away.

Presently she heard Mrs. Whitney's voice ring out the back door calling her, and then after a little Aunt Libby came puffing and panting up the stairs and tried her door, tapped stealthily when she found it locked, and whispered rustily:

"Miss Joyce! You got a young man downstairs! You better come down right away. Mrs. Whitney's all stirred up about it."

"Oh, I'm sorry, Aunt Libby, but I can't come down. I've got a bad headache and I've gone to bed."

There was silence for an instant and then Aunt Libby's distressed voice:

"You better come anyway. She's on her high horse! Here she comes!" and Aunt Libby limped away to meet her mistress on the stairs.

Then Joyce heard her stepmother's firm tread on the landing and up the flight to her door, heard her grasp on the doorknob.

"Open this door instantly, Joyce!" she demanded in a low fierce voice. "I want to speak to you. I've often told you that it isn't safe to lock doors so your family can't get in."

There was nothing for it but to get up and open the door, for the next move would be to call for help from the visitor whoever he was, or to use force on the door. And even a heavy mahogany door could not long resist the assault of so substantial a body as Mrs. Whitney's.

Joyce unlocked the door and slid back into her bed with her face to the wall. Her stepmother instantly snapped on the light and gave a swift survey of the room, not missing the pansies.

"Now, what's all this about going to bed at this hour?"

"I've had a terrific headache all the afternoon and I just wanted to get to sleep."

"Well, you'll have to wait awhile for sleep. This is no hour to give way to your feelings. Hurry and put on your clothes! Someone has come to call on you."

"To call on *me?*" said Joyce swinging around and watching her stepmother. "Whoever it is, won't you please tell them I've gone to bed with a headache?"

"Certainly not!" said Mrs. Whitney. "You don't have so many young men callers that I'm going to send the first one flying. Get up and dress as fast as you can. I'll send Libby up with some hot tea. Drink it while you are dressing, and don't you dare be long about it either. You'll be all right when you get downstairs laughing and talking. And anyway you've got to come. I'm not going to have it said that we are giving way to our feelings. They'll get us into court to testify, perhaps, if we seem to be upset. Where did those pansies come from?" She eyed her stepdaughter sharply.

"Oh, just one of the girls that used to be in my Sunday School class brought them to me," evaded Joyce.

"How silly! I suppose she thought you were suffering and

needed consolation! She probably caught you out in the woods mooning around," she said contemptuously.

Joyce did not answer. She was slipping into her garments as rapidly as she could.

"Who is downstairs?" she asked presently in a weary voice. Not that she cared.

"Why, that young Corey Watkins," announced Mrs. Whitney in pride. "It's nice of him to come. He's in the bank, isn't he? I didn't realize what a good looking young fellow he is, and so well-groomed!"

That was a new phrase Mrs. Whitney had picked up on her visit to her sister.

"Corey Watkins!" said Joyce. "What on earth is he coming here for? I hardly know him at all."

"Why he's probably coming to be kind, or to offer you sympathy. But he made the excuse that he wants you to play over something for him to sing. He says Miss Bright is off visiting her aunt, and he has to sing in church next Sunday. I told him you'd be glad to do it for him. He wants you to try it over with him, and then go down to the church rehearsal and play it there for him. He says he can't sing with that substitute organist they have."

Joyce paused in her dressing and looked aghast.

"Well, I certainly will not go down to that rehearsal!" she said almost fiercely. "I'll play it over for him once, but then I'm done."

"Now, look here, Joyce. You can't treat a young man that way! The first really eligible young man that has called on you since you came home from college! And especially at a time like this. It's very brave for him to come in the face of public opinion. And it will be a good thing for you to go down to that rehearsal in his company. People will see that you are not despised, even if your brother has committed forgery, or burglary or whatever it is."

Joyce whirled around upon Mrs. Whitney white to the lips, and with blue flames of anger in her eyes. For an instant she felt as if she must rush upon her tormentor and shake her, or throw the hairbrush at her, or something. Then she suddenly realized that fury would get her nowhere and would only do harm, and she laid the hairbrush down on the bureau and tried to speak steadily.

"My brother has not done any of those things, and you shall not talk as if he had. I shall have to tell my father if you say anything like that again. And I'm certain that I do not want anybody to take up for me on any such reason. I do not feel the need of that kind of support. I will go down and play the music over for him, but I will not go with him to the rehearsal. No amount of coaxing or commanding will make me do it."

"Look here, Joyce, don't be a fool. You aren't such a beauty that you can expect to have many more young men come around you, especially now since Jason is under the frown of the town, and you'd better make the best of this perfectly respectable young man. With your plain looks he's likely all you'll get, and you want to make the most of your chances, don't you?"

"Why?" asked Joyce suddenly.

"Well, you don't want to be a drag on your father all your life, do you?"

An angry flame swept over Joyce's face and she turned and walked out of the room.

"Well, you needn't get angry," pursued Mrs. Whitney's voice, "I'm only telling you for your own good, and who but I who stand in place of a mother to you, should do it? And a thankless task I have, too!"

But Joyce was walking down the stairs. And not until then, not until it was too late to call her back, did Mrs. Whitney notice that Joyce had put on an old morning dress, and that her hair was not arranged in its usual neat order, but barely slicked over with a single stroke of the brush, and knotted hastily at her neck. Joyce hadn't taken the slightest trouble to dress up for the young man, and she was marching down and into the front room like an army with banners going to the fray. Her stepmother leaned over the banister full of rage. Such a nice young man he was. So neat! And Joyce going down like that! And horror of horrors, she was wearing bedroom slippers! Had she done that on purpose, or just forgotten them?

She could hear Joyce's clear voice down there explaining not at all graciously:

"I'm sorry to have kept you waiting, but I had gone to bed with a bad headache. You'll have to excuse my appearance. I just slipped on something to come down and play your song over for you, since my stepmother seemed to think you were in some distress about it."

Corey Watkins was a trim neat young man with an effect of drabness. He had small hard gray eyes, drabish hair and eyelashes, a neat tight mouth, and a way of setting it that made it appear firmer than it was. He was dapper in the extreme, with close-cut hair, never ruffled from its tight satin smoothness. His face was expressionless.

"Well, I'm sorry you are suffering," he said stiffly, "but I appreciate your coming down. This really is quite important, and perhaps as Mrs. Whitney suggested, it may do you good to get out of yourself and mingle with people a little while. I thought we'd just try this over here once or twice and then I'd take you down to the rehearsal and let them see that I have my own accompanist."

"I'll play it over for you here," said Joyce firmly, "but I cannot go out anywhere tonight. You'll have to excuse me. It will be quite impossible. Is this the music?"

She took the sheet of music out of his hand and walked to the piano, sat down and began to play.

Corey Watkins had a neat tight hard voice, too, a high tenor with places in it that sounded as if he had a hot potato in his mouth. After the first playing he opened his small tight mouth and began to sing in a small tight way.

Joyce played on like an automaton, scarcely speaking except to correct a note which he had sung wrong.

At last Corey said he thought he had it, and with his hard little glint of a smile tried once more to persuade her to go down to the rehearsal with him.

"I'd like to show them what a really fine accompanist I have secured," he said with satisfaction. "They were going to force that stranger on me and she can't play accompaniments properly."

"It is quite impossible!" said Joyce lifting tired eyes a trifle haughtily.

"That was so sweet!" burst in Mrs. Whitney in a gushing voice, arriving in the nick of time with a tray of lemonade and cake and planting her substantial body in the doorway as Joyce was leading her would-be caller to the door in spite of himself.

Corey Watkins was nothing loth to sit down for refreshments, although it was little past the usual supper time of the village, and he couldn't have been in need of nourishment.

Joyce paused, hesitated and was about to beg to be excused, but her stepmother's stern eye fixed her.

"Sit down, Joycie dear," she said in the tone of an elephant caressing a moth. "Mr. Watkins will want to try the song over again after we are done, before he goes to sing it in public. A little longer won't hurt you, dear, and I've told

Aunt Libby to bring you a cup of tea. You'll feel better after you've had it. Perhaps you'll even feel well enough to go down to the church. You have such a lovely voice, Mr. Watkins, it's a pity not to be well accompanied. And we're so proud of our little girl's playing. It really does help, in singing, don't you think it does, to have a good accompanist?"

Joyce sat down but she was silent. She didn't even drink the tea when it came. She sat and listened to her stepmother, babbling on, and looked coldly at Corey Watkins, and wondered if he would ever go.

She played the song over again perfunctorily after they had finished the lemonade and cake, and then, as Mrs. Whitney had taken herself away on some pretext, she had to walk to the front door to see the young man out.

Corey Watkins stood on the piazza for a moment looking down at Joyce.

"I wish to express my sympathy, Miss Joyce, in your trouble," he said stiltedly, "and to tell you that you have my utmost respect. I shall not let what your brother has done affect my respect for you in the least. I would like to be your friend."

Joyce drew herself to her slender height and looked at him with fire in her eyes. It was not often Joyce was roused, especially before outsiders, but she was roused now.

"I do not understand you, Corey Watkins," she said haughtily. "My brother has done nothing to be ashamed of, and I do not need to be commiserated on his account."

"Ah!" said Corey Watkins sorrowfully, "then they have not told you. I am sorry that I should have to be the first to mention it. But anyway, Miss Joyce, I want you to know that I am your friend, no matter what your brother has done. I am sorry that you cannot see your way clear to put his trouble aside and come with me where I assure you you will find welcome. Anyone whom I bring is always welcome. But I shall call again when you have had time to become more resigned. Good night!"

He lifted his hat, and went neatly down the steps and out to his car. Joyce stood watching him, too angry to make reply.

After that Joyce spent a good many hours of each day in the woods, and after supper out in the grape arbor whence she could easily flee to the edge of the woodland if she should hear someone coming to call. Joyce did not want to get involved with Corey Watkins, nor to have another altercation with him. The memory of what he said had been with her every hour in the day since he came, and she had been sure from his manner that he meant to come again. Very well, when he did she would not be there!

So she escaped every evening into the twilight, sometimes going over to see Hannah, but not often, because her stepmother seemed to be especially aroused if she knew she had been there. She said it would make it bad if there was a trial, to have had the families seeing much of one another, since the two sons were involved in the trouble. So Joyce was careful to go only after dark, and quite unbeknownst to her family.

Three times the quiet persistence of Corey Watkins had brought him to the Whitney house, where each time he had waited for an hour and a half for Joyce's return, conversing meantime with Mrs. Whitney, getting very well acquainted indeed with the ways of the family and gleaning much knowledge on the side concerning Joyce and her various whims, according to her stepmother.

But Joyce was very wary. She was careful to take a distant survey of the front lawn and drive before returning, and to be sure whether Corey's car was parked anywhere about. She would not come in until it was gone.

But the third time Corey was wise and came on foot from the village, walking on the grass instead of the drive and coming to the house most quietly. However, Joyce heard voices when she entered cautiously that night, and managed to creep up the back stairs without getting caught.

So at last Mrs. Whitney decided to take a hand in the matter, and invited Corey to dinner one night.

She didn't tell her husband until he came home from the village late in the afternoon, and then most adroitly she told Nathan that Corey was interested in Joyce and Joyce always managed to be away when he came to the house, so she had invited him to dinner.

Nathan wasn't pleased, but as Corey was just driving in there wasn't much he could do about it except be most surly and ungracious to the young man. However, Corey was thickskinned, so it didn't matter. When he decided to do anything he went right ahead regardless of all hindrances, so he walked in and conducted himself with perfect ease in spite of the coldness of father and daughter, acting as if he had a well

assured basis to go on in Mrs. Whitney's alliance, as indeed
he really did. Mrs. Whitney was mistress of that house if
there ever was one.

Joyce came in at the last moment, through the side entrance. She had been away taking a walk with Rose Allison all
the afternoon, and hadn't seen even Aunt Libby, so the guest
was an entire surprise to her. As she walked into the dining
room and saw who was there a quick flash of indignation
swept over her face. But she had control of herself at once,
and came in quietly, bowing distantly to Corey, as if dis-
claiming from the start any idea that he was her guest.

During the meal she was absolutely silent except when a
question was directly addressed to her, then she answered
quietly and briefly. She was trying during the entire time to
think of a way of escape from going into the parlor after
supper, but there was no outside possibility that would not involve the escort of Corey Watkins, and she shrank inexpressi-
bly from that.

It was not that she had ever had any very strong prejudice
against him. She hadn't been much in his vicinity because of
her years away at college, and the grown-up Corey seemed to
her almost as colorless as the small boy Corey she vaguely
remembered in her girlhood. But she had been so angered by
his calm taking it for granted that Jason was a criminal that
she could scarcely bear to look at him.

Nathan Whitney ate his supper in utter silence except to
ask for more bread, or butter, and when he was done he
swung his chair around and enveloped himself in the evening
paper, having a feverish manner that denoted unusual nervous excitement. Joyce, as she watched him covertly wondered if he had heard anything more about Jason. She hoped
the visitor would not notice how nervous her father was and
report it in the town. If it had been anybody else who was
taking supper with them Joyce would have been mortified at
the way her father acted, but since it was this young man
with his unwonted persistence, she was almost glad of it,
though she knew there would be a battle between her father
and stepmother as soon as the guest was gone.

Nathan Whitney left them as soon as the meal was over
and went, paper and all, to the small room opposite the dining room which he called his office shutting himself up there,
while Joyce, perforce drifted into the parlor.

Mrs. Whitney had done most of the conversing during supper, and she was full of talk now as she turned on the parlor lights.

"Joyce, why don't you and Mr. Watkins sit on the couch together and look at your college photographs? Now that you have them in an album by themselves they are really well worth looking at. I think seeing pictures of one's friends is such a good way to get acquainted, don't you, Mr. Watkins?"

Yes, Corey said he thought it was. He expressed a consuming desire to see the pictures and have Joyce tell him about them.

But Joyce shook her head.

"Sorry," she said in a tone that showed she wasn't in the least sorry, "I loaned the book to Rose Allison to copy the head of a fancy picture I had in there. She's doing a poster for something at the church and the head gave her just the pose she wanted."

Joyce settled down on a distant chair, as far as possible from the one near which Corey was hovering, and as unrelated to any other chair as it could possibly be in Mrs. Whitney's parlor which was literally running over with little fancy chairs bursting in between large overstuffed ones.

"How vexing!" said Mrs. Whitney, looking at Joyce as if she thought she must be lying. "Well, here is the next best thing!" and she hauled out a couple of albums from a shelf in an elaborate cabinet of ornate structure.

"Here!" she cried triumphantly. "This is Jason's college album. He must have left it down here the night he had those fellows here!" and she smiled sweetly at Joyce. Just as if she didn't know that Jason never left his things downstairs! Just as if she were not aware that Jason's personal things like albums were always under lock and key!

Joyce gazed at the big gray book with a college emblem on its cover in horror. How had her stepmother got hold of that book? She knew Jason never left it out. She must have picked and pried till she got the door of his closet open. Jason had always kept that book on the top shelf of his closet!

Suddenly Joyce walked swiftly over and took the book from her stepmother's hand.

"No!" she said sharply. "Not that book! Jason would not like us to be looking over his personal pictures. He would resent it very much! Suppose he should come walking in here and find us looking through a book that he had locked away? He might come back at any moment, you know."

She turned protesting eyes toward her stepmother.

"Oh," laughed Mrs. Whitney, "Jason is scarcely in a position to object to anything we might do."

"He'll scarcely come walking in just now anyway, I fancy," said Corey with a dry cackle that he seemed to think was humor. He turned toward Joyce, but she suddenly whirled and with the big book clasped in her arms she ran swiftly up the stairs and hid the book in her own room, coming down with a large portfolio containing a number of brightly illustrated folders of foreign places that a college mate of hers who was traveling abroad had sent her.

"Mr. Watkins isn't interested in seeing a lot of college people that he doesn't know, Mother," said she as she came forward with the substitutes in her hand. "They wouldn't interest him. But here are some most gorgeous pictures that just came from abroad. I'm sure he'll like to look at these," and she smiled gravely as she handed him the folios.

Corey took the portfolio suspiciously and opened it.

"Sit down on the couch, both of you," urged Mrs. Whitney. "Joyce, you sit down beside him and tell him about them."

She motioned toward the couch and Corey followed her suggestion, but Joyce went over on the other side of the room and sat down.

"Mr. Watkins doesn't need to be told about them," she said coolly. "He probably knows more than I do about every one of those places, and one doesn't want to be bothered with talk when one has nice interesting pictures to look at."

"Well, you could enjoy them together, my dear!" gently reproved Mrs. Whitney. She never "my-deared" Joyce except when there was company present. And how Joyce hated this pose of charming companionship for the benefit of others. It didn't deceive anybody, either. Why would she do it?

"Well, I've seen them all, you know, Mother," said Joyce firmly. "Why don't you go and look at them with Mr. Watkins?"

Then as if to make the matter more decided Joyce went to the piano and sat down, letting her fingers ripple lightly over the keys, just to help her detach herself from this tête-a-tête that was being forced upon her.

They got through the evening at last, somehow, Joyce foiling every attempt on the part of her stepmother to leave the two alone, and finally the young man took himself away, and reproaches began to rain down upon the poor child's head.

"I never was so ashamed in my life! A perfectly respectable young man, and a great admirer of yours! You in your present position should be glad and grateful to have attentions from one who is such a successful person. There is a man to be proud of! Nobody suspects him of doing anything crooked. They never link his name with those of gangsters and murderers. Why? Because he has never been indiscreet enough to mix with the offscouring of the earth! And you, the sister of a boy under suspicion of almost anything, dare to treat him with disdain! Here in your own house, an invited guest!"

"He was not my guest, Mother, and you didn't even tell me he was coming. Besides I didn't treat him discourteously."

"And why didn't I tell you he was coming? Because on every occasion possible you have been running off to hide whenever he comes anywhere near here. He wishes to come here socially, to have you for a friend, and you baffle his attempts at every turn."

"I don't want him for a friend," said Joyce quietly. "I suppose I have a right to choose my friends, don't I? I'll be polite to him, but that's all. I won't go out anywhere with him."

"Yes, you think you have a right to choose your own friends. Well, I don't know about that. I suppose you'd like to go around with that Rowan Parsons. You're so thick with his plain old mother! But he's another criminal! My word! I certainly married into a lovely crowd! You turn down a charming successful young man whom everybody, simply *every-* body respects, and yet if that fellow at the next farm were to come back tonight and ask you, you'd be willing to ride around in his old shabby car in the moonlight till all hours! A criminal!"

But Joyce had borne all she could stand. She turned and flashed up the stairs and locked herself in her room, weeping her heart out, until she fell asleep and dreamed that Rowan was kneeling beside her with his arm about her, and his lips upon hers and saying that she was precious.

The days went by breathlessly for a time, everyone expecting hourly something decisive to happen. The town grew almost impatient over the delay, and the two families most concerned looked haggard and worn as day after day went by and still no news came of the two young men who had so suddenly disappeared from the home town.

Then word came from the place where the inquest and inquisition had gone on over the two Rowleys, living and dead.

But nothing had developed. The living Rowley had nothing to say, would not open his lips to answer the questions that were put to him. Not even the most severe grilling had been able to make him say anything except that he was not guilty.

It presently developed that both his and his brother's pictures were in the Rogues' Gallery, and that they had both been wanted for sometime in cases even more serious than the one back in the village where they had been in hiding from the law, under assumed names, for the past three or four years. All that time they had been working with a gang in far bigger enterprises than just the looting of a country bank and the shooting of a simple kindly night watchman. All these things were brought to light but they didn't help the two households most concerned, nor ease the pain of Mother Hannah, and the two girls, who nightly wept and prayed and tried to endure the days as if nothing was the matter.

And the suspicions were not allayed.

As the days went by rumors grew into stories that were related as truth beside firesides in country farm houses, and carried to nearby villages, and written to faraway friends, and each time they were related they grew more virulent, until the first teller would scarce have recognized even the smallest fragment of his original story. And the stories came back to the homes; they were told about in great wave lengths of sorrow and heartbreak.

And then one day, Nathan Whitney who had been growing more and more irascible, both at home and abroad, had a fight in the public square of the village with a drunken truck driver who stumbled out of a tavern next the hotel, and called out his name and taunted him in the vilest of language with being the father of a thieving, murdering gangster!

Nathan knocked the drunken brawler cold, and then stalked away to his home, leaving his neighbors to look after the man, no one who had watched the fray lifting a hand to stop him.

And when he reached the house he opened the door into the parlor where his wife and daughter sat, entertaining a couple of ladies of the neighborhood who had called to see what news they could squeeze out for the quota of the day.

He stood a second looking from one to the other, and then he opened his mouth to speak, but his lips refused to function, and twisted themselves fearfully about his face. His strong frame tottered and collapsed like a great building under a heavy blow, shattered, bowed, broken!

He fell and his fall jarred the house. Aunt Libby rushed in and stood staring at him and began to weep wildly and to jabber:

"Oh! He's had a stroke at last! I ben expectin' it, the way he's carried on. Oh, poor soul! Poor soul!"

Mrs. Whitney stood still long enough for the startled look to pass into indignant action and then she went to the telephone and sent for the doctor. On second thought she went back and sent for the other doctor, too. The first one had been her doctor, but if this was a stroke as Aunt Libby said, and Aunt Libby ought to know having lived so long in the poorhouse where they had them often, why he should have his due. So she sent for Dr. Fulton.

Joyce went at once to her father and knelt beside him with his head in her lap and her arms about him, her lips to his poor twisted face.

Then the two ladies who had been calling, drifted silently out to get their news to their respective districts as swiftly as tongues could carry them.

CHAPTER X

The whole town was stirred by Nathan Whitney's sudden stroke. For as much as two or three days they took pause again from hard words and hushed their voices when they spoke of him. They said it was sad, and ceased not day nor night to call up on the telephone and hear how he was.

Day after day the word came back that he was still alive but that was all. The doctor gave no hope of his recovery, and yet he did not know whether he would die soon or linger. The other doctor agreed. People lifted hands of horror and were aghast.

By the fourth day the wise ones among the gossips had begun to whisper about Jason. Where was he? Did he know of his father's condition? Would he try to come home? Well, if he came he would be arrested, so likely he wouldn't come home. Did the family know where he was, and were they keeping it from the authorities? What had made Nathan Whitney so unusually nervous and troubled those last few days before his stroke? Did he have some terrible news?

And then that awful word "murderer" began to creep around on its hands and knees again, stealing into the most respectable houses and presenting thoughts to unwary victims.

If Nathan Whitney died, then surely his son would be as much a murderer as if he had actually shot him to death. As if old Sam Paisley had died from the shot that was fired that fatal night when the bank was robbed.

Murder! Murder! Murder!

Murder come home to strike at the father of the murderer! The little flames of words stole here, stole there, and

114

caught on tinder minds, and flared and flamed so quietly that no one noticed at first, until it swept the whole countryside, and Joyce, listening to certain vitriolic phrases as they drifted into the house by way of grocery boys, nurses, and Aunt Libby's tearful babbling, was glad that her father was out of it all.

For they were saying now, some of them, that Jason had come by his murdering tendency naturally. That Nathan Whitney was a murderer at heart or he would not have fought that poor drunken truck driver.

Not that the truck driver was killed. No, far from it. He had slept it off with a bruise or two and a black eye, and rallied to prate about suing the Whitneys.

But Nathan Whitney was lying quietly out of it all, and safe as if he had died and were lying in his grave. They could not touch a man with his body frozen in a deathly grasp like that, a man with a twisted face and silent lips lying in the grip of a living death! Neither law nor bluster, nor the scorpion lips of his fellows could hurt him now.

And whether he was feeling anything, or thinking anything, they could not tell, nor whether the terrible vise that held him would relax at all before he died and let him speak to them all once more; nor whether he would just slip away silently without a change; they could not tell.

So Joyce ministered to him daily, and watched his tortured eyes that followed her everywhere she went. They were the only things about him that could move, those terrible eyes so full of anguish.

And sometimes he would seem to look beyond her toward the door with a kind of fright in his eyes, but then his gaze would be upon her again, and she would smile and talk lovingly to him.

In those days of her quiet ministration she came nearer to her father than she had ever come before. She told him how she loved him! She tried to soothe him. And one day when his eyes wore that look of fright, turned toward the door, she suddenly said without premeditation:

"She isn't here, Father. She's gone away to her sister's to rest awhile." He looked at her steadily as she said it over again, and then she fancied there came a relief in his eyes. Perhaps it was only fancy, but he fell asleep and slept longer than since he had been seized.

Hannah Parsons came over and brought little things that she thought he might be able to swallow. She touched Joyce's forehead lightly with her lips and whispered:

"We are praying for you, Father and I." And then she turned her eyes toward the bed and added: "And for him! Charles says he's sure he used to know the Lord, long ago!"

And after that, when the night nurse was gone and the day nurse was asleep, Joyce, kneeling by the bed would pray aloud, though very softly, for her father.

She thought he was asleep always when she knelt. But once when she was praying so she opened her eyes and saw his gaze upon her, though the light was dim. Suddenly she leaned over and kissed his forehead softly, and whispered:

"Father dear! God hears. God is here! You talk to Him, too, in your heart!"

Oh, she knew the doctor and the nurses would tell her her father did not understand her. That his mind was paralyzed too. That probably his hearing was gone.

But anyway it comforted her to talk to him, and to pray with him when nobody was around.

And once she told him that she was sure Jason was coming back pretty soon.

That night she fancied a hungry look in his eyes, and she prayed aloud for Jason when they were alone again. Prayed: "Dear Lord, take care of our dear Jason and bring him back to us soon, and let everybody know that he didn't do wrong."

Several times she said it, and when she looked at her father again she saw that hungry look, almost like a little boy who had been naughty, and now was sorry. She couldn't explain it to herself, why she had that fancy. But suddenly she stooped down and whispered in his ear:

"Father, Rowan Parsons has gone after Jason to find him and bring him back to us!"

And when she looked she saw such a light in her father's eyes as had not been there before. A real gleam, as if he was glad. As if he understood and was glad!

The next morning the drawn look in his face was decidedly relaxed. The lips were not twisted nearly so far to the side as they had been. The nurse noticed it as soon as she came on in the morning and called Joyce to look. The doctor spoke of it as soon as he came in the room and Joyce felt somehow that she had had converse with her father. Felt that he knew what she had told him, and was glad.

Charles Parsons came in to see him one day and sat and put his kindly hand upon his neighbor's twisted hand. And Joyce, watching, saw a kindling in the eyes of her father.

There had not been much neighborliness between these two for several years. Nathan had been hard to get along with, always picking a quarrel, and Charles had been sternly stubborn on his side. Charles had not approved of Jason, and Nathan had tried to put the blame upon Rowan who was older, and so it went.

But now, suddenly, something seemed to grow between the spirits of these two, a softening, a renewing of old friendship of years long gone, of eyes looking into eyes that saw a common change coming in the future, a common sorrow ripening into common interests.

It was like a silent drama that went on without words, just looks, and a tender touch now and then, just whispered words that they were not sure were heard, yet spoken the more tenderly for that!

The facing of a coming separation perhaps. Who knew? How soon?

Charles himself was looking white and tired these days. Joyce noticed it one afternoon when the late rays of the sun shone across his strong face and gave a delicacy to the flesh, an ethereal look. It startled her. Why, these two men were growing old! She had thought of them always as staying the same age forever, while only young things grew old!

But the sun's ray passed and she looked again and saw the same kind old friend, Rowan's father, just as he had been since she could remember and she thought she must have been mistaken.

Charles came often to Nathan, and one day he brought James Goodright with heartening smiles, and before they left Charles said:

"Now, tell him, Jamie, what we were talking about. I think he understands."

And the banker brushed away a tear and laid his hand upon the poor paralyzed one, and said gently:

"I'm sorry, Nate, about all this business, and when your boy comes home we're going to clear it all up and take him back into the bank, if he'll come!"

"And he's coming back! Don't you worry, Nate," said Charles.

Then Joyce, watching, thought she saw that gleam again, as the quiet eyes of the sick man looked from one to the other of his old friends.

But when they left the nurse said to Joyce,

"That man they call Charles looks very frail to me. I don't like his looks these last few days. Has he ever had heart trouble?"

But Joyce did not know, and she watched her beloved Hannah's Charles with growing fear. Rowan's father! Oh, God, nothing must happen to Rowan's father while Rowan was away! Oh, not that, please, dear God!

But Hannah saw it too.

"Father, you're very tired. I wish you would stay at home in the morning and rest a little while. I wish you'd go to Dr. Fulton and ask him to go over you and see what you need, give you a tonic or something."

"Oh, I'm all right, Hannah, just a little tired. But I'll get rested again. I always have. But I've got to go to the office in the morning. There are several important matters. And I've promised James Goodright I'll drop into the bank for a few minutes. There are some things to clear up."

So it went on from day to day, and Charles did not get the promised rest.

But one day he felt a strange sharp pain that he had sometimes felt before. He sat and thought about it awhile, and then he called his friend the doctor to see him.

That night when he came home there was something very sweet and gentle about him, and he came and sat down by Hannah's side. It was late afternoon, earlier than he usually came. Supper was started on the stove, but not ready yet.

He sat there a minute and then he took her hand.

"Hannah," he said, "I've got something to tell you that will be hard to bear! Can you take it, my girl?"

Hannah looked up with her eyes full of fear. This was the moment she had been dreading ever since Rowan went away. Some day they would come and tell her that Rowan was dead! That he had been shot, or thrown over a precipice, or drowned. She had thought it all out and promised her Lord that if He willed it so she would take it bravely. She would take it with a smile and bow to His will. They had talked it over, the two of them, and she had been prepared for almost anything like that. She was a stronghearted woman.

But when she tried to summon that smile great fear came instead and stood in her eyes and Charles saw it.

"No, dear, it's not that! It's nothing about Rowan. It's something else entirely," he said, and then when he saw a new frantic fear growing in her gaze he went on.

"It's me, this time, Hannah. Be brave now!"

"I'm being brave!" said Hannah with quivering chin and a smile among the tears like a rainbow through the rain.

"Yes, I know you are. Well, I won't keep you waiting. And it isn't perhaps as bad as it might be. But you see, Hannah, I've been having a pain in my heart a good deal lately, and I thought it was just indigestion, but lately it came back so much, and so sharply that this morning I went to the doctor and had him look me over from stem to stern, and it seems I've got a bad heart. He says I'm all right every other way and I may live for years and years yet, but then again I may go any time. I've just got to be careful and live right, and forget it, and go on. Really, Hannah, it isn't any worse than life at any stage, you know. There is always the possibility that any one of us may go at any minute."

He was holding her hand now, looking deep into her dear eyes.

"Hannah, we want God to have His way with us, don't we?"

"Oh yes, Charles—!" she managed. "Yes, of course," and the smile quivered out again, and so did the tears.

"I'm all right, Charles," she said, "I'm brave!"

"Yes, my girl! You're always brave! You've always been brave ever since we started out together hand in hand, and please God we'll be brave together to the end. But the blessed thing is there won't be any end. There may be a very brief separation somewhere, like when you went down once to visit Myra, but it won't last, and then we'll be at Home with Him!"

"Yes, Charles! But—I hope—our Rowan—can come home —before—it—happens!"

"Well, yes, that would be nice," said Charles thoughtfully. "But after all, that won't matter so much. You know I've been convinced for sometime that Rowan is off doing his duty, and that in some way God is going to use this to make our Rowan a real child of His. He had to be led. He was rebellious sometimes, and thought he knew a lot. But I'm glad God is leading him through something legitimate, and not through the discipline that comes from deadly wrong doing. I'm glad there was some good motive at the bottom. And now, Hannah, cheer up. We're living our last days down here just as happily as we ever did any others."

"Of course!" said Hannah wiping the tears and choking over the smile she flung out.

"And then there's always the thought, Hannah, that the

Lord may come before anything more happens but a few pains more or less, and maybe we won't either of us go through the gate of death. But if one of us should go first and the other remain till Jesus comes, why whichever goes first will be coming in the clouds when the trumpet blows."

"Yes, I often think of that when I lie awake at night and think how the end might come for one of us and not the other. Oh, I know it will be grand and glorious any way it turns out, only I can't somehow keep the tears back at thought of you being away. Even over night. You know I always dreaded it."

"Yes, I know, but you'll have to remember that this will be the last time, and you'll come pretty soon if I go first, and then we'll be at Home forever!"

"Yes, but oh, Charles, if it should happen—before Rowan comes back, he's going to feel it so! He's going to think that he has been the cause of it all!"

"Well, you mustn't let him feel that! You see, I had this pain long before any of this happened. Of course this last strain has been hard on me, but it hasn't been Rowan's doings. I haven't for a minute thought it was, and you make him understand that. Perhaps I'll write him a letter too, so that if I should go before he comes back why he won't have any heartaches over that. And now, Hannah, let's have supper! I'm hungry. I didn't eat any lunch down in the village today. I guess I sort of dreaded telling you this. But now it's told and we understand each other we can go on just the same as if there was a possibility I might have to go to Washington for a few days the way I used to do when we were first married."

She looked up and tried to smile and broke down in a sob, and Charles took her in his comforting arms and held her close. Two old lovers, fearful at the probability of a brief parting, but knowing all would be well when they were both at Home.

That night when they knelt to pray together Hannah said:

"You'll pray our boy will come—before—?"

"I'll pray that God may have His way, whatever it is, but Hannah, girl, don't worry if he doesn't. I somehow feel this is a long trek for Rowan, but in the end he's coming out gloriously. I haven't the shadow of a doubt."

"And there's Joyce," said Hannah. "Our Rowan loves her, I'm convinced."

"Does Joyce love Rowan?"

"Yes, I think she does," said Hannah thoughtfully. "Poor little girl! She's having a hard life. And she is very fond of you, Charles. I'm wishing so that you can stay till she has a taste of you for a father. Her own father has been so hard."

"Yes, I'd like that myself. I've always loved the child. But Hannah, her own father is coming into his fatherhood, I'm thinking. Even frozen fast in a dead body he's telling her at last with his eyes that he loves her, and she's finding her comfort in ministering to him."

"That's wonderful! But isn't it queer Mrs. Whitney stays away as she does?"

"The Lord be thanked that she does!" said Charles fervently. "It is to everybody's comfort, her own included that she stays away. She would have the sick man back in unconsciousness in half an hour if she came, if she even stepped her foot in the room, and brought her clattery tongue into the house. Oh, Hannah, I thank the Lord daily that he gave me a wife like you, with your wise, gentle ways and your quiet tongue."

She laid her face against his arm where she had so many times gathered strength, and stilled the sharp pang to think she might not have that refuge long on earth. Then she lifted anxious eyes.

"Charles, you said with care the doctor thought you might live as long as anybody?"

"Yes," said Charles with a smile.

"Then you will be careful? You will do just what he tells you to do?"

"Of course," said Charles. "Now I know what it means I'll do all I can."

"Charles, shall we tell Myra?"

"Not yet, Mother. It would only distress her, and maybe bring that Mark person around to look after my business affairs. I am sorry, but I'm afraid I don't trust that Mark son-in-law of mine. He looks slippery to me. His eyes are too little and too near together to see anything but his own interests very clearly."

"My poor little girl!" mourned Hannah. "If she could only have had a man like you, Charles! She's never known what real love is."

"Well, the Lord will make it up to her some day, so don't grieve too much over that. We can't help it now, and the time is coming when all the wrongs are going to be made right."

It was a few days later that he came home and told her that he had fixed things so that she would be taken care of after he was gone.

"You know I don't trust Mark, Hannah, and I've fixed things so he can't meddle, and so he can't control what I'm leaving to Myra. It will be in your hands, her part, till you go, and then it will be strictly hers, with a guardian, Jamie Goodright, and his son if he goes. His son is a grand man and true as steel. So you don't need to worry about property at all. That won't come into it if I go. You'll have the place, of course, to live in. I've fixed it so it's not to be sold. It's yours always and Rowan's after you. But if I were you I wouldn't say anything about money to Myra and Mark. If Myra knew, Mark would get it out of her and then he'd do something to make things hot for her, and maybe for you. Of course if Rowan were here he would prevent that. I talked to him once about looking after you and his sister if I were gone and he thoroughly understood. He'll carry on all right when he gets back, but until he does, Hannah, don't talk to the others about money."

"Father, I think Myra thinks you've lost everything in the burglary. Myra's last letter said that Mark was very bitter about Rowan having made you lose all you had, and she also said, you know, that Mark thought it was utterly unnecessary for you to have to give up all you had even if you were a trustee. You ought to have salted a good pile down so they couldn't touch it, if such a contingency arose. He said you never ought to have been a trustee. I haven't answered that letter yet, Charles, I somehow couldn't bring myself to do it right away. I felt so angry at Mark, and at Myra for letting him talk that way, and for daring to repeat it to us."

"Well, you mustn't blame our girl too much. You know she has to live with him, and she's only trying to get it off her mind. She'd like to have you deny it, I suppose. But don't worry. It's all going to come right some day. And now, Hannah, we've talked about this once and we needn't go back to it. I'll write out full directions and put them in the safety deposit box, and then if the time ever comes that you need them, you just follow them, but don't think a thing more about it unless it does. I may live to be a hundred. Who knows?"

And so the two laid their burdens down before their Lord and went forth into the coming days, strong in His strength to meet whatever He sent.

CHAPTER XI

When Jason came out of the telephone booth at Rowley's after talking with Rose Allison, somehow the world looked less sordid and horrible, and the future less impossible to him.

Before he went in there, if someone had come along and suggested suicide to him he might have been in a very receptive mood. He felt that the last hope was gone and he might just as well go to the dogs as not, yet somehow he didn't seem to want even to go to the dogs. He was the prodigal without the husks left. He had in his mind only the one wild idea that had chased itself back and forth in his consciousness ever since he had been a boy and found that people charged him with things that he had not done. He had planned then that when he grew up, if they kept on blaming him for everything, that he would go away where none of them could ever find him again.

Oh, he hadn't been perfect. He never claimed that nor wanted them to think that, but he had grown bitter as he saw through the years an increasing tendency to blame him with things that other boys did. The others hid behind him just because they knew he was too honorable to tell on them. He began presently to feel the virtue of his position. This one bit of code he kept religiously, even though he sinned in many other ways.

Sometimes he felt that perhaps it would be just as well to be what they thought him and be done with it all. Yet his conscience recognized the error of that reasoning, just as it also tried to point out to him the childishness of his cherished plan of going away sometime when things should get too

123

thick for him. Yet he still clung to that longing to start afresh, and make a new record in a place where he wouldn't have past failures tagging him constantly.

He had had this somewhat in mind when he went to college. He had battled to get away to the college of his choice. His father wanted him to go where he had gone, but Jason had wanted to go far away from home where he wouldn't be known and see if he couldn't make a record to be proud of.

In the end his father had won and he had gone to the family Alma Mater. In due time his reputation at home had seeped back to college, and then the sparks flew.

He had to admit even to himself that he had done several mischievous things in college. But the things he perpetrated himself were never found out, it was the misbehaviour of others that was blamed on him, all because of a mean little story that had come somehow from home—he hadn't yet been able to trace that to its source but he would someday.

Well, perhaps it was his fault because he never would defend himself. He had grown up with a lofty idea of letting people think what they wanted to. He never had faced this theory honestly and rooted out the source of it. He had not yet discovered that it grew not from humility but from pride, hurt pride at the thought that others did not take for granted he was blameless! And so he had let first one case and then another pile up, until that last bitter charge in college. He would have come out and denied that if it hadn't been for the fool girl who was mixed up in it; he simply couldn't get out from under and let her take the blame, even though her boy friend did do just that!

How that had angered his father! His Alma Mater! Disgrace before his own college. He couldn't blame the old man. It was tough luck and it was just because he had foreseen something like this that Jason hadn't wanted to go there to college.

He had come home and endured the whole gamut of blame from his stepmother and his father, even down to Aunt Libby in the kitchen who went around with red eyes, snuffing, her long thin nose red and dripping with frequent tears, blaming him even while she made furtive tarts for his delectation. And then Joyce. Joyce who never blamed him but who looked so sad, and who said: "Oh, Jason! Oh— *Jason!*" when he came home and told her first of all. She never blamed him but her sorry exclamation cut deepest of all.

That had been a terrible time, those months after he came home from college and lay around, and worried, and was insolent to his stepmother who kept up a continual nagging that stirred his father to habitual scathing words whenever he came around. Those were the days when he began to go to Rowley's to play pool, trying to get a little money. His father wouldn't give him a cent. Not a cent! And how could he ever amount to anything stuck down in this little dump of a village, and living on a farm? How could he get a job? His father wouldn't let him go to any other college. He said he had to get out and get to work. He would never amount to anything anyway and he was done trying to do for him.

So he had played at Rowley's and sometimes won a little money, enough to play around with the girls who came his way at Rowley's, enough to go on joy rides off to little towns away from home in other fellows' machines.

And day by day the venom of hate had worked in his soul until he was almost ready to do something really dreadful, like committing suicide, only there wasn't really any effectual way of doing it around his home. He hadn't any gun. His father wouldn't allow one. He hadn't any car so he couldn't turn it on and go to sleep. Aunt Libby was always around in the kitchen so he couldn't use the gas stove, and anyway suicide had never appealed to him very strongly. It didn't seem quite respectable, and would be so hard for Joyce to bear. He had dismissed it with a mere thought and let his mind travel on to wider schemes that included far lands. He would go away so far they could not find him, and then some day he would come back rich and successful and they would see that they had been mistaken about him. That he wasn't the scoundrel they thought him even if he did play pool for money at Rowley's sometimes, and show a girl a good time now and then with the money he got.

Then Rowan had come home from college, and he had always admired Rowan tremendously. Rowan was just enough older to be a hero in his eyes. And Rowan had been friendly.

They had gone around together a lot in Rowan's car, and he had helped Rowan plow a field, and plant corn, and pull weeds and do a lot of farm work that his father couldn't have got him to do for love nor money. But Rowan hadn't asked him. Rowan just worked, and so he worked along.

Rowan let him drive his car. It wasn't much of a car, but Rowan let him drive it. Rowan had bought it himself, and he wouldn't let his dad give him a better one. He was working to earn the money for a better one himself. Jason had decided that he would do the same. Somehow he would get a job and earn money and be a man, like Rowan. They would go out together and be buddies. Rowan didn't seem to mind that he was younger. Sometimes Rowan would even drive out and look for him at Rowley's where he was playing pool again to get money to pay the first installment on a car.

It rather amused him when he heard somebody say that it was a pity that nice Rowan Parsons was beginning to run to that road house a lot just the way Jason Whitney did. That was just the way people jumped to conclusions about him, branded him as a drunkard and a gambler when he wasn't either really. It sort of put Rowan in his class according to his crude young ideas, and made them buddies more than ever.

And then, right out of the blue, without any warning, just like a miracle had come that job in the bank. Where it came from he didn't know. Nor whose influence had got it for him. His father disclaimed any knowledge of it, and doubted if he could make good. He got no encouragement at home except from Joyce whose eyes were shining at his success. Just Mr. Goodright's wonderful note in the post office for him one discouraged morning, saying he had heard he was looking for a job and offering him a chance in the bank.

The only drawback had been that his old enemy of bumblebee days was there also, but he figured he wouldn't have to have anything to do with him, and of course the other fellow was a man now and probably had a little sense. So everything had been wonderful for several months. And then suddenly those queer things happened: each employee was called into Mr. Goodright's office and told quietly, like a warning, that money was missing. Little mistakes were discovered here and there; he knew they suspected him. It was all so subtle, it seemed as if someone had planned it. It was then he began to watch Corey Watkins. Somehow the very fact that he had always been able to get away with the mischief that he really planned himself made Jason doubly alert in watching others, and day by day he saw little things that made him wonder.

And at last, that awful morning when a marked bill was found by Corey Watkins in his locker at the bank!—planted there of course, because he had no knowledge of it. He still felt glad he had hit Corey Watkins. He wished he could hit him again. Of course that was not the way clerks were expected to behave in banks. But he raged inwardly afresh as he recalled the look in Corey's neat face as he accused him.

Jason had told Mr. Goodright the bill wasn't his and he knew nothing about it; Mr. Goodright had said all right, if that was the case they would try him again. But Jason had risen up in his old time wrath and declined to have anything more to do with the bank. It was the same old story. Other people's crimes were blamed on him. He knew now well enough where that bill came from, who had planted it in his drawer. But he wouldn't tell. He couldn't prove it, of course, though he might have created suspicion if he had gone to work in the right way. But he scorned to do that. So he held his head high and left the bank and let it be told around that he had been fired. Well, what was the difference?

Of course all his dreams of being a buddie of Rowan's were gone now. Rowan wouldn't want to be friends with a guy that had been fired after getting such a break as he had when he got in. No, he would just cut loose from everything and carry out his scheme of long ago.

He would leave at once. He would never go back to the old town. Not until he was rich and successful. He'd show them!

Bitterly he thought these things as he walked out the familiar way toward Rowley's. Not to play this time for money to carry out his schemes. Mr. Goodright had given him a whole month's pay, although he had earned but one week of it. But it was habitual to walk this road so he took it.

When he got to the turn of the road he looked back, just to get a glimpse of the old place before he left it forever. His eyes blurred a little with unwonted tears as he saw the trees and houses and all the familiar scene. There was the high school where he had gone so recently, and there the tall white steeple of the church.

Then suddenly he thought of Rose and his promise to her. Why, this was the night of the meeting, and he had meant to keep that promise. Something in her eyes when she asked him had made him feel he must do it for her, and now he must keep tryst. For a whole second he hesitated. Of course he could still go back tonight to that meeting. He wouldn't need to go home, nor to let anybody he knew see him all day, and he could sit at the back of the church. Nobody would be expecting him there, and he could leave before the service was quite over. He would be keeping his promise to Rose, and he could write back sometime and let her know he had been there.

Then suddenly he realized that he would have hard work to get away with that and not meet somebody who would tell his father and there would be all kinds of a row, and they would perhaps block him in his purpose. No, better get out while the getting was good, and not come back till he was on his feet really for keeps.

But he mustn't go without somehow letting that kid know that he had meant to keep his promise. He would go in to Rowley's and telephone. He hadn't meant to go to Rowley's at all, but now this was the quickest way and then he could light out and make his getaway before anybody had an idea he was gone.

So he went in and called Rose.

And when he came out he found himself greatly shaken. Something in her voice when she said she was sorry, when she told him she believed in him and cared whether he went away, made his heart come up somewhere in the region of his throat. Nobody but Joyce had ever spoken to him like that. Gee! what would it be if he was the kind of fellow who could go with a girl like that and take her places. What if he should go away and get to be the right kind of a fellow somehow and come back some day and go to call on her. Would her eyes light up the way they had when he said he'd go to meeting for her? Would her voice light up and get all warm the way it had over the telephone?

Walking on out of his home life Jason carried with him a lovely little picture of Rose in her pink dimity, looking up at him with her great blue eyes, eyes that had curly lashes with tangles of sunbeams in them, golden curly lashes. And hair that curled like sunbeams too. Say, she was a pretty girl. She was a honey! There weren't any girls around like her.

He thought of the wild coarse young hoydens who came to Rowley's, skinny gaunt creatures with large red lips and vivid cheeks made brighter by the chalk white of the surrounding flesh. Girls with dark plastered hair cut in queer boyish shapes. Girls with hair that seemed to have been designed by the evil one himself. Girls who looked like emaciated clowns, and acted the part. Girls with flimsy dirty little frocks, and a great deal of their skinny anemic backs showing. It revolted him that he had ever danced with them. They were coarse little things without an idea in their heads except to get as much out of a boy as they could. Girls who drank and smoked and conducted themselves in a disreputable way generally. When he thought of his desultory contacts with such girls he was disgusted with himself, as if he had suddenly found some defiling substance on his hands and knew not how to cleanse it. He hadn't had much to do with any of them, he had only danced with them a few times. They hadn't interested him. They were too low a type perhaps, though he didn't know that. He was merely getting his eyes open to himself and his own movements. It seemed that he had never really lived until now that he was going out of the environment that he knew, and going for a long time.

Suddenly as he saw all the familiar things disappearing they grew dear to him. The neat little town, the quiet countryside, the long sloping meadows where his father's cows grazed, the sunsets that flung themselves behind the hills that he could see from his window, the trim compact little bank of clean limestone where he had been so proud to work, where he had really begun to be different and act like a man and not just a kid—all that conjured up because of one girl in a pink dress, with lights in her gold hair and lights in her blue eyes, and a quiver of liking in her voice that was for him!

A strange new sweet thrill went through his young heart when he thought of her voice as she said she believed in him and she cared, and he thought back to school days and how she had smiled sometimes when he played some simple prank and nobody else knew who did it. She had a sense of humor, that girl! Why hadn't he had sense enough to see when he had the chance what a friend she would be to a fellow if he was just half decent. Of course he wasn't paying much attenton to girls in those days. He was all for athletics. He thought it was sissy to talk to girls. But now he suddenly longed for that chance back again. Why hadn't he walked home with Rose and carried her books? Rose—what a sweet name! She looked like a flower in that pink dress!

Maybe her father wouldn't have cared for a friendship between them, but maybe he would have been different if he had had a friend like Rose. Of course he had a sister like that! He raised his head proudly and walked along with his back straight, and his step firm. Of course his father was respected, and they had a nice home, and if he had started out going with a girl like that when they were scarcely more than children, likely her father wouldn't have objected. He had enough background behind him if he had only used it! What a fool he had been!

Perhaps if Joyce hadn't been away at college when he was

in high school she would have invited young people there, and Rose might have come and he would have been there having a good time with them all, and things might have been different.

But there was his stepmother. She had no time for young people. She had to keep the house so immaculate. If you just brought in a grain or two of mud it was all up with you. She wouldn't have allowed good times. She rode Joyce to death. Even now, she did. He could see that, little as he had stayed at home.

Well, if his own mother had lived, things would have been different.

He sighed heavily and walked wearily on.

There was nothing for it but to go away as he intended and try to be worth something. Probably if he ever did come back in a position to be friends with a girl like Rose, he'd find her married to some chump like Corey Watkins!

Suddenly he ground his teeth together in helpless wrath when he thought of his enemy. What a disaster that would be! Good night! If he thought anything like that could happen he'd turn right around and go back and protect her!

Only of course he couldn't, not in his present predicament. Not without a decent job.

As he thought back now he almost wished he had eaten humble pie and told Mr. Goodright he would stay on probation and show him he was all right, prove to him that he could make good. After all, Mr. Goodright had been fair. Believing as he did that he, Jason, was a petty thief, he had yet offered him another chance. But it had made him so hot to think that any man could even think such things of him for a minute that he hadn't even questioned his haughty gesture of refusal.

But that was before he talked with Rose over the telephone. That was before her voice had those tears in it about his going away in anger from his home and his job. That was before she had said she cared, and she believed in him.

Of course he could turn now and go back to the bank and tell Mr. Goodright he had changed his mind and decided to stay and show him that he was mistaken in him. But how could he? With his old enemy Corey there it would scarcely be possible. He couldn't tell Mr. Goodright to watch Corey Watkins, a man older than he was, who had gained the respect of everybody in town by his smug ways. Nobody would believe him even if he told what he knew. And it was unthinkable that he should tell. That was his one bit of virtue that he held to.

Besides, if he went back now, under a cloud, somehow it would seep out. It probably had already. And nobody would have anything to do with him, not even if he never went to Rowley's again. They had him tagged and he couldn't get away from that, not unless he went away long enough for them to forget his past, and made a new record. Then he could come home and they would probably accept him on a new basis. But if he went back now he wouldn't likely be allowed to see Rose at all. If he did once or twice he would have the whole nasty prying town talking about her, and he wouldn't stand for that. No, it was better to go on. He couldn't go back and meet his father's roar of disgust, his stepmother's contemptuous sarcasm, and his sister's sad eyes. There wasn't anything he could do but go on.

Then he thought of Rowan. That gave a wrench to his heart. Rowan wouldn't understand. Rowan had acted as if he believed in him. They had had nice times together. They were buddies. Rowan wouldn't go back on him even if the town did, or his family, or anybody. But of course he wouldn't go back and involve Rowan in a friendship that was unworthy of him, either. Rowan and Joyce and the girl, Rose! He sighed heavily as he plodded on, his eyes down. The world looked black indeed to him, and he was beginning to see that it was mostly his own fault. For the first time in his life he was seeing that his disappointments were largely of his own making. He hadn't suspected it before. He had thought that everybody else was to blame.

Perhaps if he had gone to Rowan with the whole story Rowan would have helped him work something out without this pilgrimage afar. He had told Rowan once what he meant to do sometime if things went wrong again, and Rowan had laughed at him. Had told him that the way to straighten things out was to stay where the trouble had begun and face it, untangle it, find out what was wrong and set it right.

But Jason was too proud to take such advice. Even now he was too proud. He could not go back to a girl who believed in him and face a time of ignominy.

No, he would take her belief in him as a precious talisman and he would hide it away in his heart to help him to success. She cared, well he would make her care more. He would be what she wanted him to be.

Oh, she hadn't said anything about being different, of

course, only she had voiced that one little fear when she asked him if he had done anything—no she hadn't put it that way. She had said "You haven't have you?" She had taken it for granted that it wasn't his fault, and yet she must have had a fear. Yes, of course, he hadn't given her reason to be sure about him, but he would in future. And just as soon as he got established somewhere and was in a fair way to success he would write to her and tell her about it. He would have to do it quickly too before some other guy discovered what a lovely little flower she was and tried to snatch her for himself.

The thought spurred him onward. He must hurry up and succeed.

Perhaps when he got located somewhere he'd venture to write to her. Not too soon, for he wanted to have something definite in mind. He wanted to be able to say:

"I've accepted a position with the So and So Company of Blank, and I'm in a fair way to success," etc. He wanted to tell her how it had helped him to know she believed in him, and cared whether he succeeded or not. That would be enough for a first letter, and then if she answered that perhaps they could go on and correspond, and he would feel that he had an anchor out somewhere and wasn't just drifting. It would be wonderful to have somebody you dared tell your inmost thoughts to, somebody who wouldn't laugh.

Perhaps he would write to Rowan sometime later, too. But you couldn't tell a man who was older than you were just all you were thinking. He hadn't thought ever before that you could tell any girl things like inside thoughts, not till he heard Rose's voice when she said she cared.

Of course she didn't mean anything silly by that, as some girls would mean. She meant real things, things like mothers would say, if you had a mother who cared. Things even deeper than that. Things that God made you feel. Jason wasn't very well acquainted with God. His father asked the blessing at the table in a sort of a mumble that raced along to get done; it was just a gesture heavenward; his father's life didn't seem to match up with even such a blessing. God was very far away to Jason, and dim and vague. But he guessed there was a God somewhere who made women like Rose. She was not just a good-looking body that could show you a good time, she cared about your soul.

So Jason walked on swiftly, unaware of his extreme weariness, unaware that the sun was getting lower and he was footsore and hungry, intent only on getting on.

He knew just where he was going. Back at home in his room he had a box full of steamship folders. He had spent hours in studying them. He knew where they docked, knew the numbers of the docks where these great ships that went to strange weird corners of the earth, were to be found. He had written to steamship companies, and to sailing vessels. He was full of information concerning the far countries that had lured him in his misery. He even knew what times of the month certain ones sailed, or thought he did, though of course timetables changed. But he knew their general hours of sailing. He began to calculate what he would like to do if he could make it. But he must get to New York first, and of course he hadn't any too much money to start out in life with just a puny month's salary. He must save every cent he could. He had to eat. He must get a job on the ship if possible. Any ship would do, of several lines he knew. He didn't care much where he landed. There would be chances in one place as well as another he thought. If he got a job on a ship it would save him trouble about passports and details of which he had the vaguest knowledge possible, as they hadn't seemed very important. The thing was to get to New York and find his ship. It seemed to him that of course there would be any number of them, just waiting round to take him where he chose, and perhaps actually glad to give him a job.

He walked on briskly, although now he was beginning to be aware of sudden weariness. He was glad when a farmer in an old flivver came along and offered him a lift. He climbed in beside him with almost a semblance of his old cheerful grin. Things weren't going to be so bad when people came along genially like this to help.

The farmer asked him a lot of questions which he skillfully evaded, answering them without imparting a single fact, he thought, and they jogged along in the general direction of New York.

When the farmer arrived at his destination he pointed out a cheap place to get a night's lodging. Jason got some supper, quite plain and unfrilled, served on thick ironstone china, and then went to bed. He had a good night's sleep, dreaming of a girl in a pink dress who smiled at him with dear believing eyes and waved her hand, and Jason arose refreshed, with a zest for his journey. The bitter thoughts that had accompanied him yesterday for a long time, were forgotten, and he even whistled quite cheerily as he started on his way again.

As he walked he wondered what they were thinking about

him at home. His father likely was mad, and his stepmother was making caustic remarks about him. Not that that mattered, of course, and Joyce was worried. Poor Joyce. He wished he had asked Rose to tell her that he was all right and would let her hear from him sometime. Perhaps he would mail her a post card at New York just before he sailed. He wouldn't dare do it sooner, for the family were capable of putting the police on him and hauling him back for discipline and he didn't mean to have that for a minute. He was not quite nineteen, and he knew they could if they wanted to. So he wouldn't write till the last minute.

He had several lifts on the way that day, but he walked slower each time he was let down. He was not used to such long steady tramping. A hole was wearing through the sole of one of his shoes. If that kept on he would have to stop and have it repaired. He didn't get on so fast as the day before, except for the lifts, but in each case those were only for a few miles, and night found him still quite a distance from his destination.

He acquired a map and a clean collar, and stayed at a tourist cottage that night, fairly decent and very cheap. He began to perceive that being on his own was not going to be like rolling in luxury, but he assured himself that he would soon be getting a good salary somewhere and putting away money to go home and astonish his fellow-townsmen.

The next day he had to stop to have his shoe resoled, and that set him back, so that when he actually arrived in New York City it was very late, and dark and confusing.

He had been to New York only once before. He knew the general way to the wharfs, but was not familiar with the intervening streets. He felt very tired but so excited over being near the sea at last that he walked at once to the shipping district and made his way from one dock to another, inquiring for different lines.

But it seemed to be an off-night so far as the ships he knew were concerned. They had either sailed at noon or at six o'clock of that day, or they were going to sail the middle or end of next week. He couldn't wait around to go on certain ships, to certain chosen ports. One port was as good as another, anyway. He could make good anywhere if he tried. So he wandered on along the shore, asking a question now and again of some dockman. And finally someone directed him to a sailing vessel farther down the dock, that was going out that night, or at least early in the morning. They wanted men too, were short of their crew. Did he want a job? Was he a sailor? The landsman eyed his bank-clerk suit questioningly and pointed down a long dark way with intermittent lights piercing the blackness, and a forest of masts against the luminousness of a cloudy night. It was beginning to rain, and Jason was almost at the limit of his endurance. Another day like this and he would sit down like a baby and cry to go back home. He must get this business settled up quickly, and made irrevocable, or his courage would ooze out in the night.

So he hurried down the cobbled way, stumbling over ropes and strange objects which he was too tired to identify. Down below him somewhere the black water was lapping, lapping, like a monster who had sighted him and was licking his lips in anticipation of devouring him. Strange fancy!

Back at home there was a girl named Rose wearing a pink dress and she had sunshine in her hair.

And back at home they were trying to brand him as a thief and a murderer. And the man who was his enemy, and whom he suspected, was calling on his sister.

But that he did not know, else many things might have been different.

CHAPTER XII

When Rowan started out in the darkness more than ten hours later than Jason, he was thinking more of the girl he had left behind him than of the man for whom he was going to search. This was the first minute he had had alone with his thoughts since he had left her. There had been the stealthy trip to his room to get his money, the discovery by his mother who always somehow knew his every move no matter how hard he tried to save her from unnecessary pain, the getting away from her caressing voice, and the hurried plunge down the hill in the rattly old car. But now he was out on the highroad, eastward bound, and alone in the night with his thoughts.

Such thoughts! The thrill of Joyce's lips upon his! What wonder of delight. In his highest dreams he had never felt it would be like that. Joyce's shy slender form yielded to his arms, her soft tear-wet lashes against his cheek, her clinging arms for that minute he had held her. Oh, love! Was life like this? It seemed that all the past had only been leading up to this, and suddenly he thought he knew what there had been between his own father and mother that had made the years, some of them hard years, one long dream of bliss.

He paused in his thoughts to give tribute to such a father who could love a woman as his had loved Rowan's mother, to reflect that it was a great background for himself to have, and one to which he must live up.

If in the days ahead he should be so fortunate as to win Joyce as his companion through life, he must remember the pattern set for him by his father.

He thought of his mother, with her tender arms, her frail lips against his cheek, her smile, her courage! Would Joyce be like that some day with him?

Joyce, whose lips against his still seemed warm upon him, whose slender weight seemed yet almost in his arms. What wonder! And she had been there on the next farm all this summer, and he had been too shy to go and tell her of his love, too prone to think he was not yet enough of a success to ask for the hand of any woman, especially such a woman as this.

Of course he had meant to do it soon. But he was trying to have a certain amount of money in the bank first before he took that step. He had been looking upon Joyce as a young queen who should have gifts great and precious if one would woo her. He had been coming slowly, pleasantly, up to the climax of his young life, and expecting all to be deliberate and orderly, like his farm work, and all his other plans for life, and here love had been lurking for him in the dark and had caught him when he was not looking for it.

Love! Wonderful love! Had it caught Joyce that way too, or hadn't she thought of love yet?

When he thought back he knew that his arms had taken her unaware, yet she had yielded herself. Joyce was not one who yielded herself to everyone. He had known her almost all her life, though they had never been anything more than friends before. But now he had told her she was precious, and she had not put him off. She had held her lips to his. If she had disliked him she would have made it plain even though he was just about to do a favor for her. No, she had understood his word, "precious." She must have understood what it portended of the love he had to offer her. He hadn't had time to make it clearer, but she would understand, and her attitude had tacitly responded. She had let him know at least that she was not indifferent. Oh, he loved her, and her lips had told him that she loved him, too. Thrill after thrill passed over him as he rode along in the quiet of the night. There were little creatures stirring here and there, wood sounds from the trees along the way, the whisper of a breeze in the branches, the chatter of a sleepy chipmunk protesting against some outrage of a creature larger than himself. The night call of a bird, the hoot of an owl, and once the whirr of a bat flying low into the lights of the car, but they were all familiar sounds and did not take his attention. He was going on a quest for his lady, like a knight of old, and he was lifted up with joyous pride at the thought. He did not doubt but that he would soon return and bring back her beloved brother with him.

Hot-headed Jason, to start off like that and leave town at the slightest implication. Rowan knew him well, and had talked it over many times with him.

Jason had always maintained that he would not be misjudged and blamed another time for others' faults. That he would go away, far away, to South America, where he would get a wonderful job and become a great success, perhaps do a little exploring and buy a mine, or discover a hidden treasure, something like that. Rowan had felt it was a very young attitude toward life, but yet had often sympathized with him in many of the situations through which they had passed.

But now, when Joyce had told him what had happened, he felt instantly sure that Jason had at last carried out his threat and gone to South America. He even knew the port the lad had hankered to enter, and the line of travel he meant to pursue. He had little doubt but that he would soon overtake him, even though Jason had several hours' start, and bring him back perhaps before morning. For surely Jason had more sense than to spend his small salary which was likely all he had along, on railroad fare. Besides, it was far more romantic to walk when he was out entirely on his own.

So Rowan drove confidently into the night and communed with his own heart under the stars, and quivered with joy over the home-coming he hoped soon to make.

But he did not find Jason as soon as he had hoped.

In passing Rowley's he found that the place was all dark. So Jason wasn't there. He was relieved at that. Jason had not been going there quite so much lately.

He drove on all night, thinking to find the boy trudging on the highway. He stopped at filling stations and questioned the men, but most of them were on the night shift and had not seen, or had not noticed a young man of that description footing it.

It was not until midafternoon of the next day that he stopped at a little roadside inn for something to eat, and a girl told him she had seen a goodlooking young man in a dark blue suit and a panama hat. He had come in and asked for a cup of coffee and a sandwich. He had eaten a piece of apple pie and some cheese, and asked where he could find a shoemaker.

Rowan went to the shoe shop and asked questions. He

found a voluble shoemaker who described Jason to perfection. Of course there might be other young men travelling to New York who wore blue serge suits and panama hats and hadn't any baggage, but there wouldn't be many, surely, who wore a gay little green monkey as a scarf pin, a monkey of such tiny proportions and yet with such clear features that he actually seemed to smile and had "eyes that talked" as the shoemaker said. Rowan knew all about that monkey. Jason had confided to him the storm it had raised the day he came home from college wearing it on his tie. Under his father's thundering command he had had to own to its fabulous price and the reason for its being his: that it was the emblem of a private eating club in college, a secret order to which it was a great honor to belong.

Rowan remembered that the elder Whitney had said there was no such tomfoolery in college when he was there—young men went to college to study not to eat in his day, and he doubted the word of his son. That fool organization, whatever it was, was outside his good old university, it was some town nonsense. In his time they didn't have to buy real jade monkeys to help them eat either, and he ordered his son to take it off and never be seen with it again around his home town. It was like Jason and against Rowan's advice to go right on wearing the monkey and angering his father and it was like Rowan to give advice only once and stop at that. So Jason had stubbornly gone on wearing the monkey to his father's exceeding disgust. But the monkey had done him a good turn at last for Rowan was sure he was on the right track and would soon come up with Jason.

Rowan was torn between anger at the younger man and tenderness because he belonged to Joyce. Yet when he found him he intended to mince no words but to let him know exactly what he thought of him for running off that way without letting his distressed sister know what had become of him.

He was confident as he started on again after his interview with the shoemaker that it would be only a matter of a couple of hours now before he found Jason and they started back again. Once or twice he considered the matter of telephoning to Joyce, but since he had as yet nothing definite to tell her and since the telephone was a party line he decided to wait a little longer.

So he kept on hour after hour, finding trace of his quarry but never reaching him. The monkey was something that one could not help noticing, and though Jason probably didn't realize it, it had made him a marked man. At last after dark on the very outskirts of New York, Rowan stopped at a filling station for gas and asked his usual question:

"Have you seen a young man with blue serge suit, panama hat, and a little green monkey scarf pin?" The attendant answered promptly:

"Yes sir! He stopped here for a drink of water, and caught a ride into town. Said he was going to the wharf to catch a steamer to South America."

Worn and tired and exasperated Rowan started on, looked at his watch and stepped on the gas. It was getting on toward midnight and he knew that was the time that many ships sailed. He put his old car at its very best speed, running past lights when he dared, threading his way through increasing traffic until at last he arrived at the region of wharfs and ships. He drove as near as he could to the docks, sometimes penetrating a spot where he was not supposed to be. Finally in desperation he asked a sailor who passed, where was the ship just leaving for South America. The sailor pointed down the dark cobbled way.

"Ship down there just leaving. Don't know where she's going but they need an extra hand. One of the crew is sick. That the one you mean?"

Rowan abandoned his car and plunged down the dark way indicated.

"Here, you! They won't let you leave that car there. You've gotta take it around the other side an' park it," shouted the sailor, but Rowan was gone in the darkness. And the old car stood there puffing away just as it had been left until it ran out of gas and then with a few gasps and gurgles like a dying frog it stopped dead and stood there still in the dark.

Rowan plunged on wildly into the darkness hurrying along in the direction the sailor had pointed. He was aware that it was just short of midnight now and if the ship sailed on time it would be now about loosing its cable, but he was not aware that shipping was usually carried on in such utter darkness! Yet he must go on. He must take no chance. If the ship sailed with Jason on it his quest would be long before he could keep his promise to Joyce and bring her brother back. Where was that ship? Had the sailor misled him? Then suddenly he rounded the corner of a large warehouse, and grimly against the sky he saw her masts. The dark bulky shape of the ship loomed against the sky. Only a few winking lights were aboard here and there and a single inadequate arc light over the pier. There on the grimy deck of that unholy ship under the light of a lantern that swung above his head stood Jason with a coil of rope in his hands, the most forlorn, lonesome-looking object Rowan had ever seen. Jason, leaving his home to carry out his childish purpose in a fit of anger and discouragement!

Rowan's heart went out to him and even as he recognized him he saw the gangplank hauled in and the ship begin to move darkly away from the dock. He plunged forward, pushing aside a dockhand and gave a mighty leap. He could not let Jason get away from him like that. So he hurled himself over the quietly widening dark that must be water and landed sprawling upon the deck. Almost instantly he felt the grip of a bony hand upon his collar, and a powerful arm yanked him to his feet.

A gruff sailor holding a dim lantern in his other hand stood and looked him over.

"Be you de feller we was waitin' fer?" he asked.

"I guess I must be," Rowan panted with what little breath he had left.

"You took an awful chanct."

"I hadn't time to consider that," said Rowan and it passed through his mind as doubtful if anybody would have rescued him if he had fallen into that dark water.

He was roused to the consciousness that the space between the boat and the dark spot that was the wharf was widening perceptibly. The arc light over the spot whence he had leaped was barely a pin prick in the distance now and he must do something about it at once. Where had he seen Jason? He must find him as quickly as possible and not make the ship any more trouble than was necessary to get them back to land. For the instant the leap seemed to have dazed him and he couldn't quite get his bearings but he stumbled forward in the darkness and almost fell over a coil of rope. The sailor righted him again.

"Don't know yor way aroun' do ya?" he remarked with a tinge of contempt in his voice. "You wanta find the captain, don't ya, ef yor the new man, but it won't do ya any good for he's dead drunk in his bunk. The first mate'll do, but he's Portugee. Do ya know the lingo?"

"No," said Rowan a bit bewildered, "but I'm looking for a friend. I saw him over there just before I jumped. Have you seen him? Dark blue suit, panama hat—"

The sailor laughed. "Think I can tell color on a night like this? I got all I can do ta tend ta my job. Look out there! You'll fall over that keg. Ain't got yor sea eyes yet, have ya, nor yor sea legs neither. My advise ta you is ta set right down flat where ya are an' set there till day dawn. Ef you got a friend on this blasted ship yor in luck. It's more'n anyone else has. B'lieve me you'll need him 'afore we git through this fool voyage, ef we ever do get through, which is doubtful."

Rowan stared at the man.

"But I'm not going on the voyage, you see," Rowan explained. "I came to get my friend and take him back home. I've got to find the captain or somebody and arrange about it. What is the quickest thing I can do to get us back to land?"

The man began to laugh.

"You'll do well ef you make it in a year," he said. "Ya can't tell where we'll bring up 'afore we're through—"

"But there surely is some way to get back to land!" said Rowan, startled. "I'll be glad to pay, of course."

"Young man, it would take more'n you've got in the world ta get this old wash tub ta turn back ta land. Don't ya know death waits back there in the dark fer any ship that carries a cargo like this? I'm tellin' ya!"

"What's the cargo?" asked Rowan with suddenly stern eyes.

The old man eyed him keenly by the light of the one swaying lantern for a minute, and then he spoke.

"Young man, ef ya don't know what this cargo is, it's not fer me ta tell ya. And as far as findin' yer friend tonight, there's nothin' doin'. This here lantern's the only light that's burnin', an' I'm puttin' this on the blink now. From now on till we git out o' this section we're travelin' dark an' still, an' ef you let a sound outta ya after this light goes out, you'll find yerself where ya would a ben a few minutes back ef I hadn't hauled ya in. Out there in the dark the water's slick an' even yor friend don't know yor here. So sit tight an' shut yer trap ef ya wanta keep on voyagin'. There's a pile of bags behind ya, an' ye can lay down an' shut up. This here begins the danger point and here comes the first mate. Don't let him know yer aboard yet. He's pretty well tanked up an' he might treat ya worse'n ya deserve."

With that he snuffed out the light and disappeared in the darkness and the strangest thing about it was that there wasn't a sound of a footstep!

Rowan sat down tentatively in the direction the man indicated and found the bags beneath, an ill-smelling gritty heap. But there seemed to be no choice and one couldn't stand indefinitely. He wished he had brought his flashlight from the car but if he had stayed for that he would have been too late and Jason would have been lost to them forever.

He sat quite still in the darkness and tried to think it out. It was fantastic. It couldn't be real. It simply couldn't have happened in a modern world. But if it was true and Jason was here—and he knew he had seen him just before that upper light went out. What did it all mean? What was this? A tramp steamer? Carrying—what? Contraband goods of some kind? What? Rum? Gun-powder? Arms? And what would happen in the morning? Was he foolish to lie still here in the dark and travel on and on across an unknown sea into possible danger or unforeseen circumstance? Ought he not rather to start out silently on hands and knees perhaps and search through the dark till he found Jason and rescue him? But how was he going to do that not knowing where to look? This was a terrible place. A drunken captain and a Portuguese crew who couldn't understand him, an unknown port and perhaps an uncharted sea, who knew? Suppose he had been mistaken and it wasn't Jason after all, just somebody who resembled him. What could he do? He couldn't jump overboard, it was too far to swim back and if there was a boat he wouldn't know how to lower it nor how to navigate it. Rowan was well versed in land sports and would have been equal to almost any emergency on land. But he had to admit to himself that he was up against an unknown quantity when it came to the sea.

But he had seen Jason. It was not possible that he could have been deceived. And he couldn't go back without Jason. He couldn't think of meeting Joyce and telling her that he had failed.

It was all an unreal situation and his senses were numb. He had been traveling almost continuously, with only a few snatches of sleep and nature was having her revenge. That fearful leap and the shock of that dark unfriendly boat when he had expected a great bright ship with gaiety and friendliness aboard and Jason to welcome him, bewildered him.

As if he had been given a drug, his senses swam, and his

eyes fell shut in spite of his best efforts. He tried to rouse and think what to do. It was unspeakably awful to succumb to sleep in a place like this and let himself and Jason be carried further and further away from everything real and human and desirable and yet he couldn't hold out much longer. He opened his eyes and stared up at a metal sky where wild clouds were hurrying in throngs like an army of outlaws going to battle, grim and gray. An alien sky in league with the alien boat that carried him away from Joyce, with his quest only just begun! And where was Jason through it all?

At last he slept with the stench of the mouldy bags coming up to his nostrils like sickening heathen incense. But he slept and dreamed of Joyce, dreamed that he stood by the old farm fence with her in his arms and her soft lips against his, dreamed that he whispered to her softly that he would never come back until he could bring Jason with him. So he slept and under a leaden sky and over a leaden sea the dirty old hag sailed on bearing him farther and farther.

The days went by one by one for Hannah and Charles. Charles was being very careful and Hannah had grown used to the thought that there was nothing more to dread now than there ever had been. Always there had been the possibility that either might be called out any moment and they had lived on happily for years knowing that fact. Why should it be any different now? That leaky heart might last for years.

"My times are in His hand!" Charles would say with a smile and Hannah would look up bravely and smile and their eyes would cling like a close embrace.

But the looming possibility had served to take their minds somewhat off their anxiety. They were living for each other just now and all other things seemed to take second place. But they were a great comfort to Joyce. Almost every day Charles went over to see Nathan and sat by him and talked, gently, sometimes brought his Bible and read a chapter and then knelt and prayed.

One day when Joyce was sitting in the room he began to talk quite simply to Nathan exactly as if he thought he could hear and understand.

"I'm going to leave you pretty soon, Nate," he said. "They tell me I've got a bad heart and I can't last much longer. But it's all right. I'm ready to go whenever the call comes and Hannah understands. She'll be brave. But I wanted to let you know, old friend. If I don't come over some day, you'll know

I've got my morning glory on. 'Joy cometh in the morning,' you know, and His glory is going to be very wonderful. Then, too, it just might be that the Lord will come soon for Hannah and the rest of His own and I'd be coming with Him of course—all of us to share His morning glory! I just wanted to tell you, old friend, so you would understand if I didn't come any more and so you'd be ready to go Home with us all when the Lord comes. It doesn't take long to get ready, you know, all the preparations are made by Him. All you've got to do is accept—you know the way. You've always known—"

Joyce was sitting quietly with the tears running down and a tender look in her face. He had wanted to tell her, too, she knew, and he had taken this way to do it. When they both looked they saw a slow tear trickling down old Nathan's cheek. He had understood!

CHAPTER XIII

At the end Charles went quite suddenly.

The winter was well on its way, Charles had been most careful, and Hannah had watched over him at every step, lovingly, not ostentatiously. Hannah was one of those rare women who never nagged with her attentions. Her tenderness was more like the overshadowing of a bride for her beloved, than the fussing of an elderly married woman over a sick husband. Charles never felt from her manner that he was a sick man and needed utmost care.

The time was almost like a second honeymoon for the two. Such tender affection, such oneness of thought, such radiance of loving harmony! It was perhaps as near as one can approach on this earth, to what the heavenly love is to be.

And each of them, for the sake of the other, put aside the anxiety that would have been natural for their beloved son. They had learned to trust him utterly in the Father's care, and to feel they must not mar these last days of their life together by any care about him. Since he was in the Father's care, all would surely be well with him, in God's good time. They had found assurance that this experience, whatever it was being to him, was to bring him somehow into closer fellowship with his God, which was what they desired above all else for Rowan. And so they prayed, trustfully, thankfully, for the answer to their prayers which they were sure was to come whether they were here to see it, or there! Even radiantly, not with tears. They would not grieve each other with tears now. If there were to be tears afterward for a while, so be it, but God would wipe them away.

So the days had gone by, lived like a time of waiting.

Then one bright morning Charles went out, well bundled because the air was sharp, down to the bank. Hannah said:

"Do you have to go today? It's pretty cold."

"Yes. I'm afraid I must. Some more trouble has broken out in the books- and the cash. It's a strange thing! There hasn't been a sign of it since the robbery till this week. I promised Jamie I'd come down and we'd try to work it out between us. Oh, I'm all right Hannah. I'm feeling fine!"

She watched him go down the path to where a neighbor's car was waiting to take him to the village. He didn't drive much now Hannah had persuaded him not to. She said it was a nervous strain to drive. He laughed and said there was nothing the matter with his nerves, but he humored her whenever he could.

They brought him home two hours later. He had had another attack The doctor was with him, and Jamie Goodright.

Hannah saw them getting out of the car. They had telephoned her and she was ready. Not a tear was in evidence. She had been making preparation for him. Her heart had been on its knees while she worked Her face was calm and sweet, and he looked toward her in his pain and smiled, and she smiled back Those who saw it said afterward that it was like two angels waving farewell while each went on a separate errand.

They had a few minutes together by themselves before the nurse arrived The doctor was in the other room. Hannah sat by him and held his hand. She smiled when he opened his eyes.

"It's—all—right, Hannah," he said, and that heavenly smile went over his face again.

"Yes,—it's all right, Father!" and there was a ring to her voice almost like triumph.

"Say good-bye to—the—children! Don't—let them—grieve. Tell them I'll be watching!—Tell them—to—get ready —to come Home—forever!"

"I will."

"No more pain!" He pressed her fingers and his lips hovered in a smile. "No—more—tears!"

"No more tears, Father!" Hannah's voice did not falter.

He was quiet a moment and then spoke once more:

"Tell—Rowan—I'm—proud of him!"

Hannah's eyes lighted and she touched her lips softly to his fingers.

"Tell him to look out for you—and Myra! Dear—little—

girl! Tell Myra not—to grieve! Tell her—it—will—all—come
right if—she—trusts God! And the little Olive—our girl's little girl! God bless her—and lead—her Home!"

He closed his eyes and Hannah thought he slept, but he
opened them again.

"Look out—for Joyce—our Rowan's—Joyce! Love her—
Mother!"

"Of course!" said Hannah with her lips against his hand
again.

Then he really did sleep, so quietly Hannah wasn't sure he
was still breathing. The pain seemed to have left his face and
only peace was there.

The doctor stole in and looked at him, turned to Hannah
and whispered, with a misty smile in response to Hannah's
own:

"He'll probably not waken again," he said. "He'll just wake
up in Heaven." And Hannah nodded. It was all right.

But still she sat and held his hand, and then, he did open
his eyes again, and into the quiet of the room his voice came
clear and tender, almost triumphant.

"The call has come! I'm going to leave you, Hannah dear!
Good-bye! It won't be long! Joy cometh in the morning, and
glory! Sunrise glory in the morning."

Then he was gone. As definitely as if a chariot had stopped
at his bedside and carried him away, Hannah knew that he
had left her. She stooped and kissed his lips, looked into the
face that was so dear, and turned away, his last words in her
heart. Sunrise glory in the morning.

Myra came on at once. She looked old and worn. She
seemed almost older than her mother. She sobbed continually. Hannah had a moment's sudden anger when she looked
at her child. This was not like Myra, this utter giving way to
emotion. Myra had been sweet and controlled as a girl, never
hysterical. It is true that Myra had always been more wilful
than Rowan, more insistent to have her own way. But Hannah
could not help feeling that living with Mark had shattered
her nerves. She did not seem in the least like herself.

And she was continually moaning about the last time she
had come, the things she had said to her father in her passion
about Rowan.

"It's all right, dear," soothed Hannah. "Father understood
that you didn't mean half you said. Father felt sorry for you,
dear. Your name was almost the last on his lips, 'Dear little

girl,' he called you. Now sit down and let me tell you what he said."

But Myra would go off into sobbing again and Hannah could give her no comfort. She kept berating herself for worrying her father, and then she interspersed it with berating her brother for going away in such an awful way. Sometimes she called him a thief and hashed the whole thing over again and again, with all that Mark had said about him, until Hannah was nearly at her wits' end. Finally she said:

"Myra, dear, if you have got to think those things yourself I can't stop you, but you're not to mention them again in this house. And I don't want to hear any more about what Mark says or thinks. Your father and I knew all about Rowan and we were not troubled about his absence. Some day you will understand it yourself, when he gets back, and then you will be ashamed. But until then, please don't mention such a thought again."

"Well, if you and father knew all about it I think you ought to tell and not let people go around saying such rotten things about my brother."

"There, there, Myra, that will do. I don't want to hear anything more about it."

They were trying days, those three before the funeral. And on the second one Mark arrived. That was worse yet. He undertook to run everything.

Hannah had quietly and competently made her arrangements, the arrangements that she and Charles had calmly talked over, and everything was moving along calmly, when Mark came on the scene. The first thing he did was to ask about the undertaker, and try to discover whether Hannah had gotten estimates from different ones. He said he had a list of the best and cheapest ones in the county and she had better let him take the matter over and arrange everything. But when Hannah told him that everything was arranged he went determinedly down to find out just what she had done.

When he returned, just at dinner time, he told her that he had looked everything over and told the man to make several changes. He spoke harshly about her selecting such a handsome casket, and said that in her position she had no right to go into debt for something that was to be buried under ground. Father was dead now and it couldn't possibly mean anything to him.

Hannah looked at him wide-eyed and calm, a mild surprise in her eyes.

"Just what do you mean, Mark, 'in my position,' " she said.

"Why, I mean that you being alone in the world now and having just lost nearly everything you possess, probably through the machinations of your only son, and you having no earning power whatever, will have no money to pay for a costly layout. We shall have to keep you, of course, and we can't afford to let you mount up bills which will be more than we would care to help you pay."

"Oh, I see," said Hannah thoughtfully. "Well, Mark, you can put aside your worry about that. I still have enough to pay for the funeral as it has been planned. I shall not come to you to help in any way."

"Yes, but don't you see that even if you have enough in the bank at present to pay for this, that you ought to save as much of it as you can? It will help buy what clothes you have to have. We can feed you, of course, and give you a home, but we can't afford to spend much on frills."

Hannah smiled.

"Well," she said soothingly, "I shan't need many frills."

Myra suddenly got up and went toward the kitchen. She had turned deadly white at her husband's first words, and now she was on the verge of tears again. But Mark was angry now.

"Myra, sit down!" he ordered. "I want you to hear this, too. It is better that we all understand each other. Mother, I told the undertaker to change the order. I went over the whole thing, and cut down as much as possible."

"Yes, I know," said Hannah steadily, "He called me up and told me what you had done. I told him I wished things to go on just as I had planned them. This is my affair, Mark, not yours, and you will have to keep out of it!"

Myra left the room then in earnest in a burst of tears and Mark stormed loudly, but Hannah presently got up herself and went upstairs.

"Now that Rowan has chosen to take himself out of the picture," shouted Mark after her, "I am the head of this household, and you will have to learn that you can't carry on with a high hand and spend just as you please. I can't afford it!"

But Hannah had shut her door, and even a man of Mark's furious temperament cannot carry on an argument when his opponent and audience have both removed themselves. So Mark went outside to look around and appraise the various farm implements and tools and calculate how much they would bring. No, those days before the funeral were not pleasant days and Hannah was glad that they would soon be over.

Joyce came over several times, slipping away from her father when she could, but Myra seemed to resent her presence.

"I don't think she has very fine feelings," she said haughtily. "She must know it was her brother's fault for getting Rowan into this mess. It was her brother who led him away to that awful Rowley place, they say. I've been down to Mrs. Lamb's cottage and she's been telling me a lot."

"Yes, she would," said Hannah quietly. "Myra, you've been away from home too long to be a good judge of whom to listen to. If I were you I wouldn't get my facts from Widow Lamb. Now child, forget all this for the present. Sometime I'll tell you all about it. Rowan and Jason and everything, but not now. I'll tell you, too, what your father thought of Joyce, and I'm sure the day will come when you will love her as much as I do. Now, just don't say any more at present."

Myra wept all through the service and caught none of the comfort that Hannah found in the precious words from the Book that Charles and she had read so often together.

But after it was all over and they had come back to the cleared-up house and Hannah was getting supper, just as she had always gotten it, just as if she were not terribly conscious that dear Charles' body was laid away in the cemetery, and she would not see that precious face again until she beheld it in the Morning, in glory, Morning Glory!

It was while she was fixing the fried potatoes the way she knew Myra loved them, and trying not to think how Charles had loved them too, that Myra came to her.

Myra had the look of one who was almost glad that the terrible time was over and she could get back to real living again.

"Mother," she said, and her tone was quite practical, "Mark says he wonders if you could get packed, your personal things, you know, and ready to start by day after tomorrow. He wanted me to ask you yesterday, but I wouldn't trouble you. He says he is awfully busy this time of year and he can't spare much time. We have the car here, of course, so it won't cost anything to take your baggage. You can use the trunk for your things. We only brought a suitcase, thinking there would be sheets and blankets and things that you would want to take with you. How about it, Mother, do you think you could get it all done in one day, or would it take two? I'll help you, you know."

Myra's face was white and anxious. She was evidently longing for an answer that would satisfy Mark.

Hannah looked up in surprise.

"Why, child, I've no notion of going home with you. In fact, I couldn't think of it. There are things that I must do at once that have been neglected. And besides, I don't feel that it would be wise for me to make you a visit just now. I'd better just stay here and get used to things. That's what Father would have wanted me to do."

"Mother!" wailed Myra. "You can't stay here alone! You'll come to us now, and I shall be so glad to have you!"

"Would you dear?" said Hannah, almost beaming on her child. She had sometimes felt that Myra was almost weaned from her. "Well, dear, that's nice. But I don't think it is wise, do you? Mark and I don't seem to think alike on most things, and I think it is better for you to get along the way you are. I'm afraid my coming would only bring discussion and worry for you."

"But Mother, we can't keep up two households. You know Mark can't afford it. He's doing well, of course, but he thinks it's wrong not to put away a certain amount each year. We've got to think of Ollie, you know."

"Why, my dear, there's no need to talk like that. I never expected you to keep up two households. I expect to go on living in my own home just as Father planned."

"Well, but Mother, Father isn't here to run the farm, and what would you live on?"

"Why, my dear child, I'm not utterly penniless as you seem to think. I've enough to get along on—" she smiled and added "for the present. And Mr. Hollister will carry on the farm just as he has done for the last ten years. Of course Rowan will take it over eventually when he gets back!"

"Mother! You're not still expecting Rowan to come back are you? I declare I can't understand it."

"Yes, I'm expecting Rowan back. He told me he was coming and I know he will."

"Well, you're only storing up trouble for yourself. Rowan won't come back, not with the record he's left behind him. Perhaps you don't know all that's said about him."

"Yes, I know all," said Hannah, "more than all!"

"Well, Mother, you've simply got to come home with us. I can't stand it if you don't."

"My dear! My dear! I didn't know you cared so much. If that's so I'll try to get in a visit before spring."

"No, Mother, I must have you now. I'm worn out! I've been counting on your coming home with us, and I just can't stand it any longer without you."

Myra put her face down in her mother's neck the way she used to do when she was a child, and her mother's heart went out to her. Poor child! Maybe she wanted her mother. Her heart was sore over the loss of her father. They used to be such comrades before Myra was married. Maybe the child needed her mother for a little while. Maybe she was wrong. Maybe she ought to go.

She folded her arms about Myra's neck and patted her head.

Dear child! Dear child! But Myra continued to weep as if this was the bitterest trouble of all, and at last Hannah said:

"Well, dear, if you want it so much I guess I'll have to go for awhile. There, there! Don't take on any more. Mother'll go and visit you awhile. Now cheer up. We'll have some nice times and get acquainted all over again."

Myra was ecstatic. For the first time in years she acted like herself, and seemed to continually rejoice that she was to have her mother again.

"When will you go? Can you be ready by day after tomorrow?"

Hannah considered.

"Yes, I guess so," she said with a sigh, looking around on her beloved home. It seemed ruthless to leave it this way so soon after Charles was gone. There were little tender sweet things she wanted to do, his things to put away. Things that nobody else could do but herself.

"Yes, I'll go, day after tomorrow."

So Myra went happily to Mark to tell him that Mother had given in and was going to do as he wanted her to.

Mark was cheerful at supper. He ate a great deal of the yellow tomato preserve and said he guessed he'd have to see about boxing what she had of it, that it went right to the spot, and would save putting up much else. Hannah shut her lips and tried to make the line of them look pleasant, but she didn't say anything, except that she was glad he liked it.

After supper Mark came in from wandering around the

place again and said, "Mother, suppose you let me see what of Father's clothes are worth taking to town. I might be able to wear some of them myself, though I'm not so tall as he was. Pity Ollie wasn't a boy and Myra could cut the pants down for her. But I'll take the best of them back to town and see what I can sell them for. You get good prices, sometimes, for clothes if you know how to jew the men down. Are his clothes up in his closet? Shall I go up and look at them?"

"No," said Hannah, speaking sharply for the first time. "I would rather you would not go up. I do not wish to dispose of Father's things. I have other plans. And Rowan will want some of them, of course. I will look after all that."

"Well, but Mother, that's being sentimental, you know. And as for Rowan he won't be back. You might as well make up your mind right now about that. Rowan knows good and well what he'd be coming back to, and you needn't think he doesn't. Rowan doesn't deserve consideration!"

Hannah turned with dignity and faced her son-in-law.

"Mark, though you are my son-in-law, if you speak that way again about Rowan I shall have to ask you to leave the house. Rowan is my son, and I understand a lot of things that you don't know about. Let us leave Rowan out of the conversation until he returns!"

Mark laughed.

"Until he returns! I like that! All righty! We'll leave him out till he returns, and that'll be never. Well, it suits me. I never did care to talk about him anyway. It was you who brought the subject up, remember! And as for your knowing more than I about Rowan and his pranks, don't let 'em kid you. You don't know the half and it's just as well you don't. But how about those clothes of Father's. I'm only trying to be helpful and it's always best to get such things out of the house as quickly as possible. We don't want any sob-stuff around."

But Hannah had walked silently upstairs and closed and locked her door, and before she slept she had put every one of Charles' precious garments away most carefully under lock and key, where Mark would never find them. Mark did not know of the secret closet Father had made to hold the valuables. Its sliding panel was behind the bureau in their room. Charles' garments were not silver nor gold, but she did not want Mark's irreverent hands handling them and disposing of them.

So when Mark took advantage next morning of her being

down cellar and went into the room to look over Charles' things in spite of her, he found not so much as a trace of anything in closet or drawer or press. Vexed again he came out of the room and slammed the door with a bang. Then he went up in the attic and looked around, but every chest was locked. He could not find a thing. While he was up there he gave a casual glance around and decided the old cradle would probably bring a neat sum. He'd remember that when he got back to the city and see where he could sell it to the best advantage. But this time he would keep his mouth shut till the sale was sure.

Hannah went around silently all day putting things away and getting ready to go. Myra came to her once with troubled eyes.

"Mother, Mark says it is foolish for you to plan to spend money coming back here to pack up when the house is sold. He says you'd better do now what you have to do, once for all, even if you have to stay another day, and then he can come up with a van and bring away whatever he thinks is worth while to be sold."

Hannah faced her child almost majestically.

"Myra!" she said, and the sternness in her voice made the younger woman stop in wonder, "It is time you understood that I am not to be managed by Mark! You may be under his thumb and in terror of what he thinks and says, but I am not and never could be. Now, understand this, too. This house is not going to be sold, and I am not going to let Mark come back here and pack up or manage my things at any time. If you say any more I will not go with you tomorrow. I am only going because you look sick and I think you need me for awhile, but I'll stop right now planning to go unless you give up all this nonsense."

Myra resorted to tears again and left her, and sorrowfully, silently, Hannah toiled on through the day. She was ready to go with them in the morning as she had promised.

"You don't mean to say this is all the baggage you have," asked Mark unpleasantly, the next morning, when he saw the one large suitcase Hannah had brought down, and a small handsatchel. "Now, Mother, do be reasonable. If you don't take everything you need you'll be wanting to trot back all the time to get things."

"This is all I need," said Hannah with finality and climbed into the back seat of the car.

Mark was disagreeable about it all the way home. He told

her several times that she was just bound to make all the
trouble she could for them, and Myra was distressed and silent. Several times Hannah felt as if she would like to get out
and walk back. She was sorry she had come. If Myra wanted
her so badly she could have stayed with her awhile. She
could have sent for Olive and stayed. That would have been
nice. Without Mark around underfoot perhaps in time Myra
would calm down and be like her old self.

But the journey at length was ended and Hannah went up
to the alien bedroom and unpacked her few neat things that
she had brought with her. A Sunday dress, an afternoon
dress, four clean cotton working dresses, because she expected to spend the most of her time in the kitchen relieving
Myra, some warm undergarments. There were no furbelows
nor frills to take up room.

She hung up her two best dresses on the two hooks that
were not filled with Ollie's clothes.

"There isn't any closet in Ollie's room," explained her
mother, "so I put them in here. I thought of putting up a
shelf over there with a curtain around it for her, but Mark
has got it in his head that he wants Ollie's room for a kind of
office so he can work at home night. Would you mind so
very much, Mother, if I put Olive's little bed in here? She'd
be company for you. I know I used to love it when you let
me sleep in your room when I was sick some nights. I know
she'd enjoy it to be with you."

Hannah doubted it, but thought perhaps it would make a
better feeling between herself and her grandchild if she could
win her, and besides she was going to stay only a few days
anyway, so she said:

"Why, of course, put her in here if you want to. I'm sure
we can move things around and make it quite comfortable."

Olive, however, was of another mind two or three days
later when the change was inaugurated. She set up a terrible
to-do about it.

"I want my own room. I don't wanta go with her. I don't
like my grandmother!"

Hannah slipped away down to the kitchen so Myra
wouldn't be mortified by her child, and prepared a nice supper, making Myra's specialty, graham gems. But unfortu-
nately it happened that they were not Mark's specialty. Mark
expressed his dislike at once. Said they were not fit to put in
the human stomach and told Myra he wished she would not

eat them, that she would be sure to be sick in the night. Incidentally he remarked:

"Mother, you better ask next time before you plan to make things whether we like them or not. It's a pity to have good material wasted making up things that nobody will eat."

Then Olive, who had been enjoying her gem, and had demanded a second, suddenly flung it, butter and all, across the table almost into Hannah's face, spattering hot butter down the front of Hannah's gray traveling dress.

"It's nasty!" she yelled. "I won't eat it!"

Mark chuckled.

"Smart, isn't she, Mother?" he said. "She gets onto a thing right away." But Myra coming into the room from the kitchen just then where she had gone to cut more bread for Mark who wouldn't eat the graham gems, turned white, and walked her child away from the table into the sitting room.

"Now, Myra, don't be too mad. She was only rubbing it in!" and he gave his disagreeable little laugh again and picked up his evening paper, which he habitually read through all meals whenever possible.

Hannah was glad when she lay at last in her bed upstairs, with the little rebel Olive sleeping sweetly in her bed on the other side of the somewhat small room. It wasn't going to be a bed of roses, her visit here, she could see that. But if she could in any way lighten Myra's load and help her to get a little rest in her strenuous life she was glad to sacrifice herself for a little while. Anyway it would all be over soon, and Charles was now in the glory he had talked about, and pretty soon the Morning would come, sunrise and the glory of the Lord. Morning glory!

"Dear Lord, send Rowan home before long! Please, if it be Thy will."

CHAPTER XIV

When Rowan awoke the daylight was stealing over a gray sky and meeting at the edges with as steely a sea as had rolled between him and the boat the night before.

He was still lying on the dirty bags and their stench filled his nostrils. Someone stood above him looking down. Perhaps it had been a familiar voice that had wakened him, he could not tell.

"Rowan! Rowan Parsons! How did you get here!" He thought he heard the echo of such words hovering in the air about him.

He came to himself quickly, out of the mist of dreams that his weariness had gathered.

"Oh, I've found you, Jason!" he exclaimed. "And it was really you I saw when I jumped. I was afraid I had been dreaming. I was afraid I was off on a wild goose chase, but you are really here!"

"You're right I'm here, Rowan," said the boy with a grave voice, "but it's not so hot as you may think, and I'm all kinds of sorry that you're here too. I never thought of their sending you after me! Oh, Rowan! I've been an awful fool, I suppose, I found that out last night. But I never thought I'd get you into a mess too."

"Don't worry about that, Jason, let's talk about how we can get back the quickest way possible. Your sister is breaking her heart about you, and I can't say what my mother and father think about me by this time. I hadn't time to explain. I just came off and said I'd be back as soon as I could. I didn't even tell them what I was going for. So it's necessary to get back at once. How do we make it, Kid? I tried to get something done about it last night, but the only man I could find put up such a bluff about noise and danger that I thought perhaps I might do you some harm if I went ahead and disobeyed his orders, so I kept quiet. He shoved me down here, and I was so all in that I just stayed. I never meant to go to sleep. I was going to steal out when all was quiet and hunt for you. Now, what's next, boy? It's too far to swim home, and it's not exactly a nice looking sea either. How do we get back?"

"I'm afraid swim is the only answer," said Jason solemnly. "This is an awful place. I never knew what I was getting into or I would have swung off and risked getting picked up near shore. I hadn't been on board but a few minutes before we sailed. I couldn't seem to find the captain. I heard they wanted a hand and I didn't know any other way of getting away, hadn't money enough to go far enough, so I took the job. But I wish it was yesterday and I wasn't here."

"Oh, Kid, it probably isn't so bad as it seems. Cheer up, we'll find a way out. There'll be a port somewhere and we'll get off. Where is this boat bound for?"

"That's it," said Jason with troubled eyes. "Someone on land told me they thought it was going to South America and I like a fool took it for granted and got on board. But I can't find out where we are going. No one will tell me. That is, no one who can speak English, the rest are all Portuguese or something queer. There's something phoney about this boat, Rowan, and I'm not kidding. I saw and heard a lot of things last night, but I don't dare tell them now. Someone might overhear, and the mischief would be to pay."

"Well, that's bad, but we're both here, so that helps. We can think a way out somehow, I'm sure."

"I wish we could, but—I'm afraid. I saw enough last night to make me plenty sorry I came. There's a guy on board who came for his health. He's poor and has the t.b. and some fool doctor sent him for a sea voyage—and he got stung here, too. He didn't have money but he heard they wanted a man to help and he took the job. Don't look fit to stand up, but he's got all kinds of courage. He put me onto a few things, all he dared. It was plenty."

"All right!" said Rowan with a firm set to his lips that made him look like his mother. "Then tell me, what do we do now? Where do I fit into the picture so I won't do harm to you and the other fellow?"

"Well, I guess you'd better just sail in and tell 'em you are the other man they were waiting for. Nobody hired you, but you are. So am I. They'll tell you your duties. Maybe we'll get different hours and can share the same bunk turn about. They're lousy dirty and that's the truth, but I guess between us we could keep one fairly decent. It's going to be rather unbearable you know. This isn't a regular boat. It's queer. It's weird. But—you'll find that out soon enough."

"Don't you know what the first port of call is?"

"Isn't any as far as I can find out. Looks like they were playing hide and seek with some pretty powerful party, and they won't tell what they're doing."

"Well, then, brother, we'll just sit tight and wait for developments, and don't get blue. Perhaps we'd better not be seen too much together till we get things straightened out. How about it?"

"Good idea!" said Jason. "When you get a chance you go aft and look for the sick guy. You can't miss him. He looks as if a breath would blow him away. He'll give you a lot of dope, and then perhaps there'll be another chance for us to talk. There comes the second mate. You'd better go see him. The first mate jabbers Portuguese. I've got to get on with the job they gave me. So long!"

Rowan walked to meet the second mate, trying to put on an assured air.

The second mate sighted him as if he had been a reptile and pausing before him said with an ugly challenge in his eye:

"Who in hell are you?"

"Is this hell?" said Rowan. "I was just wondering."

The second mate looked at him narrowly a minute and then laughed a hard bitter laugh.

"Smart, ain't ya? Well, who are ya."

"Why I'm just a new man. You wanted men on your crew, didn't you? Well I'm here now!" laughed Rowan good naturedly. "I'm reporting for service, sir. Do I report to you?"

"You report to the captain when he wakes up. He's pretty well stewed just now, but he'll be around before night. He better be."

"Well then, what shall I do till I can see him?"

"Mind your own business. That's the first lesson they have to learn on this tub. Mind your own business!"

"Yes, well, is that all? You see I don't have much of it with me at the present time. Is there anything else that I can do?"

"Well, ya might swab this deck if yer spilin' fer work—that's what they used ta do with greenies when I was young—but don't go no further than the hatch there!"

"Yes, sir. Where do I get the tools?"

"Find 'em in the locker if there is any. If there ain't you'll havta use yer necktie," he said leering at Rowan's neat attire.

"Oh, that's all right by me," said Rowan yanking off his tie. "You see I didn't have time to stop for my working clothes, but these will soon season down to the surroundings, I imagine."

"Smart guy!" said the second mate. "But you'll get took down all right, I expect. Get along there to work, an' ef ya need anything, go find Softy. He's below. You'll mostly find him layin' down, but he's all right, what there is of him!"

So Rowan sauntered nonchalantly about as if he owned the boat, feeling that a certain amount of assurance would carry him a longer way than an attitude of uncertainty.

He found a dilapidated mop and a bucket for water, but there remained much to be desired in the way of working paraphernalia, and Rowan finally found the person designated as Softy.

He found him on the after deck mending a sail.

He was slim as a splinter with a face that looked ethereal and a body that was active like a live wire in spite of his frailty. He had eyes that burned deep with a spirit fire that was almost luminous. He looked up alertly as Rowan came near. There were spots of color on his lean white face that might have been fever. He looked at Rowan keenly, almost startled to find one like him on the boat. He thought he knew the whole population.

"I'm Rowan Parsons, and I was told to find you and ask you what it's all about," Rowan introduced himself.

The other cast a quick wary look about.

"Not so loud, my friend, when you say things like that," he warned quietly. "I'm Carl Kinder. Glad to see you. What do you mean, 'it's all about'? Who told you to come?"

"My friend, Jason Whitney."

"Oh, he didn't tell me he had a friend on board." Kinder looked him over cautiously.

"He didn't know it till a few minutes ago. You see, his people felt pretty badly at his going and I came after him to stop him and bring him home. I didn't get here quite in time. I just made it. The water got too wide for us to walk back,

and I haven't been able to make other arrangements yet."
Rowan grinned.

"I see," said the other with an answering gleam in his eyes.
"Well, I'm afraid you'll have some trouble in doing so for the
present. If you should discover a way I'd be glad to go with
you. So far I've only been able to discover two ways out of
this boat, the way down, and the way up!"

Rowan looked startled, but tried to grin.

"Yes? Well, that's a pleasant outlook. Just how do you
figure this outfit?"

"I haven't figured it yet. I've only been on board a couple
of hours more than you have. I signed up in good faith because I hoped it was a possible way for me to get a bit of
health back, but things got shadier and shadier and I was
about to make a break for shore again when I found we were
under way. I think they must have started as soon as some of
their important men got back. They were mighty worried
about something, I'm sure of that. There's something crooked
here of course, and there's nobody to ask. For some reason
they wanted more men and when they got them they slipped
away in the dark. You must have been the last of the
number."

"It looks that way," said Rowan. "They certainly lost no
time in moving when I came in sight. In fact they almost
went without me. If I hadn't seen Whitney on deck somewhere holding a rope I wouldn't have been here myself. But
then they hauled in the gangplank and I jumped. Someone
grabbed me by the collar or I would have taken the way
down right then. But meantime, here I am and what in your
opinion ought I to do?"

"Get busy doing something. My brief experience has
taught me that if you appear to be busy at something, no
matter what, nobody will bother you. I've figured it out that
except for a neat little gang who run this thing, they are all
strangers to each other and most of them talk queer lingoes.
Perhaps most of them don't know any more than we do. I'm
not sure of that, but I think so. Everybody seems to be suspicious of everybody else. You and your friend Whitney are
the only decent men I've seen so far. The captain hasn't been
on view yet. They say he is drunk, but I have my suspicions
from a few words I overheard that he's been in a fight and
he's pretty well banged up. If you ask me I think he'd been
pretty badly hurt. There was a sound of shots in the distance
a few minutes before we sailed, and then there was a hubbub;

they were carrying someone aboard. That Portuguese first mate seems to be all there. He kept me busy on the far side from shore till we started. Perhaps they thought you were in pursuit when you jumped. Though I should think, if so, they would have flung you into the water."

"Perhaps they thought I'd swim out and give information," said Rowan thoughtfully. "Well, I guess I'd better walk pretty circumspectly if there's a possibility that I'm under surveillance."

"I guess we're all that. Have you talked with anyone else yet?"

"Yes, one sailor besides Whitney. I slept on a pile of unpleasant bags all night, too much all in to protest. The man who picked me up from the deck and flung me there advised me to keep still till morning and then he put out all the light there was and left me This morning that second mate said I could swab decks, but he didn't seem to care much what I did except that I was not to go beyond the hatch."

"Yes. That's it! There's something queer beyond that hatch. Well, this isn't exactly the garden of Eden, but it seems to have something that corresponds to the tree of the knowledge of good and evil in that hatch, so I guess we might as well keep the rules There comes somebody. I hear footsteps Better get busy about something and not appear to know me But I'm glad you're here. It's great to know there are two decent fellows on board, anyway."

He put out a hand and grasped Rowan's quickly and released it, but in that quick brief clasp Rowan was suddenly aware that the man he had been talking to was a sick man. The hand he had touched was burning with fever, and looking at him more closely he saw the white ethereal look in his face. Poor fellow! He ought to be home in bed with his mother or someone dear nursing him! And he was here in all this filth and terrible uncertainty! Well, if he could take it with fortitude, it ill-befitted anyone else to make a fuss.

So Rowan went back to his futile scrubbing, for it seemed a hopeless task, at least with the few implements at his command, ever to hope to bring cleanliness out of the filth of years.

Eventually Rowan had an interview with the captain. His arm was in a sling and his face was badly bruised, but he had little piercing eyes that looked through Rowan. He asked a number of sharp quick questions, and Rowan felt like a mere butterfly who was being fixed with a pin by a collector.

The captain was a man who used oaths as crutches to get him from one word to another and he let Rowan have a good exhibition of what he could do oratorically. When he had finished with him Rowan had no desire to go beyond bounds set, nor to call attention to himself by asking any more unnecessary questions. He had not been able to find out where he was bound, nor how long he would be gone, and he had a notion he never would find out till he got there, perhaps not even then. He came away from the interview convinced that the only help must come from Heaven, as human strategy would be vain.

He had been assigned few duties. He gathered that the time that his services would be most needed was not yet come, and that when it did it would be useless to refuse to obey. Obedience would be at the point of a gun. For the rest, his duties were merely nominal. The captain asked him if he had ever been to sea before, and when he said no, he waved him away with a kind of contempt that made him stiffen insensibly and shut his lips in that strong line that reminded of his mother, and resolve to show that captain that he was not afraid to work, and had as much courage as anyone. So he set himself the task of getting the deck clean, as far as he was allowed to go. It did little good however, for no one on the whole boat excepting Jason and Kinder attempted to keep it so, and the grime was not easily removed.

As the days went by and the scene continued to be a grimy boat on an endless tossing leaden sea, with leaden skies overhead, and a fearful cold beginning to grow about them, the future looked dark indeed, for the three young men who had by common consent drawn together and formed a close partnership.

But they had little opportunity for taking the comfort of each other's company, for it seemed to be a part of the plan of their captain that they should be kept apart as much as possible. Perhaps he suspected that allowed to herd together they would become a formidable foe at some time when he needed them under his power. So though they tried to arrange to occupy the same quarters, with the hope that they could at least have a clean place to sleep, it was refused them, and so it was seldom that the three could talk together undisturbed.

It was on one of the first of these occasions that they hovered together behind a sheltering pile of canvas at dusk. They had been discussing their desperate situation and Kinder suddenly said:

"Are you fellows Christians? Are you saved?"

Rowan looked startled.

"I'm a church member," he said thoughtfully.

"Yes, but that won't save you. Are you saved?"

"I used to think I was," said Rowan. "But that was before I went to college."

"Well, college and all they teach there won't help you now. You're here on this boat with all this ocean between us and any help but God. Are you saved, friend?"

"Well, what they taught me at college didn't really bother me much as far as belief is concerned. I had too wonderful a father and mother at home to doubt their God. But college made me forget a lot. I'm just beginning to remember it now, these long nights lying alone in that dirty bunk, without even any stars overhead to help. I've been wondering if I was ever really saved."

"I guess it's too late, for me," said Jason speaking up wistfully. "I've had plenty of chance to be good, but I was just a fool. I see it now. I don't suppose I could be any better if I ever do get off this blasted ship and get home again. I've tried sometimes to be really good, but—I can't!"

"That's where God comes in," said Kinder, flashing him a yearning look. "There isn't a soul on earth who can be good enough for God, Whitney. That isn't what I mean by being saved. God planned the way of salvation just for sinners like you and me, who want to be good and can't of ourselves. He sent His Son, Jesus Christ, to live a perfect life here, so that He wouldn't have to die for any sin of His own, and then God took your sin and mine, and the sin of the whole world, and put it on His Son and *put Him to death for it!* Then God raised Him from the dead to show that He was satisfied. So you and I never need bear the punishment for sin. Do you see? And it's believing that He did that for you that saves you. It's accepting Jesus Christ as your Saviour."

They stood thoughtfully looking out into the dark billows for a moment and then Kinder said earnestly: "Won't you two take him that way, now?" Without an instant's hesitation Rowan said, "I will!" and turned and knelt beside the canvas.

Jason looked his new friend hungrily in the face, and said humbly, like a little child: "Why, of course! I didn't know He did that for me!"

There in the stern of the filthy old boat with only a weird lantern swinging low amidship, they knelt and prayed.

Kinder prayed first. Such a prayer. It took Rowan back to his father's hearthside, and the old days of family worship, and suddenly he felt that God could be here on this ship in the darkness, was here, as much as He had been at home.

Then they had to scatter suddenly, for the first mate was roaring toward them with orders. There was sound of thunder, and lightning shivered across the wide heavens. Sails must be tended and orders must be carried out. But they went out, those three, with a feeling that now they were in God's hands in a different way from ever before, and come what might, they were safe.

The days went by, each one seemingly worse than the other, because of the awful monotony, and now terrible cold had settled down. It searched the crannies of the old ship, and hurtled through their inadequate clothing. Jason and Rowan felt it worse than the others for they had absolutely no extra things with them, and were obliged to take the filthy blankets from their bunks and wrap them up for garments or they would have perished.

Kinder shared his sparse wardrobe with them as far as they would let him, woollen underwear and socks. They did a washing every day to the vast amusement of the rest of the crew who treated them almost with contempt because of their cleanliness.

Whenever possible Rowan and Jason snatched a few minutes with Kinder, while he read to them from his little Bible, and talked of the Lord Jesus, and then they all prayed together.

Rowan had prayed before, often in his younger days, had in fact led young people's meetings at home when he was in high school. But his prayers had been worked out with words, heretofore. Now they came from the heart and breathed a spirit that was genuine.

Jason had not done much praying since the days when his mother, and later, his sister Joyce had made him kneel at night and say his prayers. But now he took his turn with the rest, praying like a child, simply, earnestly, as a soul prays who is in great need and very humble.

As the days went by it became evident that Kinder was growing weaker all the time. When his friends touched him they drew back frightened at the hot hands, the burning head. He did not eat enough, either. The coarse food was revolting to him, though he resolutely swallowed some whenever it was time. Rowan and Jason tried to save the best morsels for him if anything of the uncouth fare that was dealt out on that ship could be called best. They had grown to love him like a brother, and their every thought outside the actual duties of the ship was turned toward helping Kinder. They insisted on doing most of his work, they were continually sending him to rest.

And now the rest of the crew began to notice that the young man who had come among them so strangely out of another world as it were was not long to stay with them. They ceased to call him "Softy" and gave him Kinder instead, speaking it almost gently sometimes, giving it its true meaning, as if he were a little child and they were calling him so. It was incredible that most of these rough men should suddenly soften. Even the captain came in to see him one day, after he had lain for hours in his bunk, coughing and racked with pain and fever.

And finally he gave the order that Kinder might be moved to a place with his two friends, for in spite of their precautions the ship had come to accept the friendship between the three and set them apart from themselves, as they would have set another race.

Tenderly the two boys carried their friend to the bunk and prepared to nurse him, hoping against hope that he might get well. Tenderly they worked over him night and day as he lay there weak and sick, but brave and smiling.

The captain finally turned him over unreservedly to the two who were his own kind, and all hands were relieved. Perhaps the captain thought it would keep them out of the way, for he held many grave councils of war these days, and he wanted those three otherwise occupied so that they would not be likely to suspect what was going on or to overhear words or see anxious looks on the faces of the officers, nor yet to notice signals from an accomplice craft.

So, as Kinder grew worse, the two did not leave him at all except when they had to, and they tried to make that little bunk room where he lay as neat as they could.

It had been a great shock to Rowan to discover day by day in spite of his earnest efforts to do his share of the work on the ship, that he was not as popular as he had always been in every other group of men among whom he had been thrown. His shipmates generally resented his gentlemanly ways, and his ability to understand quicker than they did what was expected of him and to do it more intelligently. They had nick-named him "Smarty," and he was more chagrined than he cared to admit. Sometimes he had difficulty in concealing his contempt and disgust at the whole crew.

In the same way they had called Jason "Sonny," though not with quite so much animosity as they seemed to have to-ward Rowan.

Sometimes as Rowan sat on watch with their sick friend he would get to thinking of Joyce. Would he ever see her again? Would he be able to take her in his arms and feel her soft lips against his? Would all this living horror ever be gone and he be back with home and friends and able to tell Joyce of his great love for her?

He thrilled to think how glad she would be if he might only let her know that he had found the Lord. She was a wonderful Christian. He had always known that. She seemed almost like an angelic being.

Then suddenly as he was thinking such thoughts, while he sat beside his friend, he saw the vermin walking about on the pillow.

He sprang up angrily and went for the evil little creatures. He had thought that at least from this small spot where his friend lay he had exterminated them. He had hoped that his vigilance would prevent their coming again. But now here they were, bold as an invading host, marching across the poor pillow for which Rowan had bungled a pillow case made from an old flour sack begged from the cook.

"This place is unbearable!" he exploded. "It is filthy every-where. If there is one thing I never could stand it is dirt of any kind! I've never been used to it! It's an awful come-down, I tell you!"

His lip curled and he held his head high as he remembered his immaculate home.

Kinder looked at him with a gentle pity.

"It's no more of a comedown than it was for the Lord Jesus Christ to step into this world from Heaven," he said. "It must have been hard for Him to stand sin all about Him for thirty-three years, and then to take it all *on* Him."

Rowan stared in amazement. Then he looked out at the sea for a long time. Kinder, as he watched him, could almost read his thoughts. He saw the pride begin to melt away from his face; wonder took its place. Then shame came and sat in his eyes until sorrow brought a look of almost tears.

At last Rowan turned back to his companion. His voice was low and broken.

"I never thought of *that* before!" he said earnestly. "And I suppose *I* look like this to Him!" He waved his hand toward his vile surroundings. Then he sat down on the edge of the bunk and his head sank into his hands. "I always thought I was pretty good," he murmured sadly.

" 'We are *all* as an unclean thing,' " repeated Kinder quietly, " 'and all our righteousnesses are as filthy rags' in His sight, friend. It's pride in all of us, and an evil heart of unbelief that looks vile to Him."

"I suppose that is true," mused Rowan. "I thought I was fit to be an example to that young kid Jason, and I had visions of leading him out of a life of failure to nobility. But I suppose I'm not a bit better than he is, if as good. He didn't have half a chance in his home. I have a wonderful father and mother!"

Rowan choked back the wave of homesickness that swept over him at thought of them.

"Well, the whole trouble is that most people count goodness as a state of not doing obviously wrong things," said Kinder. "With God nothing counts except our personal relationship to Jesus Christ." Kinder's voice was very earnest now. "When once a man takes Jesus Christ as his Saviour the personal relationship must be kept close and vital at all costs or that man is going to show a mighty inconsistent Christian life to the world, besides grieving his Heavenly Father."

Rowan looked thoughtfully again at the lighted face of his friend.

"Yes, I can see that," he said, "and that's what makes you so different from any man I ever met except my father. You are like Jesus Christ. Everyone on this ship sees it! You let them see *Him* all the time. That's where I've failed miserably," he added humbly. "I think I really took Christ as my Saviour when I was a little kid, but I just took for granted that once I did that, my part was to live the best I could. I didn't see *Him* this way. I didn't see that He has to do it all, and I'm just here for Him. Oh, if I'd shown Jesus Christ to Jason as you do, we wouldn't have to be here. But God had to send me out *here* to find all this out!"

"I'm mighty glad He sent you, friend,—sent you *both*," he added as Jason entered the place. "What would I have done without you?"

Kinder reached out a feeble hand and laid it on Rowan's. "I've wondered sometimes why He let me come out here to *die*, for I've known almost from the first it was going to be death, not life for me—not this life. I've wondered why it had to be, but now I'm *glad!*"

Then he closed his eyes, too weary to talk more, and was racked with a sudden fit of coughing.

That night Kinder died.

Rowan and Jason were with him to the last, hearing his last word, watching his radiant face.

"We'll meet—over There!" he said, looking upward and trying to lift his weak hand to point.

"Dear friend," said Rowan, "we may be there before long ourselves. There's no telling what will happen on this ship. You said there were only two ways, down and up, but they may turn out to be one and the same for us. Perhaps we'll go together into His presence!"

Kinder smiled, a rare sweet smile, but shook his head.

"I think He's going to leave you behind for awhile—to witness—" he said faintly. "I think that's why He's saved you! You must go home—to—*live*—for Him! Good-bye! See you in the Morning!" and he was gone!

The night came and many of the ship's crew gathered with hard blanched faces for the burial. Dark water, dark sky overhead without a single star, dark faces in the light of the swaying lantern that would be put out as soon as this was over!

At the last some of the men had been almost gentle with Kinder, bringing him little things they hoped he could eat, offering to sit up with him, though Rowan and Jason kept that privilege for themselves, knowing that Kinder would rather have it so.

They wrapped their friend's body in a piece of clean sailcloth that Rowan himself had washed, and they gathered to give him the last respect and consign him to the sea. But the captain had no service to read and told Rowan he might do or say what he liked. So Rowan read some of Kinder's favorite passages of scripture from Kinder's Bible, and he and Jason sang a hymn the three used often to sing together, though their voices broke and they could scarcely finish it.

Rowan was about to pray when Jason put up his hand.

"Men!" he said and his voice rang clear and young, "I want to say a word for the man who is gone. I know he would like you to know he prayed for every one of you by name every night, and he wanted you to know God as he knew Him. He wanted you to take Jesus Christ as your own Saviour. He died for your sins and mine you know—and I had plenty! Kinder told us he'd meet us in Heaven, and I know he'd be glad if you were all there, too. It's just since I've known Kinder that I've taken Jesus for my Saviour, and now I'm beginning to get acquainted with Him. Oh, He's wonderful! I wish you all knew Him, too! That's all!" And Jason stepped back.

Then Rowan prayed, and here and there among the group a man brushed tears from his eyes.

They lowered the body into the sea, and Rowan was thinking of the verse that Kinder had read them about the time when the sea should give up its dead.

When it was over they all turned away and hurried off, leaving Rowan and Jason together alone, looking out on the dark waste of water. Would Kinder's words come true? Would they be allowed to live and go home to testify?

That night a wild, fierce storm swooped down from the northeast and tossed the dirty old boat about as if it had been a toy. The boat that had weathered so many storms, and gone so many evil errands for wicked men, was beaten and wrenched and flung on an uncharted rock, its sails torn like bits of paper, its great masts twisted and snapped like pipe-stems.

Rowan and Jason looked about on the wild waste and thought of their friend who had gone Home. Would they go too, pretty soon?

CHAPTER XV

The rest of the winter had not been a happy time for Hannah, nor perhaps for anyone else concerned.

It was not just that she was grieving, for she was bearing her great grief royally, almost radiantly, but it was that she was so lonely and homesick.

She had hoped in coming to visit Myra that she would have a tender renewal of their other days together, and that a sweet companionship would grow between herself and her little granddaughter. But things did not turn out that way. Hannah began to realize that they could not turn out so in the house where Mark was dominant and kept up a continual tumult about everything that went on. She came to realize also that Myra was driven from morning to night by the whims of her husband, and was in constant terror of one of his overbearing outbreaks. Poor Myra! Her dear little girl! To think that they had let her marry into a life like this!

And yet Mark was not a bad man as morality goes. He was just mean, stubborn, conceited, determined to rule everything about him. He wouldn't let his own little child even love her mother. He put thoughts into her mind like seeds, and wildly they grew, so that Myra had no ally anywhere, not even her own baby. And Hannah saw that she did not dare to turn to her mother. Indeed Hannah presently perceived that her very presence in the home instead of being a comfort to Myra had become a distress. Mark was continually nagging and criticizing her, or telling her it was her fault that Myra was so silly and set in her way whenever he had a difference of opinion with his wife.

The only thing that she could possibly do for Myra was to

relieve her of some of the heavy housework that Mark demanded and even then he was never quite suited.

But she was at least able to give Myra a chance to go off with her husband in the car now and then, though she wondered sometimes when she saw the look on Myra's unhappy face, if that was, after all, such a good thing. It almost seemed as if Myra would have been glad of an excuse to stay at home.

And so as the spring came on Hannah began to plan to get away very soon. She mentioned it once or twice to Myra and brought on such a storm of pleading and sharp words combined with tears, that she had put it off from week to week. But now things were really coming to a crisis.

They left Olive with her one day, with strict orders that the child must stay in the house because she had a bad cold, but Olive, as soon as their back was turned put on her hat and coat and started to go out to play with some of her little friends.

Hannah called her back, indeed drew her forcibly into the house and took off her coat and hat while Olive kicked her and screamed wildly.

"I don't have to mind you, you—old—*thing!*" she said with a kick at every word, until Hannah's ankles were smarting from the little heels. "You aren't my father and mother! I don't have to mind you! You're old! You're a mean old thing! I HATE you!"

Of course she was little more than a baby but the words hurt Hannah more than the kicks had hurt her sensitive flesh. Olive, her own baby's child, talking that way to her!

She was worn out, almost sick when at last she got the child somewhat subdued. She had tried giving her something nice to play with, a precious picture book of her mother's that she had tucked in her suitcase hoping there would be a chance to give it to the child sometime and rouse a little interest in her mother's childhood. But Olive turned the pages savagely, and then suddenly tore the book from end to end, stamping on it and saying: "It's a nasty book. I hate it!"

And suddenly Hannah was filled with a spirit of the past, and great and righteous wrath, and with almost superhuman strength she took the sturdy little girl in her arms, sat down with her wildly kicking and screaming and laid her firmly over her knee, administering a rare and thorough spanking.

The child was utterly astonished. No one had ever dared lay a chastising hand upon her person before, and when she discovered that neither kicks nor screams nor angry thumping little fists on whatever portions of grandmother were available did no good to stop the punishment, she suddenly sank her sharp little teeth in her grandmother's leg.

An hour later when Olive was at last lying in her little bed in her grandmother's room, still shaking with the sobs of the first defeat of her life, but sleeping the sleep of exhaustion, Hannah lay down upon her own bed, too exhausted to do another thing until she rested. She lay and looked at the ceiling and did some very thorough thinking.

Downstairs the pies that she had started to make did not get made. When Myra came in she gave a startled look of wonder at the table where the makings lay and then a questioning one at her mother.

"Olive was very naughty," Hannah explained in a low voice. "She was determined to go out and play in the wet with the children, and I had to spank her. I didn't get much done."

"You spanked her?" said Myra, aghast. "You really spanked her, Mother? Did she let you?"

"Did she *let* me?" said Hannah lifting astonished eyes. "Yes, she let me!" she said closing her lips firmly on any other revelations she might have offered. No need for Myra to be worried about the ugly swelling on her leg where Olive had left the marks of her sharp little teeth.

Myra looked at her mother with a strange expression of relief and triumph.

"Well, I'm glad," she breathed with a little sigh. "She never would me. But—don't tell Mark!"

"I won't," said Hannah, "but Olive will, I suppose."

"Oh, I suppose so," breathed the child's mother. "And there'll be a terrible time."

"Well, we'll have to weather it," said Hannah grimly. "Now, let's forget it while I hustle some supper on the table. You set the table."

"Supper not ready yet?" glared Mark coming into the kitchen just then and looking around. "Seems to me you've had time enough."

The two women did not answer. They flew around and had a meal on the table in no time.

And strangely enough Olive didn't say a word about her spanking. She came down to dinner all smiles.

"We had a nice time together, didn't we, Grandmother?"

she said sweetly, looking up into her grandmother's face placatingly.

Myra just saved herself from gasping aloud in astonishment, and Hannah looked at her grandchild with authority in her eye, and a distant smile that promised several different things.

"Very nice!" she said distantly, and Olive dropped her eyes in a strange new embarrassment. So it seemed that Olive was afraid of something. She was afraid that her grandmother would tell what she had done! So it seemed that Olive could be subdued if one had the courage, and the time and the strength.

Nevertheless Hannah decided that it was about time for her to go home.

The next time Myra was out of the house for a little while Hannah packed most of her things, all except the working dress that she would need. When the time came she wanted to be able to go quickly. It wouldn't be pleasant to have Myra weeping, of course. She must plan how to do it comfortably if possible so Myra wouldn't feel so badly. Maybe she would get Joyce to write her a letter saying that things at the farm needed her attention, or something like that.

That night at dinner Mark came in in a most complacent mood. He joked them all and was almost gay, for Mark.

After the dinner was well under way he said:

"Well, Mother, I've at last succeeded in getting a purchaser for the farm. It's taken sometime to find the right man who was willing to give my price and be willing to pay cash. You know when I was up there at the funeral I went over everything carefully and set down just what everything was worth, implements and furniture and the like, so I was firm about how much I wanted. He's ready to settle within two weeks, if he's thoroughly satisfied after he sees the place. And I guess he will be. He says he knows the country round there and knew Father by reputation, and he's pretty sure the farm is just what he wants. He stuck a little at the price, but he's agreed to it at last, and I'm taking him down tomorrow morning to look everything over. Suppose you give me the key tonight, so we won't forget it in the morning."

Hannah paused to pray in her heart for quietness and strength before she spoke.

"But I'm not going to sell the farm, Mark."

"What? Oh, yes, you are! There's no use your having illusions about that. We're going to get every bit of money together for your old age, Mother, that we possibly can. It isn't as if Myra and I were rich, you know. We can't afford to keep you entirely."

"No?" said Hannah quietly, "I wouldn't think you could. Not the way I would care to be kept—that is, if I was willing to be kept by anyone."

"Now, look here, Mother, that isn't a very Christian way to talk. That's not like you. Of course when one has to be kept they have to be kept, that's all, and it's best not to mince matters. Just have everything above board. Mother, suppose you go up now and get that key for me and then I won't have to keep it on my mind."

But Hannah arose and began to clear off the table. She answered not a word.

"Mother!" called Mark sharply. "Get me the key at once, won't you? I want to have everything ready for morning. We're going down in the man's car and I'm not sure how early he'll be coming for me. Eight or nine o'clock probably, and I want everything ready tonight. Just let Myra clear off that table tonight and you go up and get the key."

Hannah turned mildly on her son-in-law and gave him the look that had finally quelled Olive.

"Mark, I am not going to sell the farm. That is final. Father did not want me to. He arranged everything for me. So if you don't want to be embarrassed you'd better telephone that man tonight not to come. The farm is not for sale!"

Then Hannah took the vegetable dishes and walked calmly out into the kitchen.

But Mark followed her and put up a tremendous argument. He was quite calm and mealy-mouthed at first. But Hannah just went calmly on working and presently he waxed hot and began to storm. Still Hannah went on washing dishes. And as the storm continued she finally hung up her dishtowels and marched upstairs.

Mark hung around at the foot of the stairs for a few minutes, and then he went to Myra.

"Has your mother gone up for that key?"

"I don't know, Mark. She didn't say anything to me."

"Well, go up and bring it down to me. I want it where I can get it at a moment's notice."

"Mark, I don't think Mother wants to sell the farm. I don't think you ought to spring it on her in this sudden way," ventured Myra.

"You don't think! You don't think!" shouted Mark so loud that every word reached upstairs to Hannah, right through the register that passed through the parlor near where Mark was standing. "What have you got to do with it! That farm is going to be sold whether she likes it or not. It's ridiculous when I've got a perfectly good purchaser for it who is willing to pay my price. We'll have enough in the bank to pay her board and keep for the rest of the time she lives and won't have to worry. If you get into this I'll teach you where to get off, and I mean it! I guess you know I mean what I say!"

"Yes, I know," said Myra excitedly. "Of course I know. Oh, God, why did I ever—" the rest of the words were drowned in tears, but Hannah's heart was wrung.

The next words she heard were Myra's again, pleading.

"Mark, don't bother Mother any more this winter. She hasn't got over Father's death yet. It hurts her to think of parting with the farm!"

"Sentimental twaddle!" shouted Mark.

"But you can't bully Mother into selling it. She won't be driven. I've told you that before."

"Well, we'll see whether she won't be driven. She'll find out who's the head of her family! I've got her in my power and she can't help herself."

"Mark! You can't sell her farm unless she signs the papers!"

"She'll sign all righty!" boasted Mark. "I know how to make her sign. I'll just tell her that we'll take out papers that she isn't of sound mind and we'll put her in an asylum if she doesn't do what I tell her."

"Mark! You wouldn't do that to my mother!"

"Wouldn't I? You just watch! I'd do it so soon you wouldn't know what was happening. We could you know. Rowan isn't here, and nobody knows but he's dead. There's only you and I, and I could certainly make you sign anything I told you to. You don't think after all the trouble I've taken to get this buyer that I would be balked just by a little thing like that, do you?"

The conversation ended in more tears and cries and sobs, and amidst it Mark stalked out of the house slamming the door behind him. But presently, just as Hannah had expected, a chastened Myra with scared assumed smiles stole up to her room and knocked at the door.

"Mother!" she called, "I want to talk to you."

But Hannah lay still on her bed where she had laid herself when she first went upstairs and locked her door.

"Not tonight, dear. I've got a sort of headache, and I thought I'd lie down awhile and maybe snatch a bit of sleep. Good night, dear. Ollie's all right, sleeping soundly, so you needn't worry about her. Good night."

She heard Myra give a soft sob and wait a minute. Then she said, "All right, Mother!" and went slowly to her room.

By and by it was all still in the house and then Mark came stamping in. He came straight up to his room and woke up Myra and asked her if she had got that key yet.

"No," said Myra. "Mother is asleep. She had a headache!"

"Well, she deserves to have one, the way she has acted up! And you coddling her! It wouldn't have made her headache any worse to wake her up and ask for that key, would it? If you won't do it I'll do it myself!" and he stalked across the hall to Hannah's door and knocked good and loud, and then tried the door.

"Mother! Wake up and give me that key right away! I'm going early in the morning!" he called. But Hannah answered not a word.

"Mother! I say wake up!" shouted Mark, shaking the door! "What right has anybody got to lock a door in my house, I'd like to know!"

"Mark!" called Myra in distress. "You'll wake Ollie up and you know how hard she is to get to sleep again!"

"Well, I don't care!" shouted Mark. "I'm not going to be defied in my own house."

But Hannah lay very still and did not answer, and presently Myra got her man stilled till morning. Poor Myra!

After the house was still again Hannah made her plans. In the silence of the night she took off her shoes and her working dress, and moving without a sound she hung up the dress in the closet and fumbling about found her traveling array and put it on, moving as lightly as if she were a leaf on a tree.

All in the dark she got out her hat and coat and gloves, and her hand bag. She folded and laid her other things in the small bag. Then she stole step by step across the room to the bureau where she gathered up the few things left there, and packed them. There was a ball of cord in the upper drawer, and she slipped the end of it through the handle of her suitcase. The window was open. She could let her things down in the early morning.

Then, with everything ready, she went back to her bed

with a pencil and paper. Taking one of Ollie's picture books
for a desk she wrote a letter in the dark very carefully. There
wouldn't be time in the morning.

Dear Myra:
It's best that I should go now. You needn't worry, I was going
in a day or two anyway, and you will be happier if I am not here.

Don't forget to spank Ollie if she is naughty, and if Mark makes
a fuss, spank him too, somehow. Men do need it sometimes, you
know, not literally, but in someway. I should have taught you that.

I'm sorry to run away, but it's easier for us both this way. I love
you, dear, and you can write to me.

> Lovingly,
> Mother

Hannah put this note in a drawer where she knew only
Myra would find it, and then she lay down on her bed, but
she did not sleep much. She spent the time in praying, asking
her Heavenly Father to keep her calm and help her through
this hard way and keep Myra, too, and save her from pain
as much as was in His will.

At the first hint of dawn in the sky Hannah was up,
though even Ollie in the same room could scarcely have
heard her she moved so quietly She was in her stocking feet,
and she went to the window and lifted her suitcase and bag
one after the other, and slowly let them down to the grass in
the back yard by the loop of cord through the handle Then
she dropped one after the other, her coat, hat, bag and shoes
softly after them and with a sad, tender look at her obstrep-
erous little granddaughter whom she loved in spite of her
naughtiness she opened her door, the hinges of which she
had oiled the first day she had been in the house, and slipped
silently, slowly, down the stairs, making less noise than a
mouse would have made.

Outside at last with the kitchen door locked behind her she
sat down on the back doorstep in the early dawning and put
on her shoes, her hat, coat and gloves Then she picked up
her bag and suitcase, and walking on the grass she carefully
left the premises with no echo of her footsteps left behind to
stir early consciences.

It was a hard panting trip to get that baggage to the corner
and around another block out of sight. During the last lap
she had to set them down and carry one at a time a little way
and then go back for the other. She was rather worn with the
excitement of the night, and she found her heart pulling

pretty hard, but she made the corner at last where the trolley passed, and to her relief saw it coming in the distance. If she could only get to the station, and on a train, even a way train, surely she would be safe. She wanted to get home to her own house, and now that she was on her way she had time to think back to those awful words that Mark had spoken. Maybe he didn't mean them but it was bad enough that he should even have thought them, that he should have dared to speak the words to her own child. That he would put her in an insane asylum! That was what his words had practically meant. He said they would swear she was not of sound mind!

Well, of course they couldn't do that, even if Mark tried. But she would feel more comfortable when she was back among her old friends and neighbors, and in the stronghold of her own house, the house that Father had left to her, and to Rowan after her.

She was glad she had never hinted to Myra that Father had left her some money too, even though it was well guarded so that Mark could not force her to use it for his own purposes. Well, the Lord would work this all out somehow. But oh, if Rowan would only come home!

The trolley conductor was very kind. He helped her onto the car, and carried her baggage for her. And she didn't have to wait long at the station for the first train. She sat back thankfully and closed her eyes when she was moving along at last on her way back home. She mustn't let herself think of the happenings of the last few hours. It would unnerve her, and she must not be unnerved when Mark came after her as he surely would if what he said about having a purchaser for the house was true, and it likely was. Mark was itching to get hold of any money that could be grasped. Poor Myra!

She slept a little on the way home, and dreamed of Charles. The vision of his face steadied her. She thought of his calm assurance in the face of death, of his word that he had left everything all right for her. Charles had sensed what Mark would do. She must not worry. He had fixed it.

When she got home it was so good to see familiar faces on the street. The day had just begun. Her heart gave a sudden stab. It almost seemed as if Charles must be there to meet her. But she put on her self-control as a garment and went out into the street. The one taxi of the village was not in sight anywhere, but a neighbor was going up her way and took her, setting her down at her own door, and promising to stop at the farmer's cottage and send him over at once to see if there was anything he could do for her. Maybe she would like him to start a fire to take the dampness out of the house, though the day was not chilly.

So Hannah entered her own door; her baggage was carried in for her to her own dear wide hall, and the neighbor departed.

Then, first of all Hannah shut and locked her door and knelt down by Charles' chair and gave thanks. After that she went to the telephone and called up Mr. Goodright asking if he could come over for a few minutes and talk with her.

He promised to come at once, and Hannah went about making it cheerful in the parlor. A fire on the hearth. She could compass that before the farmer came. There was wood in the woodshed, and kindlings.

She had the fire burning brightly, and had washed her face and combed her hair and made herself tidy before the banker came.

By this time the farmer was on hand, welcoming her heartily, and promising to make a fire and bring some supplies, milk and butter and eggs. It seemed like living again.

Then she found that Mr. Goodright knew all about Charles' fears and wasn't in the least surprised at Mark's behaviour.

"Don't you worry, Hannah," he said. "Charles has fixed it all. Mark couldn't sell this farm if he tried. It is all tied up. It belongs to you as long as you live, and then passes to Rowan, and if so be that anything happens to Rowan in that time it is held in trust for Myra and her children, but never passes into Mark's control. Charles was very careful about all that."

"Oh," said Hannah with relief, "he told he had done something about it but I didn't remember what it was. But I wonder just what I ought to do if Mark comes after me, and brings this man along with him? Should I lock him out? I don't exactly like to do that. He might even break down the door if he got angry."

"Well, Hannah, if he comes, you just send him down to me. Or, if you prefer, suppose I stay here with you."

"Oh, no, I couldn't think of letting you do that," said Hannah. "I'm not afraid of Mark. If you are behind me, I'm all right."

"Well, you just telephone me," he said as he left. "Telephone me at once if you want anything. I'll be in the bank all the morning."

So Hannah went about getting ready for callers.

It was almost noon when Mark arrived with his buyer. The buyer hadn't turned up as soon as he had expected, and Mark was boiling with irritation when he finally knocked at the door.

They had had to come on a surmise that Hannah was here. Myra hadn't found the note yet. She hadn't tried very hard to find one knowing that she would have to show it to Mark if she did so she refrained from looking very thoroughly until Mark was gone She was not surprised at her mother's action. She felt a kind of triumph that Mark had been frustrated. It was so seldom that he was. He always forced people to do what he demanded, by hook or by crook. He seldom had to make even a gesture of carrying out his threats. he knew how to threaten so effectively that people were simply paralyzed into yielding without an attempt to get free. It made him furious that his mother-in-law was the only woman so far who had frustrated him, and he couldn't seem to put over a thing on her.

But he meant to now. He had her all right this time. The idea was in his eye when he knocked at the door. with the interested eager buyer beside him. He had already accepted a small sum to bind the bargain He had managed that on the way over by effective salesmanship, making the man sure there were other eager buyers who might claim the priority. There was no denying that the buyer was eager.

Hannah opened her door as calmly as if she had been established in her home right along all winter An air of well being and warmth and pleasantness rushed out with a spicy odor of something baking in the oven, was it Johnny cake or gingerbread? Mark was hungry and it smelled good. He ignored the past night and their differences.

"This is Mr Edwards, Mother." he said, exactly as if it had all been planned between them. "He's come to look the house over as I told you last night he would."

But Hannah stood in the doorway. acknowledging the introduction pleasantly. yet not inviting them in.

"You'll have to excuse me," said Hannah to the stranger. "My house is not on exhibition I have just returned from a visit and am about to do some cleaning. It wouldn't be convenient for you to see around today, even if there were any reason for it. I'm afraid. Mr. Edwards, that you are under a misapprehension This house is not for sale and never has been. My son-in-law has made a mistake in thinking it was. I'm sure you will understand."

The prospective buyer's face went down several degrees. He turned to Mark in indignant amazement and Mark gave him a knowing wink.

"What does this mean?" he asked.

"That's all right, Edwards," said Mark with assurance, "Mother here just doesn't understand. It happens that I'm the head of this family now, and I know that this house has to be sold. Mother naturally is fond of her old home and she hasn't yet come to realize that it will have to be sold, but it will be quite all right. Mother, you don't realize that Mr. Edwards has paid a sum down to bind the bargain, and that the place is practically sold to him already. I'll just have to trouble you to let us pass you. We haven't much time and Mr. Edwards has to get back home tonight. We won't bother you long."

"Well, I'm sorry, Mr. Edwards, to have to disappoint you," said Hannah. "It does not suit me to have anyone go through my house now or at any other time, and if you wish to find out anything further about the matter I must refer you to my banker who is looking after my affairs. I am sure he will make you understand the matter."

Hannah spoke with dignity and finality, as she half closed the door and stood firmly in it. Then she turned to her son-in-law.

"Mark, I'm sorry not to invite you to come back to dinner but you know I've just got home and there wouldn't be much to eat in the house. I think you can get something in the village. There's a very nice little restaurant."

Then she went in and shut the door, and she heard the chagrined Mark say as she slipped the bolt soundlessly:

"Sorry, Edwards, she's a pretty stubborn old woman, and not quite right in the upper story, you understand, but we'll just run down to the bank and get it all straightened out. I hadn't an idea she would act like this."

So Mark went down to the bank and had an encounter with the stern banker, for Jamie Goodright could be stern upon occasion.

When Mark went away he was thoroughly convinced that it would do no good to try to break Father Parsons' will. He had it all tied up so thoroughly that Mark couldn't even get what belonged to Myra except through her mother, and the guardians of the estate, so he went home a sadder and a wiser man and took it out on Myra. Hannah had been afraid he would do this, but there wasn't anything she could do about it.

CHAPTER XVI

Joyce came over that afternoon and Hannah held her in her arms and wept over her. It was so good to see her. It seemed to bring real living back again. It brought both Charles and Rowan nearer, and for the first time since the death of her husband, she had a good cry in Joyce's arms.

It only lasted a minute or two and then she was herself again.

"But oh, my dear, I am ashamed!" she said wiping her eyes and putting her glasses back on again. "I entirely broke down when I saw you. So many things have happened, and I've had to be going on so hard and keeping up so calmly there hasn't been a chance for a tear. But I'm that glad to see you, child. And how are you, and how is your father?"

"Just about the same," said Joyce, "that is, he holds his own, the nurse says. I don't think his face is quite as much twisted. The nurse thinks it is gradually relaxing, and he seems to take more interest in what I say. I truly do believe he understands. The other day I tried him. I asked him if he knew what I was saying to close his eyes, and he looked at me a minute and then he closed them and opened them again, slowly, so I knew he was doing it of himself."

"Oh, my dear, how wonderful!"

"Yes, it is a great comfort," said Joyce. "I didn't have a chance to tell you before you went away, but for the first few days after your husband died he kept watching the door, about the time for him to come over and call. And finally I told him. I said, 'He is gone Home to Heaven,' and I pointed up and he looked at me a minute and his eyes got full of tears. I wiped them off for him and there seemed to be a new look in his eyes, as if it comforted him for me to touch him. It was the next morning that we noticed again that his face wasn't twisted so much. The nurse said sometimes a shock or emotion did that for one who was paralyzed. But he is a little better, I really think he is. Oh, it would be such a comfort if he could get so he could speak, and I could be sure he understands."

"Yes, dear child, I know. Perhaps it will come yet. Has your—has Mrs. Whitney come back yet?"

"Not to stay. She comes and she goes. She says her nervous temperament won't stand it to be around Father, and I think it's just as well. Although of course people are talking. But somehow—well it seems as if God had put me above talk, and it doesn't matter. And I think it's easier for Father when she isn't here. She always fusses so when she goes in there, and sits around and weeps and bewails. She won't believe it that he can hear her, and see her, and understand it all. And all the time she is here his eyes look so distressed."

"Too bad!" said Hannah wondering why God's dear children, frail little ones like Joyce, had to have so many severe trials.

"Well, have you heard anything more about the bank? Have they heard anything through the Rowley man that was arrested? Did they have a trial? No one has written me about it."

"Yes, they had a trial, but it didn't amount to much. They condemned him to a long term in the penitentiary. They had plenty of evidence against him, fingerprints and so on, and they found out definitely that his brother, the one who was shot by the policeman, was the one who fired the shot. They found the gun, and seemed very sure he was the one who shot poor old Sam. Sam didn't die, you know. But he doesn't seem to get well. He has been so weak that they haven't dared to question him much about the robbery. But do you know that every time they have spoken of it to him he has declared that neither Jason nor Rowan were on the street that night. Isn't that grand?"

"Yes, it's just like our Father to let him be able to tell that. But you look so tired, dear. Don't you get out at all? You ought to get away a while each day and get a little rest from bearing burdens."

"Well, I don't want to get away," said Joyce sadly. "Father's all I've got left, now Jason is gone and—" she hesitated —"Rowan," she added with a shy little apologetic laugh. "I haven't even a friend left. No, I shouldn't say that. I have Rose. Rose Allison. She comes over quite often and brings me a flower or a little cake her mother has baked or something. She is a sweet child. Did you know she knew Jason? She did, just a little. They went to school together but they never had much to do with one another. But it seems that the last week Jason was home she stopped him on the street and asked him to come to some young people's rally or something, and he promised he would, and then, the day he left the bank he called her up and told her it was going to be impossible, that he had had trouble in the bank and was leaving town. She got worried because they were talking so about Jason and she came to tell me about it. There were several things he said to her that made it almost sure he couldn't have done the things they said he was doing."

"She is a dear girl. I have often watched her in church," said Hannah. "She is the kind of girl who will grow into a wonderful woman. I'm so glad she gave you comfort."

"Yes, she is," said Joyce thoughtfully, "and she's praying for Jason too. Oh, how wonderful it would have been if Jason could only have stayed at home and gone to that meeting. Then people would have known he wasn't that kind of a fellow."

"Don't worry about that, dear. Just one meeting wouldn't have changed Jason's reputation, and when a town begins to talk you can't stop it so easily. But dear, I feel sure that God is doing something more wonderful for our two boys than even bringing them to one meeting. Father felt so. He felt sure that God was in this matter of their going."

"Yes?" said Joyce. "I'm glad you told me that. If he thought so, too, it must be so. I've held onto that, and I've been praying it might be so."

"You dear child! You are a precious child!" and Hannah looked at her lovingly. The girl that Rowan had seemed to like best of all girls! How her heart yearned over her!

And Joyce remembered with a thrill that that was the word that Rowan had used toward her, "Precious," and now his mother had called her that! She came over and kissed Hannah tenderly.

"You are such a dear mother! Very much like my own mother as I remember her. I was so lonesome while you were away. I missed you so. I don't seem to have anybody! And I've been so annoyed with that Corey Watkins. I think

Mother is inviting him. He comes whenever she is here, almost every night, to ask how we are, if nothing more, and he is always trying to coax me to take a ride with him. I don't want to ride with him. Do you think I need to? Mother says I am rude and disagreeable to him. I don't really mean to be, but that is the only way I can get rid of him, just to walk out of the room. I simply can't stand him. Do you think a girl ought to have to go with young men she doesn't like, just to be polite?"

"Of course not, dear!" said Hannah. "You have a right to choose your friends. In fact it is misleading if a girl accepts invitations from a man she doesn't want to make her friend."

"Well, that's the way I feel. But Mother has made my life miserable every time she comes home. She invites him to dinner, and she insists on my hanging around and showing him this and that, and she puts me into situations where I simply have to sit down and talk or seem just awfully rude. She keeps telling me that I can't afford to turn down a young man like that, so well off and so successful and charming, that I may never get another chance, and all that! Oh, I oughtn't to tell you this and burden you with my annoyances, I know. You have enough troubles of your own."

"You are not burdening me, dear. I'm glad to be an escape-valve for you. And I'm so sorry you have to listen to such talk. But what does she think your father would do if you were married?"

"Well, she says the doctor says he won't live long anyway. Yes, she says just that! Isn't it dreadful! My dear father who is just beginning to love me the way he used to do when my own Mother was alive! I'm sure he does. His eyes have grown to be loving eyes. Ever since that day when—when Mr. Parsons prayed with him!"

"Call him, 'Father Charles,' Joyce. He would have liked that. He loved you, child! He wouldn't have wanted you to put him so far away as 'Mr. Parsons.' "

" 'Father Charles'! What a dear name! I will!" and her heart gave a faint little thrill of delight. The name seemed to bring Rowan nearer to her.

"Father used to think the Lord would come very soon," mused Hannah. "He spoke of how he would be with Him if he came while I was living. It's been very beautiful to think about!"

"Oh, wouldn't that be wonderful!" said Joyce. "If the Lord

would come my father would get well, wouldn't he? He'd be changed in a moment. How I wish I knew! But I'm going to read to him about the Lord's coming tonight. Do you know, I always read in the Bible to him every night, and he lies and watches me with his eyes wide open, and an almost eager look in them. And then I kneel down and pray a few words. I'm going to tell him how Father Charles was saying the Lord might come and bring him back with him to get us. And oh, Mother Hannah—may I call you that?—My own mother would be with Him, too, wouldn't she? How wonderful!"

When Joyce was gone Hannah stood watching her away across the meadow, and thinking how dear she was. Then the stinging thought came that she was more loving than her own Myra. Poor Myra! But she used to be loving! She was just harried now beyond endurance. And Mark wasn't a Christian man. That made all the difference in the world. Oh, he went to church usually, once on Sunday, but that was all the interest he took in religious matters. How careful parents ought to be to teach their children not to have fellowship with unbelievers, not to choose their intimate friends from among them, not to marry them! Oh, how could Myra ever have happiness in this world? And she wasn't paying much attention to the next world either, that was sure. Poor Myra, weeping over disappointments and not looking up for God's way and God's appointments! Well, even that, too, might be brought in His good time to a solution. She must just leave it to God!

Then Hannah set to work to make her home look like itself and make pretence that she was getting ready for Rowan. It was only a game to keep her cheerful. She had been through so many hard things! And she had promised Father she would keep happy for Rowan! But it was so hard to keep the tears back! At every turn there was something to remind of the loved ones who were gone! Myra and Rowan and Father! How blessed it was that one didn't have to stay in this land of sorrow and pain forever, and that over There, there would be no more parting!

Myra, poor darling Myra! She had to trust her with God too. Why was it so much harder to trust Myra with God than even the other two who were gone from her? Father who was at Home with God, Rowan who was off in some unknown, unthinkable place, Myra who was in a home with her husband and child? Well, God was as much with one as the other, and she must trust and not be afraid.

So that night she lay down in her lonely house, in her lonely bed, alone for the first time since she had come a bride into that house. But she looked up and said:

"It's all right, Father, Thy will be done!"

CHAPTER XVII

The storm raged for three long days and nights, and when at last the wind and drenching rain ceased to slant across the stricken ship, and they looked about them there was nothing but tempestuous water on every hand; their frail bark was tossed like a bit of flotsam in its mighty power.

The men were strangely grim and silent. They watched and waited, and kept apart from the two who were of a different world. Not even now was the vigilance relaxed that kept them away from the hatch that marked the line of separation. Rowan wondered idly why they cared any more, since all would likely perish in a little while. They could not navigate with broken masts, and rent sails. They had no motor, and surely the boat must have sprung a leak, for it seemed to his landsman's mind that no boat could stand the shocks that this one had and live through. They were at the mercy of the sea.

Silently the crew stood about, helpless. Only Rowan and Jason went calmly on trying to do the useless duties that had been assigned to them when they first came on board, just to keep them sane and trusting. The other men watched them curiously, but said little to them. For a time fear showed in their eyes, but as night drew on the two noticed that the look of stark fear was gone, they had lost their apathy, and in its place was a tensity of strain that was almost expectancy.

Rowan and Jason went to their bunks early, as soon as their evening rations had been served. They had noticed that the portions were greater now than they had been for the last two days. What was the idea? Was the captain getting reckless? Did he think they were going down in the night, perhaps, and that they might as well enjoy one last meal. But they had got beyond trying to fathom the thoughts of their captain.

They were worn out with the long nursing of their friend, and exhausted by the days and nights of the storm. It had been impossible to sleep much when the masts were snapping and each moment seemed that it might be the last. But now they slept heavily, almost as soon as they lay down, and did not hear strange noises, nor voices that did not belong to their crew.

Vaguely Rowan roused once, and was aware of something unusual, hurrying feet, falling of metal objects, weird lights that flashed back and forth like a code. But as much as he thought at all he felt it must be a dream, and turned over with a sigh, thinking he heard Joyce singing.

Later someone roused him, waked Jason too, and a voice commanded. Was that the captain? Yes, the captain was shaking him awake.

"Can you row a boat?"

"Oh, yes," said Rowan, instantly himself. "Sure I can. Is the ship going to sink?"

"Yes, the ship is sinking. It won't be long. Put on all the clothes you have, and take your blankets. Go out and get into that boat alongside!"

Rowan roused Jason and they hurried their few things together, taking their blankets as they were bidden. They took also what warm things of Kinder's they could reach with a single motion and then they were out following the captain. Two of the crew who could not speak English were standing by the rail holding ropes. A small lifeboat was bobbing down there in the mighty sea, like a cork on a billow. It was barely discernible in the thick darkness. There were oars at rest on its gunwales.

"But I thought we had no boats," protested Jason looking down in wonder. "I thought they were all torn away in the storm."

"There's the boat," said the captain roughly, "get in, and be quick about it if you want a chance for your life."

"But is there room for everybody?" Rowan hesitated. "I can die as well as anybody else. I forced myself upon you. I don't want you to give up your chance of life to me."

"Get in!" was the grim command. "Everybody's got a place."

Rowan and Jason were lowered into the boat, and then instead of following after them the captain disappeared.

"Pull away!" someone commanded. They couldn't identify the voice, and Rowan thought a weird shape like the ghost of a ship loomed on the other side of the old wreck. But just as he sighted it the lights everywhere went out, and they were alone, they two in that little boat out on a wide sea in the dark! In a frail little boat that looked like an eggshell. But of course it must be a dream.

Just to prove it was, Rowan sat down and tried an oar, but he might as well have dipped a feather in Niagara. He shipped it quickly and made sure it was fast. There was no use rowing in a sea like that. They must just drift.

Morning revealed the fact that there was food in the bottom of the boat, enough for several days. Then the captain had set them adrift on purpose alone! He had meant to get rid of them! They looked at one another in the ghastly morning light, with those green towering walls of water about them. They looked at the oars that seemed so fragile, and then they looked up.

The sky was clearing. Calmer weather might come, but were they ever going to be able to row that boat on the sea? It was heavy and neither of them had ever had experience on the water.

Gradually they thought back into their dreams and began to piece out the story of the night. Those must have been guns, signal guns that were shot off, and they had dreamed they were thunder! And that had certainly been another ship standing by! A sister ship, perhaps, out to search for the lost after the storm. Their own boat must have been carrying something precious indeed to be searched for so carefully in such a storm! And what were those strange noises in the night? Precious metal being moved, or arms? They could not tell. They probably never would know. And now they began to be aware that they had been sent away so that they could not tell what they did know.

A curious thing, they had been on that ship for weeks, and yet they had never found out just what it was about it that made it fantastic; they had never been able to figure out what wickedness it was carrying out, that perhaps should have been revealed to the powers that be, whoever they were.

"We were dumb, I suppose," said Jason. "We certainly were dumb. Get as near as that to mystery, and crime perhaps, and then be set adrift without finding out."

"We weren't meant to clean up the universe," said Rowan. They talked about it a few minutes, theorizing, and then because their own fate was even more interesting than the ship with its unknown cargo, they discussed the possibilities of life and death.

"Well, if we can't navigate," said Jason at last, "I move we lie down and finish our sleep."

So they lay down, but somehow they could not sleep.

"Rowan," said Jason suddenly, "I want to talk to you. I've got a girl back at home and I begin to think I love her. Do you think that's wrong?"

"Wrong?" said Rowan. "How would it be wrong? What kind of a girl is she?"

"Oh, she's a wonderful girl! She's far too good for me. She has eyes like the sky, and hair with the sunshine tangled in it, and she wears a little pink dress. She has a lovely smile, and dimples in her cheeks. Her name is Rose. Do you think it's wrong for me to be thinking of her all the time? She doesn't even know I love her. But I got to thinking that here we are probably about to die, and I'd like to think she was here and I was talking to her. I'd like to think she kissed me if I was dying. I guess I'm getting a fever, don't you think, or I wouldn't talk this way, would I? I guess I'm wandering or I wouldn't be thinking of such weird things."

Rowan looked at his friend tenderly.

"No, Kid, you're just lonesome, you're not out of your head. Who is she? Does she care, too?"

"Yes, she said she cared, but I guess she just meant she cared for me to stay at home and make good or something like that. It's Rose Allison, the minister's daughter! Now, do you think I'm crazy? Loving a girl like that? I never had anything to do with her, either, only just saw her in school, till a few days before I came away."

And then Jason told him the story of how he had talked with her on the telephone.

When he had finished Rowan looked at him lovingly.

"Well, brother, I guess I'd better confess, too, since you've told me this. I love your sister Joyce, and before I came away I took her in my arms and kissed her! I wouldn't ever have told that to you till I'd seen her, and found out if she really cares for me. But now it looks as if we were on our way to Heaven and it can't hurt for us to have the comfort of knowing each other's hearts. I've been thinking if it should so be that you are saved somehow and should ever get home, I'd like to have you tell her that I love her, and that I've been thinking of her and loving her ever since I left her. Of course, I don't know whether she cares for me, but she won't mind hearing it if I'm gone, anyway."

"Sure, she loves you," said Jason confidently.

"How do you know that?"

"Caught her looking out her window watching you drive away to college, and weeping all over the place. Sure she's loved you, since ever I can remember. Brothers can tell."

Rowan considered this gravely, then he said, "Thanks awfully for telling me that, brother! I can call you brother now, you know."

"It's been about the biggest thing in my life for a long time to think that some day maybe you would be that!" The boy's voice was very gentle as he said it, and then, even in the midst of their intimate confessions he felt embarrassed and hurried on.

"But say, brother—" he stopped and grinned lovingly, "if it should be the other way around and I'm called and you get home, would you sometime tell Rose Allison for me that I loved her, and that her saying she cared and would believe in me about saved me from suicide when I first started out. I kept on thinking I'd make good and come back and show her, and right then I began to know I loved her, and I've thought about her and dreamed about her ever since. You tell her, too, how I've been saved, and maybe it was her asking me to meeting that helped in that, too. Will you do it, Rowan?"

"I surely will!" promised Rowan solemnly.

"Well, then you pray for us both, and then let's go to sleep. I can't look at those green walls any longer."

So they lay down side by side, expecting most confidently that they would wake up in Heaven.

And the little boat went drifting, drifting, guided by an unseen Hand!

CHAPTER XVIII

There was great excitement in the village. Corey Watkins had been taken to the police headquarters between two policemen and nobody could quite believe it, though the rumor had been well authenticated.

Nothing had been given out officially yet, but it was said that James Goodright and some other officials of the bank not named had caught Corey at work on the books in the night!

Later it came out that the Watkins home had been searched and they had found a false partition in Corey's den, behind which was a capacious safe in which they had found the rest of the papers that had been missing since the robbery, papers that were more valuable than anything else that had been lost papers that established without a doubt. the fact that Jason Whitney had nothing to do with the robbery. They were the papers that Jason had handled the last thing before he left, having been sent to put them into the safe. And when they could not be found suspicion was at once fixed upon him.

But there were none of his fingerprints on the papers, and now that they were found, of course *he* could not have stolen them. Now that they had caught Corey a good many things in the past were explained.

But though suspicion was removed from Jason in the matter of the valuable papers, and though Sam Paisley had at last recovered and exonerated him from any part in the night raiding of the bank, the fact remained that Jason and Rowan were still missing, and the town could not bear that. They wanted to get the facts in orderly array and clean up the whole matter.

So a committee waited upon Hannah and offered to get up a posse of trained police and detectives to go out west and search for the two young men. It was supposed the men who escaped from the law when the Rowleys were taken, had fled there. To that end, they begged her to tell all that she knew of Rowan's departure.

Hannah thanked them with her habitual calm. She even found tears in her eyes that these hardheaded, quick-to-believe-and-suspect, self-righteous neighbors of hers had come with this belated offer. But she declined their help. She told them all that she knew of Rowan's going was that he had felt that Jason had gone out discouraged and rather desperate perhaps, because things seemed against him, and that Rowan had hurried after him to bring him back. Where he had gone she did not know, but he had promised to return, and told her she could trust him. She was confident that something was detaining him beyond his power or she would have heard from him. She was sure that he had not gone with the Rowleys and she had never felt that they had had time to kidnap the boys and take them along. They wouldn't have any reason to do so. She was trusting in God to bring them back in His own good time. She thanked them for their kind intentions and sent them away rubbing their hands in self-satisfaction that they had made such a noble gesture.

Then the town settled into its routine calm to await the next excitement, meanwhile whetting its tongue on occasional exclamations about poor Mrs. Watkins. Saying, "Just to think that such a nice young man as Corey, so well fixed and all, could have been such an awful hypocrite!" Though some said they had always thought he had sly eyes.

CHAPTER XIX

The little boat drifted for two long days, and the two boys had given up hope of rescue. Their food and water was almost gone, and they were trying to face starvation bravely.

There were the same waves tossing them about, waves that made any idea of navigation impossible, although they tried from time to time, only to have the oars slapped back at them as if the sea would have no trifling thing like that to interfere with its motion. It seemed that they were hemmed in on every side by dark green water. The wonder was that their frail bark stood the strain of the constant battering.

Occasionally one wave higher than the rest curled over them and drenched them, and they had to bail out.

"I wonder why we keep on doing this?" said Jason wearily as he bent to the task again after an especially large avalanche of water. "I wonder why we don't just let it go ahead and sink? Sooner or later the end will come and why not let it be sooner?"

"Now, brother, you know better than that!" said Rowan with a weary smile. "We're bound to do all we can for that witness we've got to give at home, in case God wants that."

"Yes, I know," said Jason, "but somehow it seems so useless!"

Then the next morning they woke to find the sun shining and the sea as calm as a summer morning! Like a miracle a new world had dawned, or else during the night they had drifted into a different clime. And there on the edge of a pearly-colored dawn they saw a phantom ship.

It was only a sailing vessel bearing a load of rubber, but it hung on the water like a dream of home and mother.

Frantically the two picked up their oars and fell to rowing with all their might. not quite sure it was not a mirage, but determined. if there was any chance that it was real, to reach it before it vanished into other seas.

Anxiously they watched, and their hearts bounded with joy when they saw that they were actually making some progress toward it.

A little later a small boat detached itself from the larger one and started toward them and then they set up a shout of joy, and bent to their oars in earnest.

It was almost like getting to the outer vestibule of Heaven to be taken on board that clean boat. It wasn't much as a boat, but it was clean, and there were friendly faces on board and smiles even if they were rough men And there was food and warm clothing given freely. with good will.

Oh. they presently found out. when they were rested and refreshed. that it was a very slow sailing boat indeed, and it might still be weeks before it landed in the native land, but they were on their way! And there was nothing mysterious about this ship Everything was hearty and aboveboard.

It was little they could tell about how they came to be adrift Their knowledge was all suspicion But the men who rescued them were simple incurious people. and took them frankly at their own representation. that they had been on a wreck and were set adrift in a life boat from another ship that evidently had come up to offer help while they were sleeping from exhaustion They did not know even the name of their own boat. They did not know their location and they had drifted perhaps a long way from the wreck. What use to say more?

So they worked and helped to pay their passage, and in due time they did arrive at a port in their native land.

Rowan and Jason had little money left of the small sums they had taken with them. and they were dressed in ill-fitting garments that the friendly crew of the rescue ship had given them to replace the rags they had been wearing, but they felt happier than they had ever been in their lives as they set foot on their native land.

They worked a day on the wharf helping to unload the ship and earned enough for railroad fare to the city not far from their home. They could walk it from there if some friendly car didn't pick them up. So they started on their way.

But when they reached that city so near home they grew

suddenly shy. The long months that stretched between their going and their coming might have wrought changes!

"And we mustn't frighten Mother!" said Rowan.

So they used their last dime to telephone.

Hannah was sitting in her dining room reading her Bible when she heard the ring. By common consent it had been the Parsons' number and not the Whitney one they had called up. Hannah's hand trembled as it always did these days when she took down the receiver. Would this be some word about Myra? Or—?

"Yes?" she said alertly, anxiously.

"Mother!" said Rowan. "Oh! Mother!"

"Rowan! Oh, my dear boy! At last I hear your voice!" Hannah wanted to shout. She wanted to cry and to laugh.

"Yes, Mother. I'm on my way. We'll be there in about two hours. Tell Joyce I'm bringing Jason. It's been longer than I thought but we're almost there now!"

"I'll tell her!" lilted Hannah. "Come straight here. I'll tell Joyce to come over. Her father is sick, and it's better for you to come here first!"

"Yes, that's what we'd planned to do. But, sick! I'm sorry! Oh, Mother, are you and Father all right?"

Hannah hesitated and there were tears in her voice as she answered.

"Yes, dear, both—all right—but—Father's gone Home!"

"Gone Home?" said Rowan. "You mean—?" his voice trailed off and stopped.

"Yes, Rowan. He's gone Home! God called him. But it's all right. He left a message for you. He believed in you! He said he would see you in the Morning!"

The boys tramped on through the bright home country that was just beginning to show signs of spring, and it was all so good to weary sea-fed eyes. But they did not laugh and joke now. For the father of one was sick and the father of the other had gone Home.

Back in the farmhouse Hannah hung up the receiver and stood looking up.

"Oh, God," she said, "Thank you! Thank you!"

Then she took down the receiver and tried to make her voice steady as she called the Whitney number.

"Is that you, Joyce? Well, can you come over a little while? Can you be spared?"

"Now?" said Joyce. "Yes, I can come. Has—anything— happened?"

"Nothing bad, dear," said Hannah. "I'll tell you when you come."

So Joyce was there when finally they came walking in. She hid in the parlor until Hannah had taken her son in her arms. And then from that long embrace Rowan stood back and his eager eyes searched the room.

"Joyce! Isn't she here?"

Joyce came rosily out from her hiding, and then to her utter and sweet confusion she was folded close in Rowan's arms, and his lips were upon hers.

"I've brought him back, dear!" said Rowan lifting his head and looking down into her face, thrilling with the dearness of her. "I've brought your brother back. It took longer than I thought, but we're here."

Then Jason gave his sister a bear hug and a resounding kiss, and Hannah had her boy again, his arms about her this time, his sorrow for his father's absence in his gaze.

They sat down around a little supper that Hannah had prepared and Hannah told them about the last words of Charles, and the glory that was to come in the Morning.

She told it simply, shyly, not sure it would meet with response, but she was almost overpowered with the light that came in the faces of both the wanderers.

"Oh, but Mother, that's wonderful!" said Rowan. "And you don't know our best news yet. We've both come to know the Lord, yours and Father's Lord! We had to be sent to the other side of the world to learn because we wouldn't learn from our own Christian folks at home."

Hannah's eyes were suddenly alight with a more than earthly radiance.

"Oh, my boy!" she said. Then turning to Jason she said, with a smile, "My boys!"

She got up and came around and kissed them both, and then folding her arms about Rowan again she said:

"It's just as Father said it would be. He said God had taken you somewhere to draw you nearer to Him. He said it was going to be all right!"

A few minutes later Joyce and Jason went across the meadows to their home, walking hand in hand, Joyce telling of her father's illness, having more sweet sisterly converse with Jason than she had had in many a year. Not since they were children had they been so close.

As they approached the house Jason said:

"Joyce, do you know anything about Rose Allison? Is she—" he hesitated for words and Joyce broke in joyously.

"Yes, I know about Rose! She's my dearest friend! She's sweet. We've been together a lot all winter. She's sweet, Jason, and she"ll be so glad about you. She's been praying for you every day. She came and told me, when she heard all the things people were saying, how you had telephoned her."

Jason's hand tightened on his sister's arm as he helped her up the steps.

"What do you mean, all the things people were saying?"

"Oh, you don't know, do you? But it doesn't matter any more. There was a bank robbery the night you went away. The Rowleys were at the head of it, and they tried to connect you and Rowan, too, with it for awhile, but it's a long story, and we haven't time for it now. Only it was that that brought Rose to tell me, and it was sweet of her. I should have gone crazy thinking maybe they had kidnaped you or something, only she told me you had gone away because you couldn't get a square deal here, and she set my mind at rest about—you *both!*" she ended shyly.

Jason stooped down and kissed his sister almost reverently.

"Rowan told me about you and him," he said gently. "One night when we thought we were going to die pretty soon. But that's a long story, too, that will wait. He told me, and I'm glad! He's great. It will be wonderful!"

Joyce was startled, covered with wonder!

"Rowan told you about us!" she said. "But there wasn't anything to tell—not that he knew—nor that I knew!" she laughed. "That is—he only kissed me good-bye!"

"I know," said Jason gently, "he told me. He wanted me to tell you in case I got home and he didn't; he wanted me to tell you he loved you!"

"Oh!" said Joyce softly.

Presently they went up the stairs together, arms about each other, reunited as they had never been united before Jason went away.

Joyce slipped into the room first while Jason waited outside the door.

"Father dear," said Joyce going up to the bed quietly, "Jason has come home! Would you like to see him?"

She watched his face eagerly. Would he understand?

But she was not prepared for the great light that came into his eyes. And suddenly the lips that had been dumb all those months, dumb and twisted, untwisted themselves and spoke.

"Jason!" he said. "Jason!"

Oh, it was not his old forceful speech. It was a halting, lisping attempt, but Jason understood it, and came close at once.

"Father! Dear Father!" he said bending down and kissing his father. He had not done that since he was a little child. And the poor twisted face suddenly assumed a look of radiant peace, the hands that had been so rigid and gnarled, relaxed in Jason's strong ones, and the demon that had held the man's body in its tense grasp so many months, began to let go its hold. The nurse and Joyce stood looking on in wonder, and then the nurse hastened away to telephone the doctor. The doctor said his patient must have immediate rest and quiet and he would come at once. So Jason kissed his father again, bringing a faint shadow of a smile to the stiff features, and he and Joyce went out. "See you in the morning, Dad;" waved Jason in his old dear way. And then the sick man closed his eyes, and there came a look of peace upon that tempestuous old face. It was as if the sunlight had suddenly touched a mountain-side where storms and tempest had long been raging.

"I'm going to Rose," said Jason with a light in his eyes. "Do you think I could?"

"Yes, go," said Joyce, her face all joy.

So Jason went down the hill to the village and down the street till he came to the church.

But there he saw the church was lighted, and the little parsonage next door was dark. He remembered it was Wednesday night. The door was open and many people were inside. Rose would be there! It was another meeting, and he would keep his promise to her now and go to meeting.

So he slipped into the open door and took a back seat. Presently he spied her.

She was sitting near the front with her mother, and the dress she wore now was blue, the color of her eyes. He feasted his glance upon her sweet face. They were singing a hymn and he watched her lips as they sang. Sweet lips! Would he ever dare to lay his upon them as he had reverently dreamed away off there on the sea?

The meeting went on and they were calling for testimonies. There was a silence. Nobody spoke. Then suddenly Jason rose to his feet.

"Friends, I want to testify what the Lord has done for me!" The congregation stirred and turned and stared in as-

tonishment. Jason Whitney! He had come back, and he was
testifying in a meeting! A miracle was happening in their
midst! They listened and thrilled to his words. Rose sat beside
her mother, trembling with joy, and trying not to look as if
she had ever heard of him before. Jason! Her Jason! He had
kept his promise and come! Her prayers were answered. And
she mustn't show people she cared!

But nobody was looking at Rose, not even her father, who
knew. They were all looking at a new Jason with a clear ring-
ing voice.

"I went away from this town out of sorts and bitter at the
world. I was angry at God and I didn't care where I went. I
went aboard the first ship I could find sailing from New York
and found it an awful place of dirt and filth and vermin and
sin. But there was a man aboard that knew God, and he
taught me about my sin and my Saviour. I had to go to the
ends of the earth and endure hardship and peril and come
near to death. Our ship was wrecked and we were in a little
open boat for three days and nights alone in a tempestuous
sea. Rowan Parsons was with me, my friend! He came after
me, and got there too late to save himself from that awful
voyage. But God was with us every minute of the time and He
was precious. I'm glad I had to suffer now, because there
probably wouldn't have been any other way for me to get to
know Jesus Christ. He saved me and let me come home to
testify what a difference He has made in my life. I'm glad for
this chance to tell you right at the start. I'm trusting in His
power and grace to keep me, for there is nothing in myself to
do it. I hope you'll pray for me."

The minister could just control his voice to start a song:
"Praise God from whom all blessings flow," and the congregation were so stirred they sang as they never had sung before.

They gathered around Jason at the close and greeted him
with so much true Christian fervor that he was embarrassed.
He had not known his fellow-townsmen could be like this.
He grew shy and as soon as he could he hunted up Rose and
they slipped away.

"Rose," he said when they were alone on the street, "Rose,
I love you. Perhaps it's too soon to tell you so. But you don't
know what you did for me, telling me you would believe me.
Telling me you cared. I've kept you with me all the way of
that awful journey, and sometimes if it hadn't been for you
I'd have died. Until I knew the Lord you were the only thing

that there was in the world to care for, you and my sister Joyce. Are you angry with me, Rose, for talking like this? I know I ought to wait and be more decorous about it. But it's so good to see you. You won't be angry with me for telling you this? I'll wait as long as you want me to, if I've been wrong, but I had to let you know what you are to me!"

He looked down at her anxiously, and she looked up, her face luminous with joy.

"No, I'll not be angry, Jason," she said with a lilt in her voice, "because you see *I care*. And now that you belong to my Lord Jesus, there's no reason why you shouldn't tell me."

They were walking along the street near the parsonage. Maple trees were just coming into full leaf, and the moonlight was sifting in lacy patterns on the pavement. Suddenly Jason drew her to him and holding her close kissed her again and again!

And the people were coming away from the church!

"My! I was embarrassed!" said sweet little old Miss Pettibone guardedly, as she told her sister about it when she got home. "But my dear, it was sweet! Those two dear children!"

The sister sat grimly listening, melted in spite of herself, and finally said:

"Well, *I* think they might have waited until they got into the house!"

"Then I wouldn't have seen it," chirped Priscilla, " and it was so sweet!"

Back at the Parsons' farmhouse the fire glowed bright on the hearth that night. Rowan and his mother and Joyce had been having a beautiful hour of converse together, and Hannah had been telling them all about Charles' last words, and the glory that was to be in the morning. Then they knelt together in the firelight, hand in hand, the three of them, Hannah on one side of Rowan and Joyce on the other, while Rowan prayed.

"Lord, we thank Thee for the hope that Thou hast given us of that glory in the great morning. Ours to look forward to, our sunrise! The glory of the Lord."